BANDWIDTH

ALSO BY ELIOT PEPER

"True Blue" (A Short Story)
Neon Fever Dream
Cumulus

The Uncommon Series

Uncommon Stock: Exit Strategy
Uncommon Stock: Power Play
Uncommon Stock: Version 1.0

BANDWIDTH

an Analog Novel by
ELIOT PEPER

47N RTH

Published by 47North, Seattle

www.apub.com

Amazon, the Amazon logo, and 47North are trademarks of Amazon.com, Inc., or its affiliates.

ISBN-13: 9781503954427 (hardcover)
ISBN-10: 1503954420 (hardcover)
ISBN-13: 9781503954601 (paperback)
ISBN-10: 1503954609 (paperback)

Cover design by The Frontispiece

Printed in the United States of America

First edition

To all who taste the cynic's bitter draft, and instead choose hope.

CHAPTER 1

Dag Calhoun sipped his third macchiato and considered that fickle bitch, power. The creamy sweetness of the steamed milk cut the earthy acidity of the espresso. A solo bassist plucked jazzy scales in the café behind him. A balmy spring breeze ruffled Dag's thick brown hair, the gust an unexpected blessing in this country ravaged by the twin specters of drought and violence.

From his seat at one of the sidewalk tables, Dag gazed at the professional dog walkers escorting the pampered pets of Mexico City's elite. The park across the street was one of the verdant oases that made the wealthy La Condesa neighborhood feel completely isolated from the rest of the hustling megalopolis. Dapper professionals strode back from lunch meetings as preschoolers in color-coded smocks clustered around teachers in the dappled green shade.

History was badly plotted and written by committee. It lacked the narrative structure, moral fiber, and cathartic transformation that even the crassest feed serials took for granted. Visiting Distrito Federal never failed to remind him of the delicate, capricious cascade of events that had shaped the geopolitical fortunes of the Americas. That was why he was here after all, to rest a finger on the scale, to give history a nudge in the right direction. Or in his client's direction anyway.

Sighing, Dag took another sip. Sometimes there was nothing for it but to revel in the ephemeral bliss of a perfect cup. This balanced roast teased his palate with notes of blackberry, tamarind, and maple sugar. His feed displayed the supply chain all the way through from the estate of origin in Aceh to the local microroaster. He made a mental note to tip the barista again on the way out.

His gaze slipped back to the elderly couple seated a few tables down. The woman had lustrous skin and elegant features that hinted at Mayan heritage. Her lanky partner's high forehead, short-cropped beard, and dated-but-classy attire made Dag think he might hail from Ethiopia. But what really caught Dag's attention was their dynamic. There was too much ambient noise for him to eavesdrop, but they exuded an intimate authenticity. His earnest enthusiasm. Her lopsided smile. The attentiveness with which he stirred two spoonfuls of sugar into her coffee.

Dag selected a toothpick from the small dispenser on his table. Then he spread out a napkin and dipped the end of the toothpick into the dregs of his macchiato. With utmost care, he lowered a single drop of milky espresso to the napkin. As soon as it touched, the fibers sucked up the droplet like a sponge. With a series of quick strokes, he used the tip of the toothpick to push, pull, and tease the liquid as it was absorbed. Then he dipped into his cup for another drop.

Trust emanated from the couple like scent off a rose. The generous, warm, unselfconscious trust that bound together people who gave more than they took. Dag tamped down a budding ache of jealousy. In his business, the vulnerability that trust required was anathema. It was a target painted on your back, a point of leverage others wouldn't hesitate to exploit. He knew, because he exploited people for a living. Ambition did not tolerate exposure.

Chewing on the toothpick, Dag admired his handiwork. The lines were blurred, edges ragged where the liquid darkened the coarse weave of paper fibers. It was as distorted as a long-forgotten black-and-white photograph, warped by age and water damage. Nevertheless, something about the couple shone through the rough medium. Though it lacked mimetic detail, the sketch captured something essential about their rapport. The corner of Dag's mouth quirked around the toothpick as he imagined the piece framed on the wall of some cosmopolitan gallery, effete hipsters hoping to impress each other by lavishing praise or ridicule on it as prevailing social conditions demanded.

Connection, coffee stain on napkin.

A shout from down the block caught Dag's attention. A golden retriever was charging up the sidewalk, big pink tongue lolling out of its mouth, leash slapping freely against the pavement with every bound. Sliding out of his seat, Dag stamped down on the end of the leash as it whipped past, whistling to the dog so that it turned toward him in time to save itself from a violent jerk to the collar. As Dag knelt to retrieve the leash, the irrepressible retriever licked his face with instant affection.

A young boy sprinted up, put his hands on his knees, and gasped for air.

"¡Muchas gracias, señor!" he managed after a minute.

Dag handed over the leash and wiped the slobber from his face. "No se preocupe," he said. "¿Escapar es vivir, no? Es un perro muy lindo."

After scratching the beast's head once more, Dag returned to his seat. It was past time. He crumpled up the napkin, tossed the toothpick, and scanned his fellow patrons. In addition to the loving elderly couple, there were a group of scruffy students working on some academic project, a pair of sleek housewives complaining about their respective au pairs, and his two bodyguards with their slick hair, tight-fitting suits, and hard eyes. They had swept this place before his arrival. And, as a matter of professional pride, Dag had arrived forty-five minutes prior to the designated meeting time. Hence the jittery thrill of overcaffeination. But the café now felt like home turf, and that slight psychological edge sometimes made all the difference in a negotiation.

There. A black SUV rounded the corner and pulled to a smooth stop in front of the café. A new duo of bodyguards emerged, heads swinging left and right, eyes hidden behind reflective sunglasses, weapons barely concealed beneath their chic blazers. Dag gave them a jaunty wave, which they ignored with professional stoicism as they cased the joint. Satisfied, one took up a position on the street corner while the other opened the back passenger door to let their employer out into the afternoon sunshine.

Federico Alvarez emerged, blinking away the glare as his eyes adjusted to the world outside the tinted cocoon of his vehicle. Once a professional soccer player, he'd let his body go to seed as his political star rose. Now not even his Italian tailor could hide his paunch. But he still moved with an athlete's confidence, and his open face concealed his cunning.

Dag rose and smoothed his tie.

"Federico," he said, grinning. "I was starting to think you had been sucked into the black hole of your beautiful city's infamous traffic."

They shook hands and embraced.

"Oh, Dag," said Federico with a sad shake of his head. "One day I hope you're able to set aside your obsession with punctuality. I swear that every time I visit those United States of yours, I fear that the entire population is living on the brink of cardiac arrest thanks to their uncompromising calendars. Cálmate, amigo. Estás en México. Relájate."

They ordered a round of coffees—Dag starting to regret the volume of his previous espresso intake—and settled into the comfortable meandering banter that preceded any weighty discussion in this particular capital. Federico's daughter had inherited his love for the beautiful game, and he described her recent victories in lavish detail. There were rumors she was in the running for a midfielder slot on the national team. His son was completing a degree in philosophy at Oxford and upon graduation would surely enjoy a fast track into the bureaucratic elite. They commiserated over the widespread destruction the latest hurricane had left along the Yucatán peninsula and traded self-deprecating anecdotes about romantic conquests long past.

Two café au laits and a croissant later, Dag made his move.

"You know why I'm here," he said with an apologetic shrug. "The goddess of Silicon Valley is getting anxious. She wants to see progress." Federico's forehead wrinkled. "Patience, my friend. Haste does not equal efficacy."

"As you said before, we Americans have an unhealthy preoccupation with promptness." Dag leaned forward. "And we cannot afford to lose momentum on this initiative. It'll transform the country, empower your constituents. Think how much better prepared residents in the Yucatán could have been, and how much faster the disaster response time could have been, if the program had been in place."

Federico was a favorite on the field and in the feed. His storied career as a striker gave his personal brand as a politician an optimistic-populist sheen. Dag liked him. Federico was gregarious and well-intentioned. But what made him key to Apex Group's strategy was the larger narrative that Federico's legacy fit within: the story of a new tomorrow for Mexico, working toward a brighter future rather than returning to a mythical past. That paired well with Commonwealth's campaign to expand its full-stack service offering here. Federico was moderate enough to be taken seriously and bold enough to set things in motion.

Dag's employer, Apex, was the premier Washington lobbying firm serving major blue-chip clients like Commonwealth. Dag had spent more than a year cultivating Federico, advising him on political strategy, shaping the finer technical points in his proposed legislation—all on Commonwealth's dime. The return on that investment would be extending its fiber-optic tendrils into one of the few countries that maintained independent and outdated telecommunications infrastructure.

"You know I want it as much as you do." Federico's tone was quiet, sincere. Bass notes dribbled out of the café as thick as molasses. Dag's heart tap-danced a caffeinated syncopation. "But you know what's at stake here," Federico continued. "Getting this through despite . . . them—it takes time. And money."

Dag arched an eyebrow. "We've provided plenty. Even you have to admit that."

"Sí, sí," said Federico, drumming his fingers on the table. "Of course. I don't mean to come across as ungrateful. But a coalition is a delicate thing, and we have to go about it slowly and carefully, lest we invite retribution. I wish it were otherwise, but—"

"I'm here to deliver an ultimatum," interrupted Dag, impaling Federico with the glacial intensity of his pale-blue stare. "We need to find traction. This is happening, one way or the other." He held a sympathetic smile and understanding murmurs in reserve. Land the blow, then salve the wound.

A pained expression flashed across Federico's face before he could replace it with the politician's mask of professional neutrality. "Okay," he said, "I'll do—"

But Dag was no longer paying attention.

Behind Federico, the bodyguard posted on the corner dropped into a crouch as three ancient motorbikes accelerated out of the traffic surrounding the park and onto the café's side street, tires squealing on blacktop. Belatedly, Dag saw that each motorbike had two riders and all wore ski masks. Even as the bodyguard's hand darted toward his holster, a staccato burst of submachine-gun fire turned him into a bloody marionette.

"Get down!" yelled Dag as the world exploded into chaos.

He threw himself sideways, trying to put the parked SUV between him and the motorbikes. His shoulder hit the ground, knocking the wind out of him. The gunmen opened fire in earnest, turning the café into a thundering kaleidoscope of screams and shattered glass.

Adrenaline avalanching through him, Dag reached up and yanked Federico's arm. The big man toppled from his chair, landing beside Dag on the cement. But it was too late. Federico's chest was peppered with bullet holes. He had a surprised expression on his face, and when he opened his mouth, all that emerged was a large bubble of blood.

As bullets pulverized the concrete around them, Dag returned for a fleeting moment to his speculation on the nature of power. All he had wanted to do was his job. But perhaps he had been navigating its dark alleys and dead ends for too long.

The bubble burst.

CHAPTER 2

Water burbled in the stone fountain in the lobby of the hotel, rivulets coursing down the bodies of an entwined pair of granite naiads. Staff murmured in low voices behind the reception desk, and a lone tuxedoed pianist stitched together languid chords in a far corner.

The series of disasters this afternoon resurrected memories Dag would rather have left buried. A frigid thirty-six-hour race through the scarce icebergs of a thawing Arctic to reach the relative safety of Canadian waters, while airborne and submarine drones from half a dozen countries and multinationals hounded their boat the entire way. Four nights on the run through Tokyo suburbs trying to evade yakuza enforcers. Two weeks spent in the mountainous backcountry of the Golden Triangle negotiating with half the opium warlords while dodging raids from the opposing half. Most of his work was hints, whispers, and three-piece suits. But if he was honest with himself, Federico's untimely demise was only the latest in a string of operations that blurred the line between lobbying and espionage.

Across the expanse of marble floor, elevators stood ready to whisk him up to his well-appointed room. He should shower and collapse into bed, sneak in a few hours of shut-eye before his early-morning flight deposited him into the inevitable conference-room fire drills that awaited him in San Francisco. But hours of tense interviews with lawyers and police investigators had driven him to an exhaustion beyond the reach of sleep.

Dag looked down at himself. His jacket, soaked in blood and caked in dust, had disappeared hours before. In an unusual display of customer care, the security firm had supplied him with a fresh shirt and pair of slacks. His shoes were scuffed but serviceable, and the acrid whiff of sweat and propellant was faint.

He turned from the elevator bank and made his way to the hotel bar. Dark wood and low lighting gave it a classic feel. Botero prints lined the walls, sensual curves hinting at humanity's oversize opinion of itself. A few well-dressed businessmen debated hotly in a booth off to the side. A woman in a scarlet dress nursed a cocktail at the bar. Dag ordered three fingers of Casa Dragones and found a seat at a small table out on the balcony.

Cicadas sang, and Mexico City spread out before him in an enchanting, dangerous, putrid sprawl that reached from horizon to horizon. Starlight didn't have a chance in hell of piercing the ceiling of smog and city glow, which heightened the impression of the city existing as a world unto itself. This valley had once been the swampy seat of the Aztec empire. Philosophers, merchants, warriors, and *ōllamalitzli* stars mingled on paved boulevards and drank from expertly engineered aqueducts. Cortés besieged and razed the city, claiming it for the Spanish crown even as the viruses and bacteria stowed away in the bodies of his crew eviscerated an entire nation. European and American populations, separated after exodus from the African motherland, reunited in violent turmoil compounded by variegated microbiology. Such was the way of the world. Dag swirled the glass, the silver tequila leaving healthy legs on the sides of the tumbler as he inhaled its grassy bouquet.

Something had to give. The wonkish joy of political science graduate school had long faded. He remembered dense conversations on lengthy strolls around the muggy Georgetown campus, seminars and research papers brimming with insights into the incentive systems that shaped the world. Politics was a vast game that he and his classmates dissected with enthusiasm and hubris.

But none of their clever theories or analytical models had saved Federico. If only Dag could have reacted half a second faster, enough time to drag the other man to the sidewalk with him before the *sicarios* blasted him beyond the reach of even the most skilled Aztec priest. But had he succeeded in the rescue, perhaps the attackers would not have been run off so easily by return fire from the three remaining bodyguards. Maybe Federico's death had bought Dag his life.

He took a sip. Pepper and cloves enhanced the semisweet flavor of agave, and the fire in his throat reeled Dag back to the present like a trout on a lucky fisherman's line. He summoned his feed and saw exactly what he expected to see. The media was piling on to the afternoon's assassination with as many crazy theories and hot takes as bandwidth would allow. The fire hose of information and opinion gushed with irrelevant detail and heedless grandstanding.

This was his fault. He should have remembered his training. They should have been more careful. That café had been too exposed, too difficult to secure. He had underestimated the cartels. Legalization had dried up the demand for black market narcotics north of the border, wiping out their entire business model. Now drug lords with private armies and billions in offshore accounts were scrambling to reinvent themselves, seeking to monopolize that most potent and scrupulous of opiates, bandwidth.

While most countries enjoyed the bounty of communication infrastructure Commonwealth provided, Mexico, China, Thailand, Russia, Iceland, Ethiopia, and France sacrificed connectivity for control and ran their own internet pipes. Commonwealth countries accessed the feed with unsurpassed reliability and security, while user experience in the Prideful Seven varied according to local infrastructure. Mexicans could still access the feed, of course, but at frustratingly slow speeds. Sensing opportunity, ex–narco traffickers got into the network business, seizing domestic trunk lines and jealously defending against Commonwealth's efforts to supplant them.

Even so, Dag was surprised by the decisiveness and drama of an assassination. It was still early days for this initiative. Federico had not gone public yet with his support. The cartels must already feel pressure. His fingers drummed on the tabletop. Commonwealth would be incensed. The entire effort would have to be rebuilt from the ground up, only it would be harder this time, slowed by the need for additional security and the fear this attack would kindle among policy makers who might be convinced to support their cause.

An involuntary sigh hissed through his teeth. It was going to be complicated and expensive, both of which would frustrate the Silicon Valley bigwigs. Political subtlety was antithetical to the engineer's world of flawless design, absolute efficacy, global scale, and ruthless efficiency. Sean would bear the brunt of it, and Dag would owe him. But the clients would grit their teeth and soldier on despite their bluster. There simply wasn't someone better they could go to for this kind of help. K Street was packed to the gills with suits who would happily whip up a slick presentation but couldn't for the life of them get anything passed. International was especially convoluted, requiring a different set of assumptions and a unique network of people who owed you favors.

The sheer scale of the project was at once thrilling and intimidating, awesome in the original sense of the word—precisely the kind of thing that piqued Dag's fancy. Setting modesty aside, it was just the kind of assignment he was known for. That's what had caught Sean's eye so many years ago, when the leading energy-industry lobbyist had snatched Dag up from a graduate seminar. Dag had worked his way into the fold and up the chain of command at Apex, careful not to let scruples cloud his ambition. He had ridden in like a white knight to save Wall Street royalty from regulatory castration after yet another financial meltdown. He had played the Arctic Council like a violin to secure Lowell Harding's drilling concessions to open the thawing northern climes to oil exploration. Now, finally, the vaunted title of partner was his, along with the hefty profit share that afforded him luxuries he had never dared dream of. He was drinking Casa Dragones after all.

But like so much else, the prize was diminished by possession. He had returned to Georgetown last month, an esteemed alumnus holding court in a seminar cameo. Ears perked and eyes shone as his war stories stoked students' newfound enthusiasm for the Beltway boogaloo. But for the first time, their eagerness grated, and a gulf opened between Dag and his former self. Here were some of the brightest minds of the next generation, young people with the connections and resources to land them spots at DC's most prestigious university. And they were dedicating their energy and attention to advancing the agendas of the highest bidder.

Maybe it was the shock of this afternoon's attack. Or maybe he had been reading too many essays laced with caramel-coated maxims. Find your purpose. Follow your passion. Free your heart. But right now, Dag's commitment to the job that consumed his life seemed as fleeting as a half-remembered dream.

"May I join you?"

Dag startled, just barely managing not to spill his drink across the table.

It was the woman in the dress, scarlet silk hanging loosely over porcelain skin. She looked Korean. The black hair falling down her back absorbed light as if it were fashioned from a singularity. Oversize thick-rimmed glasses framed large dark eyes so charged with latent voltage that Dag couldn't tear his gaze away.

"It's beautiful out here on the balcony," she said, looking out over the shimmering urban vista. "And I believe I've exhausted the bartender's supply of small talk."

Momentarily released from the power of her stare, Dag collected himself.

"Please, sit," he said. "Forgive me, I've had a . . . trying day."

One corner of her mouth twisted up into a half smile.

"So I've heard," she said.

CHAPTER 3

Room 412.

Despite himself, Dag's heart fluttered as the elevator ascended. She had slipped the folded napkin into his pocket as she left the table. His lips still tingled where she had brushed them with a suggestive forefinger. Anticipation welled up inside him. It had been too long.

For the second time that evening, he considered the many drawbacks of his chosen career path. There was always a wildfire smoldering somewhere in the world, and Apex was stoking or fighting it as its clients demanded. That didn't leave much time for even small pleasures. Relationships were a luxury Dag couldn't afford, so he had to content himself by himself or swing the odd one-night stand.

She was *exactly* his type. He recalled lying on the hotel bed the night before, losing himself in a porn feed. Immersed in a half-imagined bacchanal, with a flurry of strokes he had launched himself into the passing self-annihilation of orgasm. But for all the convenience of masturbation, it always left him with an emotional hangover not unlike that of MDMA. Without the presence of a lover to reconnect with en route to lucidity, euphoria gave way to a heightened sense of isolation.

If he was honest with himself, it wasn't just the job. The intimacy sex required was darkly enticing but made his skin crawl. When he worked up the courage to actually sleep with someone, he made sure to edit her out of his life as soon as the clothes were back on. Dag was usually happiest on his own.

But today hadn't been a usual day.

Visions sprang into his mind unbidden. Getting up early to prepare her an elaborate breakfast in bed. Arguing over what vegetables to plant behind their country house. Sharing a secret smile at the college graduation of their firstborn child. They'd retire on Sardinia. Or maybe Vancouver Island.

He shivered as a thought slipped into his mind like a cat through a cracked-open door. What if she wasn't who she seemed? What if she was bait? Could he be walking into a trap? He let the scenario play out in his mind before cutting it short. No. That made no sense. The cartels had no reason to play such games. If they wanted him dead that badly, they could have simply sent in another team of sicarios to gun him down. Plus, she was far too sophisticated to be a cartel courtesan. Too aware of the ebb and flow of geopolitics, too ready with witty repartee.

With a soft chime, the elevator doors slid open, and Dag stepped out into the opulent hallway. What a day. He felt simultaneously awash with energy and as if he were perched on a precipice above absolute exhaustion. He had seen combat before, but it had been a few years since he had ventured that close to mortality. Sunlight scintillating across shattered glass. The wild barks and howls of the terrified canine denizens of the park across the street. The bitter aftertaste of the café au lait. Crisis heightened the senses and rendered time as thick as honey. But the backwash of hormones and adrenaline after the emergency passed was the true system shock.

As he lifted a hand to knock on the door of Room 412, he noticed that his fingers were trembling. Get laid. Get rest. Get home. The rest would take care of itself. Death and sex were the classic literary pairing after all, a favorite of poets down the ages. What could be more important than how you were going to die or who you were going to sleep with? Federico finally had his answer to the former. Even though his ears still rang from the gunshots, Dag was determined to contribute an answer to the latter.

When he knocked, the door swung inward at his touch, registering the access she'd granted him. Dag imagined pulling the dress over her head, removing her lingerie with his teeth, running fingertips lightly across the soft skin of her belly. Would she place her glasses on the nightstand or wear them as they made love? A hard-on pressed against the inside of his slacks, and he ran his tongue along the roof of his mouth. He would worship her, taking pleasure in its giving.

"Mind if I join you? You were right, the bartender didn't have a deep reservoir of small talk," he said, stepping into the room and closing the door behind him with a soft click. The lights rose to a low glow, the illicit illumination of a speakeasy. Eager now, pulse accelerating, he moved into the room to join her on the bed, to slide under the sheets and toward ecstasy.

But she wasn't there.

Confused, he peered around the suite. Was she out on the balcony? No, the French doors were closed. Could he have arrived while she was washing up in the bathroom? But as bewilderment dissipated the haze of lust, he realized he wasn't entirely alone.

His erection wilted.

Dag was staring at himself. There on the wall behind him. A mirror, some saner part of his mind posited. But it wasn't a mirror. And it wasn't exactly Dag, or at least, not today's shell-shocked, horny version of himself. It was a photograph, a life-size photograph printed onto a poster.

Autumn leaves carpeted manicured lawns in the background. He stared at the camera with the faux male-model expression, wind tossing his hair. Gretchen had taken that picture. His brash redheaded classmate at Georgetown. It was a silly portrait. Goofing around on the quad in between lectures. They hadn't talked in years. He missed how she'd looked at him, the man he'd seen reflected in her eyes.

Dag's mind reeled. Forcing himself away from the disconcerting photograph, he saw that the entire wall was plastered with images. His senior yearbook picture. His windburned face surrounded by the fur lining of a parka hood. Blowing out a candle of a shared birthday cake at the first foster home in San Diego. Shaking hands with the president, forced smiles against hanging flags. The nurse who'd led seven-year-old Dag away from his aunt's hospital bed after she'd flatlined. Repressing a grin at Diana's antics in a command tent in Namibia. Sean slapping him on the back as they both laughed uproariously at a company barbecue. Lips pursed into an air-kiss for a selfie sent to some forgotten sweetheart. Onstage at a Wall Street press conference. Standing proudly in front of his condo in DC on move-in day.

But he wasn't the subject of every photo. Friends, clients, colleagues, lovers—all of them were pasted on the wall in a chaotic mosaic documenting every moment he'd spent on this planet, including a lurid snapshot from last night's indulgence. Not just people either. Signatures scrawled across the bottom of his client agreement with Lowell Harding next to a snapshot of the man's profile, complete with infectious grin. Redlined treaties Dag had maneuvered the Arctic Council into ratifying. Econometric analyses they'd commissioned for the final SEC appeal. An exchange with Federico's assistant organizing today's meeting. Org charts. Financial models. Topographical maps.

It wasn't just his life—it was his life's work.

Bile rose in his throat. His head swam. His teeth started to chatter. This madness was calling forth the afternoon's trauma. Afraid his knees might give way, he turned to survey the rest of the room. Every wall, even the ceiling, was covered in monstrous, damning, intimate collage. It was too much to take in, too far beyond the borders of normalcy. His mind and heart were already saturated from the day's events. Everything within him rebelled, tried to find context, any kind of halfway reasonable explanation.

His stomach clenched and vomit exploded from his mouth and onto the pristine duvet. Acid and tequila seared his tongue. A wave of dizziness overcame him, and he just managed to catch the edge of the bed, hands smearing puke across the high-thread-count cotton. He retched again but came up empty.

Sucking in a few gasps, he wiped an arm across his mouth and tried to regain control of his body. He squeezed his eyes shut for a second. But when he opened them, he saw the photo above the headboard, and his heart froze.

There they stood. Laughing, radiant, decked out in ridiculous Christmas sweaters, tossing him into the air as he screamed with joy, half-packed bags for their fateful Taipei trip in the background. His parents. The photo that immortalized them, that failed to replace the memories he'd never had a chance to form. How he hated them, how he loved them, how they haunted him. Their absence had sketched the contours of his life.

But that wasn't all. Above the photo, spelled out in enormous mismatched letters, was a question.

Who are you?

CHAPTER 4

Sailboats tacked and jibed across the sparkling San Francisco Bay, whose rising tides nibbled at the edges of coastal real estate. Even with waterfront homes lost to erosion, the Bay Area retained its distinctive charm. Dag ducked as a flock of emerald parrots flapped past, squawking and chortling as they wove their way out over the city. He sucked in a deep breath and smiled. It was a beautiful afternoon. He'd walk to see Sean.

Dag felt freer than he had in years. Between Federico's assassination and . . . whatever he had found in that hotel room, by rights he should be on a psychotherapist's couch. But there was a lightness in his heart, a sweetness on the back of his tongue, a sense of illumination suffusing his limbs.

From Mount Sutro, the whimsical houses and soaring skyscrapers of San Francisco spread out before him like a quilt. It was a rare sunny day. For once, the vast column of smoke from the smoldering inferno that was Southern California must be blowing in another direction. On his flight back from Mexico City this morning, he had peered through the window as the plane detoured around it, Tinseltown and its environs reduced to slag and embers. Years before, the conflict over water rights to the Colorado River had nearly exploded into civil war. Orange County residents fled their McMansions, refugees to wetter climes. The fire was still burning even now. But Northern California had been saved by a combination of Sierra Nevada snowpack and the liberal deployment of tech fortunes.

The clear sky lifted his spirits. Dag was buoyant as he set off down the hill, humming along with an ambient feed playlist while navigating the steep, uneven sidewalk. The deal he had devoted over a year to developing had fallen apart like a house of cards. He'd lost a trusted colleague. Their client would be livid. But the trip to Mexico City had unshackled him, at least temporarily, from the burdens of memory and responsibility. It was as if he had died alongside Federico and today was reincarnated into a more hopeful world.

Was there not room for hope? He might be mired in the weeds of quotidian politics, but if he took a step back, he couldn't deny that there had been some progress. Tax reforms were starting to mitigate America's economic inequality. Public funding for schools had finally outpaced that for prisons. Relaxed immigration and trade rules were reinvigorating a national economy that the West Coast's successive technology revolutions had been shoring up. Washington was still the clusterfuck it always had been, but once in a while, things did get done.

Slightly embarrassed by this uncharacteristically upbeat line of thinking, Dag considered his options. He needed to be prepared to work out a plan with Sean for how to assuage Commonwealth and define a road map for next steps down in Mexico. The Estevez clan was upwardly mobile and needed a bandwagon to jump on. And Apex could woo Francisco Vasquez—winning access to his billionaire aunt with her media empire wouldn't hurt either. Dag had friends at State who could help apply diplomatic pressure. A snide comment at the right cocktail party could go a long way. Losing Federico was a disaster, but disaster made their firm's services that much more indispensable. That was the beauty of lobbying. Regardless, he needed to ensure he was up on the latest news. Nothing undercut an expert's aura of omniscience more than ignorance of the latest piece of journalistic trivia.

Dag summoned his feed and promptly tripped over an exposed root. The sidewalk flew up toward him, and he barely had time to throw his arms out before he hit the cement. The impact knocked the air out of his lungs, and his effort to turn the fall into an awkward roll was only partially successful.

"You okay?" A wizened old woman set down grocery bags overflowing with bok choy and green onions to offer him a hand.

"Yes, I'm fine," he said, accepting her help and rising shakily to his feet. "Thank you."

But he wasn't fine. His heart was racing. He tasted copper and smelled propellant. His balance was wobbly. The sweat he'd worked up on the walk turned cold.

She was right there at the top of his feed, winking on a repeating three-second video loop. Her expression was perky and sly, raven-dark hair framing her heart-shaped face. The woman from the hotel. Room 412.

Forcing himself to start walking again, Dag tried to stop his hands from shaking. Blood oozed from a dozen small lacerations that the sidewalk had torn in his palms. His tongue was thick and sticky in his mouth. His unreasonable optimism of a few moments before seemed to exist in a different, friendlier universe. This wasn't a reincarnation. This was just another day in a world spiraling into madness. Those images, that suite, it had all been real. Dag was familiar with the realities of data breaches. He worked in politics, after all. He'd had to manage fallout from a half dozen different flavors of scandal. But this was different.

He pushed down another wave of nausea, violation manifesting itself in the gut. *Who are you?* The most mundane and intimate moments from his life fashioned into some kind of obsessive patchwork. It brought to mind crime-drama serial killers. But to what end? Blackmail sans directives was a poor form of coercion. The woman winked at him again and again, an infinite loop.

Belatedly, Dag realized that he had arrived.

ANALOG. The wrought iron name was mounted above bronze-bound oak doors. Burly bouncers flanked the entrance, faces blank and eyes obscured by dark sunglasses. Behind them, the windowless matte-black warehouse gave an overall impression that was more medieval fortress than San Francisco retrofit.

Dag dusted off his suit jacket and approached the entrance. The bouncers waved him through without a word. He'd been cleared.

"Welcome to Analog. My name is Nell." Nell looked like she was only here to kill time before her next glamour photo shoot. Pale-gray eyes, smooth dark skin, pageboy haircut, conservative black dress. Nell stood behind a wooden podium in a small but comfortable anteroom. Thick red satin curtains separated them from the club itself. She raised a delicate eyebrow.

"Dag Calhoun," he said, attempting to gather his wits. "Here to see Sean Bancroft."

She consulted a list. A *paper* list, Dag noticed. It looked like fine-grain 100gsm cartridge paper, perfect for pencil and light ink work. Cardboard boxes stuffed with spiral-bound sketchbooks filled an entire closet in Dag's apartment, every page covered in minutely detailed illustrations of fantasy worlds full of savagery and wonder. This place was old-school. Marking something on the sheet, she graced him with the briefest of smiles.

"It looks like this is your first time visiting us," she said. "Go on in, but have a care. Some people find it"—she waggled her head to convey equivocation—"disorienting."

With a bemused shrug, he stepped past her and through the heavy curtain. Having helped satiate the voracious appetites of half the world's oligarchs, he wasn't intimidated by whatever flavor of kink this joint might offer.

A magnificent wood bar lined the entire left side of the vast space, shelves upon shelves of exotic liquors rising up behind bartenders in bow ties and red suspenders. Oil lamps sputtered on chains hanging from the ceiling, casting everything in a warm uneven light. Booths lined the wall opposite the bar, and tables filled the space in between, legs resting on thick Persian rugs. At the far end of the hall, a trio of vizslas napped before a roaring fire in a hearth the size of a bull. One of the dogs stirred, raising its head and transfixing Dag with intelligent golden eyes. Tapestries transformed the windowless walls into scenes of ancient boar hunts and epic battles. A troupe of musicians in a far corner performed wild gypsy folk on accordion, fiddle, and drums.

But something was wrong.

There was a deeper silence behind the music. A quiet no mere noise could fill. It took a moment to register. His feed. His feed was gone. Not dimmed, not marginalized.

Gone.

Dag swayed on his feet. His window into the digital infinite, that whirling vortex of endless global conversation, had been slammed shut. It was always there in the periphery, the low murmur of the entirety of human culture, as present and comforting as the sound of waves from inside a beach house. A vast, pulsing constellation of voices, information, art, commentary, and dramas, distilled through the algorithmic sieve to the intimately relevant personal feed. So second nature that it was obvious only now, in its absence.

It was as if he had gone suddenly, inexplicably deaf.

CHAPTER 5

A hand touched his arm.

"It can take some getting used to, but I think you'll come to appreciate it."

Dag refocused his eyes, forced himself to take a breath. "I . . . uh . . . thank you . . . um . . ."

"Nell." She suppressed a smile.

"Nell, of course, I'm sorry."

She led him like a lost child to a booth near the hearth and vanished as Sean rose to wrap him in a bear hug. His thick red beard scratched against Dag's cheek. As he slid into the booth across from his boss, he was struck by how bright the older man's green eyes were.

Sean pressed his lips together. "I'm glad you're okay, kid," he said, his voice rumbling out of his barrel chest. "It was a close thing."

"Yeah, well, all part of a day's work." Dag shook his head, trying to get his bearings.

"Our little ninja." Sean grinned and twirled a finger in the air. "Wild, right? This place is an institution. They've been off-grid since mobile phones were a thing. The ultimate technocrati social club. Unplug. Defrag. All that jazz. They treat it like an acid trip. The psychedelic of disconnection. Huian Li dreamed up Cumulus in front of that fire. Mara Winkel recruited Vernon Rutherford in this very booth.

It's infamous. You know Lynn Chevalier? The investigative reporter? She's the only person to have ever successfully smuggled an electronic device in and out of Analog. The conversation she recorded brought down Vince Lepardis. To this day, nobody knows how she pulled it off."

Dag was still trying to acclimate to the stillness. They were sitting inside a manufactured anachronism, a bespoke time machine transporting them to a simpler era. The disquieting quiet was profoundly isolating.

"And you didn't think to warn me?"

"Oho, but that would take all the fun out of the experience, wouldn't it?" Sean's wink reminded Dag of the woman who had unaccountably invaded his feed. At least whatever membrane was holding back the digital cosmos had banished her apparition as well.

He shuddered, then tried to play it off. "I'm not sure how I feel about it."

"It'll grow on you," said Sean with a shrug. "Everyone's self-conscious at first. It reminded me of the butterflies I feel before public speaking. Then you sort of settle into it, feel the groove, center yourself. Pretty soon you'll be flying off to meditation retreats every weekend."

With surprising delicacy, Sean slid a tumbler across the table to Dag and then raised his own.

"Talisker 18," said Sean.

Dag raised his glass and noticed a sensual richness as the flickering light from the oil lamps and hearth made the amber scotch appear to glow from within. The fiddler improvised an extraordinary solo, soaring over the quiet murmurs of other patrons. One of the dogs twitched, chasing prey through a dream. The wood grain of the table whorled in a calming pattern. The individual stitches on the tapestry hanging above their booth were neat, firm pixels in a sprawling pastoral scene. Their glasses touched with a soft clink. He inhaled and sipped. Thick with Isle of Skye peat and brine, the whiskey evoked long, hard winters weathered in stout hovels battered by pitiless North Atlantic storms. As

Dag's cognitive dissonance began to resolve, he realized that perhaps this heightened sense of presence, the luxuriance in immediate detail, was a symptom of his absent feed.

"In one hour," Sean said in his get-down-to-business voice, "Rachel Leibovitz is going to walk in that door"—he pointed—"to tear us new assholes. With Federico off the board, what's our next step in Mexico?"

Dag grimaced. "She's coming in herself?"

"The binary baroness. The computer Khan. The cloud queen mother." Sean's bushy eyebrows waggled. "In the flesh."

"Damn," said Dag quietly. Rachel was the legendary chairwoman of Commonwealth, the group of affiliated megacompanies that controlled the world's digital infrastructure. In order to establish Commonwealth as the default infrastructure upon which the feed ran, Rachel had dedicated years and billions of dollars to assembling the best minds in cybersecurity to build what was less a command-line fortress than a resilient, living membrane around their bundle of services. The fact that the feed was so mundane and ubiquitous was a testament to Commonwealth's success at providing a reliable and secure back end. The sovereign monikers were apt. It wasn't a good sign that Rachel was coming in place of her team of corporate lackeys.

"We could rope the cartels in on the deal, but that's not my preference," Dag answered.

"Too realpolitik for the techno-optimists?"

"Incentives just aren't aligned long-term. The cartels will want to milk it, but the whole point is to expand access, not extract rent."

Sean snorted. "Oh, Commonwealth will extract rent all right, but on the back end, not the front end."

"Sure." Dag shrugged. "But the point stands. The deal would be a house with no foundation. Commonwealth is on a crusade against latency, but the cartels are trying to protect the connectivity cash cow. Their infrastructure's way out-of-date, but they won't release their stranglehold. Commonwealth servers and software power the feed for

Mexicans just like everyone else, but Rachel won't settle for anything less than jacking the country directly into its hard-fiber network. That guarantees Mexico is locked in to the Commonwealth ecosystem."

Swirling the liquor in his tumbler, Sean squinted. "Let's cut straight to the meat of your shit sandwich. You didn't come here without a proposal."

CHAPTER 6

Poise. Rachel Leibovitz exuded it like the fire gave off warmth. Her silver hair was tied back into a practical ponytail. A thick scar slashed across her wrinkled face from forehead to cheekbone, the eye it bisected dim and murky, her good eye an imperial purple. An octogenarian, she presided over the coalition of companies that provided the foundation for the digital universe that was absent only here. Her handshake, never reneged, was notorious. Dag had moved to Sean's side of the Analog booth and Rachel sat across from them in her impeccably cut suit, hands clasped before her on the table, fingers interlocked and perfectly still.

"Millions of Mexicans shell out money they can't spare for bandwidth they can't live without," she said in a voice accustomed to command. "If it were up to me, I'd have the UN classify feed connectivity as a basic human right." Dag couldn't help but think how doing so would make the world's nations even more dependent on Commonwealth than they already were. "Letting the cartels ration it out hobbles the entire country. Letting them murder our in-country champion constrains our ability to remedy the situation." She looked pointedly at each of them. "I didn't come here for explanations or excuses. I came here to find out what we do next. The cartels can hold off the inevitable for only so long."

Dag tried to control his nerves. This was the woman who had built the feed from the ground up, and he had met her only once before, on the day their firm was engaged for this project. The seat of its global headquarters, the San Francisco Bay Area had turned into an extended campus for Commonwealth, with skyscrapers and compounds eating up real estate as fast as the coalition could claim it. From high up in one of its graphene monoliths, he had pitched Rachel as they watched the fog roll in to wrap Alcatraz in its damp embrace.

More than just a tech behemoth, Commonwealth was the world leader in corporate social responsibility and worked with local non-profits the world over to address various social issues. Its reign may not have always been so benevolent, but in the lobby on that first visit, Dag hadn't been able to resist a smile as he dodged schoolkids on field trips from two dozen countries. His smile had faded only when he considered his own reason for being there, to lubricate the will to power.

Now, he smoothed his tie and began to outline the plan. Without his feed, he couldn't reference notes or figures, so he had to speak from memory. "We'll call in favors from Alejandro at Pemex," he said, "then tighten the screws by pressuring American importers supplied by *maquiladoras* and amending requirements to inbound World Bank capital. To round things out, we'll send someone to Donya Lajani's annual art auction. Everyone that matters will be there." Bidding on the fruits of human expression was a proxy for negotiating the treacherous waters of human ambition.

Rachel didn't nod, shrug, gesture, comment, object, or ask questions. She just listened. It was the most effective and off-putting interpersonal tactic Dag had ever encountered, and he struggled to maintain his own equanimity in the face of such rapt attention.

Adam's apple bobbing up and down, Dag continued. They would need to host a delegation here in California to bring new players into the fold. He bulleted angle after angle. Sean jumped in with various suggestions. Together, they constructed an exquisite choreography. The universe was malleable, as long as you defined the rules.

But even as he brought the presentation to its conclusion, Dag's mind wandered. One of the bartenders brandished a copper-plated cocktail shaker. Nell escorted another guest to a table of young women immersed in some complex board game. His shoulder throbbed from the fall. He had to blink and look away when he half imagined a glimpse of the winking woman in the dancing flames.

That video clip had had no attribution, which was impossible. That just wasn't how the feed worked. And Room 412 haunted him. Lust doused in intrigue, with disastrous implications. It was a magnet for every shred of paranoia he pretended not to harbor. His elementary school transcripts pinned up alongside snapshots of the porn he'd indulged in only the night before. The trivial details of forgotten escapades were more disturbing than the overtly significant snatches of classified trade secrets.

Who are you?

Something big was going on, but he couldn't even figure out what the ground rules were. There was evidence in that room that could sink Apex, dethrone a half dozen heads of state, and get Dag tried for treason or worse. His mind ran around in circles, trying to fit the available data into a structure that made sense. But there was no way to connect these dots. Or there were too many ways, any of which could get him institutionalized. He couldn't abstract it, couldn't see the game. But that was the thing about games. If you weren't playing, you were being played.

It was time for him to make a move.

"And that's why," said Dag, with a self-effacing nod, "Sean will be taking over this project personally." He felt Sean stiffen in the booth beside him and could imagine the shock and confusion in his eyes. Sean had his own client list, including most of the top quartile of oil executives. But Sean was also a pro with a veteran poker face that would conceal his surprise and discomfort.

"Yes, of course," Sean said quickly. Dag could hear the strain beneath his words, but they were in front of a client, and a unified front was the only option. "Dag will be involved in an advisory capacity every step of the way, but I will move in to advance the ball on the ground. It's our policy to transition in a new partner if projects escalate to direct physical violence. It keeps the opposition on their toes and allows us to complement the experience and intuition of the original lead with a fresh set of eyes and resources. We're already taking the necessary steps."

Rachel just stared at them in silence, and Dag had the sinking feeling that she might have seen through the halting improvisation he had instigated. But there was no alternative.

"Back when Commonwealth was just another Silicon Valley startup, I made a lot of mistakes," she said. "I knew what the world needed. It was obvious. Economists fall all over each other paying lip service to competition. But that's *human* logic. Computers don't care about any of that theoretical stuff. They just care about efficacy. The feed needed solid infrastructure, and a reliable feed would be a platform for a whole new generation of technology companies. I wasn't trying to dream up some grand vision. It just needed to happen."

She leaned forward. "I had a product manager, Gary. He was smart and hardworking, and his team liked him. But when his team built architecture, it was just never quite right. I knew what to do. I'd review everything and tell them how to fix it. Eventually, I started dropping in on their brainstorming sessions for new products to make sure they started out on the right track. But things got worse, not better. Six months later, Gary quit. He ended up founding another company that I had to spend twenty-seven billion dollars on in order to bring it under the Commonwealth umbrella. He could have done that happily as an employee, but I micromanaged him until he couldn't take it anymore."

There was a beat. Then she sniffed. "It was a painful lesson, but eventually I realized that building something meaningful requires you to let go of the obsession with perfection. It requires empowering others and trusting them to do their part, even if they do it differently than you might have. But trust is a two-way street. Autonomy means you're held accountable."

Her single violet eye bored into each of them, unblinking.

"You better know what you're doing," she said.

CHAPTER 7

"What the fuck was that?" Sean slid back into the side of the booth vacated by Rachel. He gripped the edge of the table as if holding himself back, and his cheeks were approaching the color of his beard.

"It's fine," said Dag, a lump forming in his throat. "She said we better know what we're doing, and we do. The plan will work."

"You know damn well that's not what I'm asking about," said Sean. "What the fuck was that? And don't make me ask a third time."

Dag swallowed. He was back in La Condesa, bullets whizzing around him, dogs barking, and patrons screaming. His hands slipped across the vomit-covered duvet as he blinked up at the uncanny gallery. He twitched as the women playing the board game a few tables over broke out in laughter. There was so much to say that he didn't know where to start. Opening his eyes and unclenching his fists, he gazed down at his bloody palms. Scabs were starting to form.

"Son, are you sure you're okay?" Sean looked pointedly at Dag's ravaged hands and then up into his eyes. "Is there something you want to tell me?"

Sean was the first person to ever really believe in him. He had plucked Dag from Georgetown and introduced him to the game-within-the-game, groomed him, taught him everything he knew about the subtle art of professional manipulation. He had challenged Dag with missions of ever-increasing urgency, pursuing ever more paramount ends. Dag had always stepped up to the plate, always underpromised and overdelivered for clients who commanded fortunes, armies, and each other.

But Dag's elevated sensitivity to the details around him was shifting into a new kind of self-awareness. Without the murmur of his feed, there was nothing to dull the sharp edge of hypocrisy. Earlier that day, he had luxuriated in a daydream of how the country was heading in a good direction. But he had made a career out of opposing those very changes and empowering incumbents to build moats around the status quo. For who but the already powerful could afford Apex's rates, the rates that made his status as a newly minted partner such a financial windfall? He helped real estate magnates carve up land beyond the coastal buffer so they could rake in the returns as erosion pushed communities to higher ground. He bartered water-rights transactions that cursed downstream towns to fade into dusty oblivion. He was a knight defending the divine rights of wealth.

There was a beat. The anger written across Sean's features transformed to a look of concern. He was a good man, a good mentor. Dag had capitalized on that, leveraging Sean to secure a steady series of promotions. Dag should tell him about the woman, the room. They were a complication. The firm needed to know, lest he put them all at risk. He was a partner. They were a team. The whole situation was just so strange, so personal, the motive so obscure. *Someone might be blackmailing me, but I don't know who or why, and there are no demands.* Is that what he was supposed to say? Yes, that was precisely what he was supposed to say. The delicacy of their work required full internal disclosure.

And yet. When Congress had subpoenaed Dag to testify about the Arctic deal, Sean had coached him through the whole process. *When facts won't do, good lobbyists lie.* He held up a thick finger and smiled through his beard. *Great lobbyists are like novelists, they use lies to tell a deeper truth.* Lowell had adored that line when Dag passed it along over bourbons after the hearing.

Dag looked Sean in the eye. "Have I ever asked you for a favor?"

Lamplight played across the hardening lines of Sean's face. "Dag, what's going on? You're our best operator, and nobody has better relationships in Mexico. Why would you do something like that?"

Dag felt a flush of pride at Sean's praise. Its rarity gave it weight. But that didn't change what had to happen next, or how much it would disappoint the firm. Butterflies fluttered in Dag's stomach.

"I need to take a leave of absence," he said.

CHAPTER 8

Leaves of absence were supposed to be fun. Blow off steam on a private jet hopping from metropolis to metropolis, picking up exuberant newcomers and dropping off exhausted veterans of a never-ending airborne sex party hosted by a billionaire princeling. Go on a backcountry trek to Bhutan where a perilous journey through the Himalayas forces you to discover new things about your own personal quest for meaning. Or maybe sit back and relax, get your house in order, and catch up on all that reading you've been meaning to do for so many years. Refreshed, rejuvenated, and energized, you return to work brimming with perspective and an unflagging sense of mission.

This wasn't that.

Dag had spent the first week of leave on an obsessive quest to root out information on the woman from Room 412. He had scoured the feed, surreptitiously reached out to law enforcement contacts, and called in as many favors as he dared. He'd even set up a meeting with Diana.

But it was all to no avail.

There just wasn't anything to go on. He had no name, no image, no address. Nothing. At random intervals, she would flash into his feed like a mosquito buzzing past your ear as you tried to fall asleep. And like such mosquitos, she seemed impossible to catch. That left Dag in a vicious spiral fueled by fascination and frustration.

It wasn't just the sense of personal violation that scared him. If even a small percentage of the contents of Room 412 leaked, this leave of absence would become permanent. Sean's career would be over too, and the way these things went, half their contacts would go down with them. Dag remembered the taste of dust on his tongue as he and Lowell drove along Northern California suburban byways scoping out undervalued acreage that the coming disasters would transmute to prime real estate. Dag had made partner at Apex because of his discretion, his capacity to handle situations that regular lobbyists couldn't, his knack for solving impossible problems without raising awkward questions. The questions raised by Room 412 weren't awkward.

They were apocalyptic.

Pushing the inbound and outbound flight manifests from Mexico City International Airport to the edges of his feed, Dag looked around the Berkeley hotel room that had inadvertently become his little command center. Sunlight glowed through silk curtains. The sheets were a rumpled mess. Stubble shadowed the jaw of his reflection in the mirror.

He should have been out of here days ago, on to the next stage of the search. Instead, here he was. Wheels spinning.

Dag stood and stretched, feeling muscles strain and joints pop. Adding a dose of stir-crazy to his already volatile mood wasn't going to get him anywhere. Maybe he just needed to get outside, force his mind onto other things so that the search could ferment in his unconscious. Maniacal focus wasn't always the best path. Sometimes you had to find a new angle, slice a problem into pieces and reassemble it again and again until something clicked.

Afternoon sunlight lanced into his eyes as he threw open the door and stepped outside. He had to blink away purple blotches and swirls to regain his vision before picking a direction at random and setting out down the street.

Berkeley was an odd town. It was a world unto itself, a quality usually limited to major cities like Shanghai or New York. Here, slightly off-kilter progressive values paired with an almost academic sense of moral superiority made up for the small population with strident advocacy. There was an unusual number of backyards featuring expansive chicken coops. "Free Tibet" placards championed a cause the rest of the world had long since abandoned. It was the kind of place where a city council meeting about zoning might be overwhelmed by an impromptu poetry slam filled with impassioned manifestos that channeled Marx with nostalgia for a revolution that had never materialized.

Dag retraced a step and did a double take. There, down a deserted back alley, a line of matryoshka dolls faced out from a grimy window. A small sign hung above the window, upon which illustrated paintbrushes formed a kind of insignia.

Curiosity piqued, Dag wandered up the alley to investigate.

The entrance was below street level, and he had to descend a crumbling concrete staircase to reach it. A bell tinkled as the door swung shut behind him, and he waited for a moment to let his eyes adjust to the gloom.

"The bathroom is for customers only!" an angry voice called out from behind a line of shelves piled with ancient turntables, record players, and phonographs. A bout of violent coughing followed this pronouncement.

"Don't worry," said Dag. "I'm not looking for a restroom."

A bent elderly man tottered out from the maze of shelves, bifocals making his sour expression almost comical. He wore a tattered tweed jacket and smelled distinctly grandfatherly. Wisps of white hair clung to the sides of his bald pate like desperate alpinists to an uncaring cliff.

"Well then." He squinted suspiciously at Dag. "What do you want?"

"I noticed the matryoshka in the window and was hoping to have a look around."

"Hmmph," said the old man, as if Dag had threatened nuclear war. "Make it quick, and don't you dare try to flounce out of here without making a purchase. This is a business, not an amusement park."

With that, the proprietor coughed again and retreated behind a small counter in the corner. Although the man ostensibly ignored everything but the pocket watch he was inspecting, Dag couldn't shake the feeling that his every move was being watched, weighed, and judged.

Dag soon discovered that this strange little establishment offered far more than retro sound equipment. It was a weird amalgam of antique and art-supply shop. There were baseball cards of minor players from the twentieth century alongside a surprisingly large array of pastels. Cast-iron tortilla presses were stacked haphazardly in a crate next to a collection of vintage frames and fresh canvases in a variety of sizes. Paintbrushes sat in neat racks balanced against a wall lined with grandfather clocks that ticked and tocked in almost-but-not-quite unison.

He found the bizarre collection of relics reassuring in a hard-to-define way. He'd always loved history, and these items were clues to a forgotten past, a whole series of worlds that would never be seen again. It was almost as if he might be able to escape the dark environs of his personal history if he could immerse himself in that of others. Like memory, history was synthetic. Humans thought of both as factual records, but study after study confirmed that they were more like dreams, narratives constructed and reconstructed by the mind to fit the demands of the present, not the reality of the past.

Whenever he came across these kinds of antiques, Dag couldn't help but imagine the father who might have gifted the set of dolls to his young daughter in far-off Saint Petersburg or the horologist who might have last repaired the clocks with painstaking precision.

And that's when it hit him. Not a brilliant flash of realization but the delayed recognition of something so obvious that its discovery was more frustrating than inspiring. It might not even work. But even the sliver of a chance was better than straining against the yoke of futile investigation in a shitty hotel room.

It must be here somewhere.

There.

An entire shelf was devoted to paper, pens, and pencils. He selected a large spiral-bound sketchbook and a set of fine art pencils before making his way to the counter.

"Leaving so soon?" The old man remained surly and gruff, but seemed to be enjoying the company. "Did you see my collection of baseball cards? I've got vintage Barry Bonds back from when people still liked him."

"You've got a great collection," said Dag. "But this'll be all."

"Hmmph." The proprietor frowned. "Well, a young man like you must need a discount, times being what they are."

"Thanks," said Dag. "I appreciate the sentiment, but I'm happy to pay full price. I found what I needed."

"Nonsense," said the old man. He reached under the counter and pulled out a jug of clear liquid and a pair of shot glasses. "Here, to fortify your health and inspire the Muses to whisper in your ear."

"Really, I'm—"

"I distilled it myself," said the old man proudly. "Quality gin. Only the best. You can't trust what you find in the liquor store anymore."

He handed over a shot, which Dag accepted reluctantly, then raised his own.

"To survival," he said in his thin, reedy voice. "If you can't beat 'em, outlive 'em."

"I'll drink to that," said Dag.

It tasted like gasoline, but Dag kept it down.

Approving the purchase via feed, Dag was amazed when the old man used an antique physical screen to process it. It was hard to remember that there were still some people who lived their whole lives as if in Analog, peering into the global hive mind of whirling information only through shards of glass.

Perhaps the worthiest antique in this shop was its owner.

CHAPTER 9

Dag lurched in surprise as a hand appeared out of nowhere to caress his cheek.

"Jesus Christ, Diana," he said, turning. "Why do you always have to do that? I could have fallen." He indicated the precipice only a meter away. They stood atop Indian Rock, the massive outcropping of gray boulders that rested in a quiet residential neighborhood of the Berkeley hills like slumbering giants from a medieval fairy tale.

"Oh, the melodrama! You're just so *cute*, I couldn't resist." Diana, surely an alias, twirled a forefinger in her brunette curls in full faux flirt. She was neither beautiful nor ugly, neither fat nor skinny, neither tall nor short. Her brown eyes and freckled face were friendly but unremarkable. She was someone you wouldn't notice in a crowd, someone eminently forgettable. That was likely why she had been recruited by the intelligence community in the first place, skipping from agency to agency like a bored toddler until she tired of the bureaucracy and struck out on her own. "You're particularly jumpy today, though. Relax. Drink a smoothie. Schedule a vacation."

Dag smothered a grin—she might be his go-to consultant when he needed a guide to the shadow world, but she was also irrepressible. She had funneled him trade secrets as they negotiated with OPEC and had made that incendiary video of Senator MacMillan disappear. She'd introduced him to the discreet security outfit they'd used for the Arctic operation, the introductory message nestled away in a secure cache but bursting with emojis. He heaved a theatrical sigh. "A holiday sounds wonderful—do you think you could help me arrange that as well?"

The ringlet of hair sprang free. "Oh, I don't think you could afford my rates as a travel agent," she said. "Haven't you heard? I'm *very* exclusive. Not for small-fry."

"Are you saying I'm small-fry?"

She rolled her eyes. "Ahh, the endless bounties of male ego. I hope this new love interest of yours appreciates your boorish attitude."

"I told you, she's not a love interest. And that's not what I meant."

"I was starting to feel jealous, but then, wow, is she out of your league. I mean, you have as much of a chance as an earthworm aspiring to win an Olympic gold. No matter how much wriggling he does, it's not going to help his triple axel. You're better off getting into figure skating yourself. My second cousin is a coach up in Minnesota. I could introduce you."

Dag stepped toward Diana, suddenly intent.

May I join you? He could almost taste the tequila, almost feel the energy in her gaze. The first thing he did upon stepping out of Analog two weeks ago was check his feed. But she was gone. In her place was footage of mass migrations from flooding Bangladesh, a dozen messages marked urgent, a report from one of his contacts in Juárez, and a self-important expert predicting the demise of yet another round of international climate change negotiations. No matter how he searched, he couldn't locate the clip. The original post had no attribution, and now it had vanished into the ether. Two impossibilities in one.

She had disappeared as mysteriously as she had from the hotel in Mexico City. He had checked it out, of course. But the staff reported that no guest had been registered for Room 412 that night and no, housekeeping had noticed no irregularities when they freshened up the suite. The local security firm that had supplied his bodyguards for the meeting with Federico procured surveillance footage, but all the relevant coverage was conveniently riddled with technical errors.

"Does that mean you found her?" he asked, unable to keep the urgency from his tone. The woman had dropped into his feed again at random intervals, even as his search intensified into an obsession. She blew him a kiss, pushed her thick-framed glasses up her nose, frowned in concentration. Every time it was nothing more than a few seconds. Every time it was unattributed. And every time it would disappear before he was able to capture any record of its existence.

"Whoa, cowboy," said Diana. "Hard to believe she's not a heartthrob, if that's how you react."

He clenched his fists. The frustration of fruitless pursuit tightened his chest. Without a name, a picture, a DNA sample, he had nothing to go on. He had replayed their conversation at the hotel bar time and again, trying to tease out any detail that might be useful, anything that could provide a chink in the fortress of his ignorance. Sean had given him a month, had promised to smooth it over with the partnership, blame it on emotional fallout from the assassination. Four short weeks to get to the bottom of this mess, unravel the tangled setup that he had somehow found himself at the center of. And two weeks had yielded nothing but insomnia and self-doubt.

"Enough games," he said. "I need to know."

"Let's take it one step at a time," she said. Opening her purse, she pulled out a large spiral-bound sketchbook and handed it over. "I made a few, uhh, improvements to your work. I hope you don't mind. In fact, I think you'll like it."

He accepted the sketchbook, remembering the harsh burn of bootleg gin.

"Diana."

"This was a highly unusual job," she said. "I mean, I'm the best in the world at what I do, obviously." She offered a wry curtsy. "So you came to the right person. But this wasn't so much finding a needle in a haystack as inventing a method for constructing a needle from its component subatomic particles." Her expression turned thoughtful. "I like a challenge—you should bring me puzzlers like this more often. Most projects are ever so boring. I mean, how many politicians have mistresses? How many bumbling executives expose themselves to data breaches? Who's even surprised by that kind of stuff anymore? Can't we all just get along?"

"Diana."

"Fine, fine. You know how to take all the fun out of a thing, don't you? There is one last thing before I give you the goods, though. I noticed you're not using the normal account."

"Don't worry, you'll get your money."

She tapped her chin. "Not on Apex's orders, then."

"I'm working independently on this one."

"Has someone been a naughty boy? I saw some unfortunate news reports from Mexico City. I'm glad we don't meet for macchiatos." She formed a pistol with her forefinger and thumb, blowing away imaginary gun smoke.

"You're paid handsomely to not ask questions."

"Oh, you don't have to worry about me spilling your beans." She zipped her mouth shut with a thumb and forefinger. "But it's my business to know my clients' business. Otherwise, you can never know what you might get caught up in. A girl has to be careful."

Dag authorized the final payment.

"There," he said. "Does that clear things up?"

"You know, Ursula K. Le Guin wrote that knowing a person's true name gives you power over them."

"And what is that supposed to mean?"

"Emily Kim," she said, raising her hands and wiggling her fingers as if in mystical incantation. "Emily Kim, Emily Kim, Emily Kim. Emily Kim."

Dag's jaw muscles bunched as he stared at Diana for a long moment.

"You found her," he said, barely able to believe it.

Diana granted him access to a secure cache of files. "Oh, she's a sly one, your portrait model, a ghost, barely any digital presence at all. But that's her all right. Once I get a scent . . . Well, let's just say that I know my business."

"Emily Kim," he murmured to himself. Opening the sketchbook, he examined his handiwork. There she sat, nursing her cocktail at the bar. Then a close-up of her expression from the first time he looked up from the table on the balcony. He had reconstructed various angles of her face from his memories of their conversation over Casa Dragones. And, of course, flashes from the clips that snuck into his feed. He had drawn every portrait in fine art pencil, the graphite lines and textures contrasting sharply against the cream paper. Holed up in the hotel room, he'd allowed himself to get lost in the act of creation like he hadn't in years. The curve of a stroke, the pressure on the page, the scritch-scratch of the pencil—it was an all-consuming thing, a black hole of attention.

Drawing was his refuge. Imagination was the one place he could find escape and absolution. It was where he retreated when the world became too painful, where he could get out from under the yoke of the demands placed on him at every turn, whether it was abusive, drug-addled foster parents or university exams. He had poured the confusion and insanity of the last two weeks into every shade and flourish, and Emily Kim had come alive on the page in all her strange, seductive humanity. Diana had taken the sketches, tunneled into theoretically impenetrable databases, and correlated her way through facial recognition and special-purpose search algorithms to track down and identify the woman who had been naught but a digital wraith.

"Whaddaya think? Can I grow up to be an artist?"

Diana had decorated the white space around each portrait with hearts, stars, and swirls inked in bright, sparkly nail polish. Dag ignored her quip, looking up from the page and out at the horizon. Across the bay, the deep-orange sun had just touched the top of the Golden Gate Bridge as North America rotated into night. Skyscrapers gleamed, the ruffled surface of the bay was liquid silver, and the Berkeley campus glowed with light that would make a photographer swoon. Dag smelled eucalyptus and watched a hawk circle lazily overhead. The smoke from Southern California was blowing north again, peppering the air with a faint scent of ash and turning this sunset skyscape into a riotous bouquet of color. Emily Kim was out there somewhere, and he was going to find her.

"Be careful, lover boy." Diana gave him an odd look, unaccustomed tenderness shining through her jaded whimsy. "I'd hate to see something happen to that cute little face of yours."

CHAPTER 10

Dag slipped on a piece of seaweed, but he took a heavy step forward and caught his fall. The gray kayak he was dragging down to the water was loaded with gear, which made hauling it awkward. The redhead at the rental shop shared a tide chart in his feed and handed him a jacket with a smile. Most tourists didn't come in for multiday rentals. The scratch of the gravel against the hull quieted as the nose reached the shallows.

Double-checking everything, he pulled on the skirt, slid his legs into the kayak, and sealed the elastic neoprene around the cockpit. The last rays of sunlight had faded from the snowy peak of Mount Baker behind him, and it was full dusk. The ocean was shifting from slate gray to black, and the San Juan Islands were nothing but shadowy humps of darkness in the distance.

Retrieving the paddle, Dag raised his arms and scooted his hips forward. Once. Twice. On the third try, the kayak slid silently into the glassy waters of Lummi Bay. In his black hooded spray jacket, he would be as insubstantial as a ghost to any passersby gazing out at the deepening night.

Reviewing the wind, current, and swell data, he dipped the paddle into the brine and glided out to sea. Once on course, he dialed down feed opacity and stared out into the darkness. Diana's cache hadn't contained everything he needed, but it had given him enough evidence to continue the chase on his own. He had peeled away shell companies like layers of an onion, unraveled the cat's cradle of offshore accounts, back-channeled information requests through inside contacts, and finally traced Emily Kim to a private island off the northern coast of Washington State that supposedly held a foundation and boarding school under her direction.

The salty air was chilly and sharp, smelling of fish, marine diesel, and rotting seaweed. Dag placed the paddle into the water at an angle that minimized noise and spray. Once the blade was submerged, he pulled strongly, leveraging his hips and back to maximize force. After half an hour, he fell into a rhythm, one stroke after another in a constant, timeless gait. There was a lot of water to cover.

When Dag was seven years old, he'd been placed in his third foster home, this one in East County San Diego. It turned out to be a foster farm, the parents harboring as many kids as they could squeeze into their squalid bungalow to collect and skim the government support payments. Now he saw them for who they were: pathetic, petty fraudsters taking advantage of a flawed system. But at the time, they had been the despots of his universe, using their flock to mass-produce handmade wooden rosaries that they sold at a hefty artisan markup via feed.

Dag still remembered the first day. Despite the experience of his previous two foster homes, he had harbored the unlikely hope that this one would be different. When the social worker dropped him off, his new guardians had said all the right things, smiled in the right places, wrapped him in sweaty but affectionate hugs.

But as soon as the checklist was complete and the bureaucrat holding it had disappeared in a cloud of parched dust, the pretense had dropped. Dag poured his desperate need for love into a trembling smile, and they had handed him a crate of unpolished wooden beads and a bottle of spray varnish. The only thing worse than his foster parents were his foster siblings. Childhood was rendered innocent only in the rose-tinted memories of adults. Something started building inside Dag like steam filling a kettle.

One day, after he finished tidying up the master bedroom, he slipped through the back door and wandered through the neighborhood until he found a bus stop. The bus ferried him through neighborhoods baking in summer heat and eventually deposited him in the beatific beach holdout of La Jolla. Even then, the rising ocean was making incursions. But the sea lions hadn't yet abandoned the rocky point, and Dag spent hours staring out at them, face pressed up between the bars of the railing bordering the sidewalk. Tourists and joggers bustled by, but he paid them no mind. His consideration was only for the sea lions. There they lay, shiny and fat as sausages, snoring and cavorting on the warm rocks like they had not a care in the world. The tang of gull guano tickled his nostrils. And then, on whatever whims flutter through the minds of pinnipeds, they would plunge off the rocks and into the surf, where the bulk and flippers that made them so awkward on land turned them into instruments of grace beneath the waves.

That had been the first thing he'd drawn, a sea lion kingdom hidden in a deep ocean trench safe from the predations of adults. Adults were the end of all good things. The lifeguard had proved that right, to Dag's dismay but not surprise. He was quite precocious when it came to fatalism. The lifeguard smiled and offered him a candy bar and promised to help. But in the end, he turned Dag over to a police officer, who delivered him back to his foster home, where retribution was exacted to rein in his wanderlust. Despite it all, Dag never forgot that beautiful things could exist in a world of hurt, or that there were beings on this earth who could nap on rocks and do underwater somersaults whenever they pleased.

A foghorn blew in the distance, and he returned to the reality of churning muscles and sea spray. What the hell was he doing out here alone in an expedition-grade ocean kayak packed with firearms and tactical gear? Why in seven hells hadn't he told Sean—whose respect he'd dedicated years to earning—what he'd found in Room 412? Dag had finally cultivated a streak of good luck. Thanks in no small part to his mentor's tutelage, he was a rising star at a prestigious firm that pulled geopolitical strings from behind closed doors.

Yet here he was, paddling into a dark and dangerous unknown.

He had never checked up on that particular set of foster parents or siblings, but he could safely assume they were dead or deadbeats. They wouldn't even recognize him now, and if they did, it might push them into the cardiac arrest they so deserved. He didn't pretend to care that San Diego was now nothing but a charcoal pit. So why had he gamely dodged out a side door after flying home from Mexico City? It wasn't like he hadn't lived through various and sundry disaster scenarios before.

Dag leaned back. It was a clear night, and stars wheeled above the Salish Sea like pilgrims around the Kaaba. He was nothing. A short-lived speck on a meaningless rock orbiting an insignificant star in a forgotten galaxy in a universe bound by the unflinching laws of thermodynamics to descend into ultimate heat death. For a moment, the veneer of paranoia that laced this excursion fell away to reveal the unadulterated curiosity beneath. Whatever was at the center of this uncanny labyrinth, he wanted to press his face to the railing and stare.

CHAPTER 11

As Dag hauled the kayak up underneath the trees, dawn broke over the eastern horizon, setting wisps of morning mist aflame. He had beached in a secluded cove on an undeveloped corner of the island, far from the main dock. The temperate rainforest was thick with brambles and the rich smell of loam. Pines, oaks, and madrones formed a gray-green canopy overhead, and the ground beneath his feet was soft and spongy.

Dag stripped off the spray jacket, perspiration evaporating off his shoulders. No mistakes this time. He tried to remember the grizzled infiltration instructor from his month of special operations training in Namibia seven years ago. Sean had called it commando camp, arranging for Dag to attend once he proved himself capable of falling into dangerous situations. Lobbyists rarely needed such expertise, but on the singular occasions when they did, it paid to have someone who could fieldstrip a gun in addition to tying a tie. Dag was reluctant, and didn't like the "ninja" nickname it earned him around the stuffy K Street office. The biggest lesson he'd taken away from Namibia was how hopelessly useless a month of training was against professionals who'd spent their lives in the shadows. On the other hand, that's where he'd met Diana, who was already working freelance and ran the cyber component of the course. Ever since, Dag had tapped her when Apex needed covert help.

Time to polish those rusty skills.

Dag kneeled and methodically unpacked the kayak, cataloging each piece of gear against his feed checklist. Once everything was laid out on the forest floor, he removed the rest of his clothing. His nipples hardened and penis shrank in the chill as he stood naked under the whispering leaves. Then he pulled on a tight-fitting base layer and a camouflaged jumpsuit, matching backpack, gloves, and soft-soled boots. He strapped a holster to his right thigh, checked the handgun, and slid it into place. He did the same to the submachine gun slung on a strap across his shoulder, magnetically held in place for snug convenience and quick retrieval.

Be careful, lover boy, I'd hate to see something happen to that cute little face of yours. Diana needn't worry. There was no private security team protecting his person on this mission, but he had come prepared. He'd had enough surprises lately. This wasn't another diplomatic cocktail party. His muscles felt like jelly when he stretched, but aside from the firearms, the outfit was as weightless and flexible as a second skin.

Kneeling, he stuffed an energy bar into his mouth and washed it down with electrolyte-fortified water. Packing the discarded clothes and backup provisions into the cargo hatch, he pushed the kayak deep underneath an enormous blackberry thicket. Stepping back, he circled the bush until he was satisfied that no adventurous hiker would stumble across the boat.

Inhaling deeply, he savored the scent of pine, sea breeze, and damp earth. Ferns sprang up in prehistoric curls, and moss turned the occasional boulders into brooding green life-forms all their own. Sunlight slipped through gaps in the canopy to dapple the forest floor like a leopard's coat. Calling up a topographical overlay in his feed, Dag confirmed his position, marked the location of the kayak, and set off along the route he had mapped out yesterday.

This side of the island was a natural reserve filled with old-growth forest and polka-dotted by the occasional meadow. To get to the other side, he circumnavigated the large hill that dominated the island's geography and whose trails offered unparalleled views of Mount Baker and the San Juans. But Dag kept off the trails, skirting meadows, dropping into ravines, and traversing ridgelines through woodland that had remained largely unchanged for thousands of years.

Reaching the top of a small hill, he caught his first glimpse of the compound through a break in the trees. An old barn sat off to one side, abutting a rolling pasture where cows chewed their cud, jaw muscles bunching as they masticated grass in the morning sunshine. Satellite dishes and antennae bristled from the roof of a large, rambling ranch house perched on top of a low rise, overlooking the entire property. Below it, chickens pecked in the courtyard of a large horseshoe-shaped building that had the same style of shingled, vine-covered walls as the house but looked like newer construction. Firewood was piled in long stacks beside a shed, and smoke billowed lazily into the air from what appeared to be an old-fashioned smoker. Beyond that, a dock jutted out from the rocky shore, and a catamaran, a fishing trawler, and a number of smaller craft were moored along it. A boathouse stood off to one side, and a seaplane bobbed at anchor farther offshore. Everything matched the latest satellite imagery, which Dag found vaguely disappointing.

Descending the hill, he headed west and slowly circled the property from the cover of the trees. This was a private island, and the compound was the only development. Forest blanketed the rest, interrupted only by hiking trails, deer paths, and the occasional gravel utility road.

Approaching from a new angle, Dag dropped to the ground and slithered up into a tight cluster of saplings that gave him a view of the grounds. Zooming in, he scrutinized the compound. From this vantage, he spotted a few new details. Rotors drooped from a helicopter resting on a pad that had been hidden by the main building from his previous outlook. Bees buzzed and orbited around a long row of hives. A neatly organized grid of raised beds grew enough produce to feed a small village. Pigs nuzzled for fallen apples in a small orchard nestled behind the barn.

All of a sudden, the central door of the main building burst open, and Dag's hand twitched toward the submachine gun before he assured himself that there was no way he had been spotted. Instead of the heavily armed security officers he was expecting, at least two hundred children of various ages poured out into the courtyard, laughing, shouting, and pushing each other. A pair of younger ones—Dag estimated them at six years old—chased after the squawking chickens until an adult in a tweed jacket and horn-rimmed spectacles stuck his head out of a window and shouted them off. The crowd migrated over to the open grassy knoll that led down to the dock and split off into smaller groups, sitting on the grass, talking loudly, and chasing the occasional Frisbee.

Dag's heart pounded in his chest. He summoned an overlay of the data he'd dug up on Ms. Kim. This was the only geolocation he'd been able to tie her to. The island was officially designated as the headquarters of her charitable foundation and attached boarding school. But after sifting through so many shell companies and offshore accounts, Dag had assumed this was just another piece of clever misdirection. Foundations and private schools were notorious covers for large-scale money laundering, and this must simply be another domino in whatever scheme Kim was running. But actually hosting two hundred laughing, mischievous children on-site was extravagant prestidigitation.

The alternative, that this establishment was legitimate, was even more unsettling. If Kim was indeed the executive director of a nonprofit and principal of an exclusive boarding school, then what had she been doing in Mexico City and why had she ambushed Dag with Room 412? It didn't add up. The inconsistencies dividing the idyllic scene from the disturbing memories made his palms sweat.

A bell rang from the main building, which Dag now thought of as the school, and the students reluctantly started to make their way back inside. Some of the smaller kids chased each other all the way up to the courtyard, unwilling to forfeit their game of tag. The teenagers hung back, lagging behind the throng, clearly considering whether they might be able to skive off and get away with it. But within ten minutes, everyone had returned to the mother ship.

As the sun climbed to and descended from its zenith, Dag continued his remote observations of the property. The students emerged every couple of hours for a break or exercise. He counted 245 of them. A number of adults moved around the property as well. Teachers took lunch breaks and crossed the courtyard between classes. People ferried back and forth between the ranch house on the hill and the school, sometimes taking shifts tending the animals or the garden. A boat arrived with supplies, and a motley group of older students carried the crates up. A grizzled old man split firewood with an ax, a sheepdog snoozing next to him in the sun.

By the time dusk fell, Dag was struggling to keep his eyes open. He hadn't slept in more than thirty-six hours, and when he blinked, he slipped into staccato increments of sleep. When he forced his eyelids open for too long, sparklers went off in his peripheral vision. Unzipping a pocket, he popped a gel into his mouth, letting the rush of sugar and caffeine buoy his flagging body.

Had this trip been nothing but a waste of time? Was this month of leave a monumental mistake? He should be back in La Condesa wooing new allies to Commonwealth's cause and racking up billable hours. This might be the stupidest thing he'd ever done, risking his career on a wild-goose chase. He hadn't caught a single glimpse of Kim—maybe she wasn't even here. She could be halfway around the world messing with the mind of another hapless victim. This might be the only physical place he could connect her name to, but that didn't tell him anything about her current location. It was even possible that her connection to this island was fabricated, carefully engineered into the tortuous trail of digital debris attached to her identity.

But if he had learned anything from Sean and his worldly intu-ition, it was that nobody was squeaky clean. And if he had learned anything from Diana and her irreverent hypercompetence, it was that nobody was perfect. Everyone had a secret, and nobody could ever keep them, so there was always a way in. If this was all a setup, then it was a supremely sophisticated one. It was far more likely that he was teasing a thread. He might not yet see the full pattern, but it would start to unravel soon.

Pushing himself up onto stiff legs, Dag slipped through the trees toward the back of the property. It was almost midnight, and the lights in the dorm wing of the school had long since gone out. A few windows in the ranch house still glowed, but he needed to get moving, to do something instead of just watch. There was something here he could use—there had to be.

Jogging along in a low crouch, he crossed the gap between the forest and the pasture, and vaulted over the fence. The barn blocked the view from the house, but even if someone was looking, he would be just another shadow. He dodged fresh cow pies, glowing green on infrared, as he slunk across to the barn, aching muscles grateful to get loosened up.

The barn door was barred but not locked. Raising the wooden beam, he opened the door and slid inside. It smelled of hay, manure, and livestock. Soft grunts and the sound of large animals shifting on their feet made the place feel alive. The cows shone in his night vision, resting in their stalls. Nothing appeared out of place. This barn was just a barn. Sensing Dag, the nearest cow swung its head to the side and lowed. He stepped back outside and barred the door before any more of the animals woke and drew attention with a bovine chorus.

Keeping his gait steady and feet light, he moved along the wall of the barn and struck out across the grounds toward the next building. Staying in the shadow of the long row of stacked firewood, he snuck up to the shed. This was where the old man had labored with an ax in the late afternoon. No lock here either, and no animals to give away his location. The shed turned out to be a full workshop. There were band saws, work tables, additive and subtractive 3-D printers, wood chisels, laser cutters, a micro clean room with a chip baker, and all manner of raw materials. A cornucopia of tools hung in neat rows according to size and function. It looked like a skilled craftsperson could fashion almost anything in here, from a dovetail joint to an integrated circuit. Dag moved silently around the room, running his gloved fingertips along the blades of power tools and carefully twisting his feet in the fine layer of sawdust so as not to leave clear tracks. Once he had mapped the place out in his mind, he stepped back out into the night.

It was hard to keep the dozens of theories flitting through his mind at bay. He was in data-acquisition mode, and fitting a thesis to a limited data set could blind you to the most important clue. For now, he needed to keep his thinking open and his touch light. Only when he had uncovered a critical mass of evidence could he draw useful conclusions. But he couldn't help but think that this was a fool's errand. He was infiltrating a boarding school as if it were a secret military installation. Instead of bypassing heavily armed patrols and dodging drones, he was slinking around barns and toolsheds. Maybe he should abort this whole misadventure, try to forget Room 412, and get back to work.

He crossed the lawn, steering well clear of the school, and descended the slope where students had played Frisbee that morning. Waves lapped against the barnacle-encrusted pilings of the dock. The sharp saline tang of the sea filled his nostrils. He imagined how its rising waters had encroached on the island's shoreline centimeter by centimeter, year after year, until the beaches were submerged and salt had withered the roots of the outermost trees, the bathtub of the world's oceans filling to reclaim every island.

The boathouse wasn't locked either. Dag considered how safe the island's residents must feel to leave their structures unsecured. This was a world away from the urban milieu he inhabited, where victims were often scoffed at for gullibility and a coffee meeting might mutate into a gunfight. Inside, it smelled of tar and diesel. Loops of rope were piled in a corner, folded sails stacked beside them. There was a marine-engine repair station with all the requisite equipment. A few small sailboats were dry-docked and midway through a maintenance regimen. Wet suits and scuba gear filled one corner, along with every conceivable kind of fishing accessory. Like the barn and the workshop, this boathouse appeared to be well equipped but innocent.

Then Dag's heart leapt into his throat, and he blinked rapidly to clear his vision. He strode across the room with no deference to tradecraft. His hand found the grip of the submachine gun. Anxiety sent tremors through every nerve ending.

There, resting contentedly on a rack, was his kayak.

CHAPTER 12

Emily Kim came out to collect firewood the following morning.

Dag was positioned in the same copse of saplings overlooking the ranch house. Adrenaline and caffeine gels had fueled his vigilance through the night. Thoughts ebbed and flowed. How had they located his stash and retrieved his only mode of transport on and off the island? The thermal blanket folded away in his backpack had helped stave off the chill, but he was still shivering.

Her appearance stunned Dag. He had lost faith that she was anywhere close to this island, had decided that his best chance was to find a clue here that would reveal yet another set of tracks to follow. But there she was, flannel shirt over faded jeans, the cold morning turning her hot breath into puffs of condensation. She scooped up a generous armful of firewood and returned to the house, wiping the dew from her boots before opening the back door and stepping inside.

As soon as the door shut behind her, Dag realized his error. He had missed the perfect opportunity. It was early, and nobody else had yet appeared anywhere on the property. She had been less than twenty meters from him, so close he could see how her overlarge glasses steamed up when she exhaled. He couldn't have hoped for a better chance. He bit his cheek and tasted blood. All this planning, all this preparation, and he had lain there shivering and ogling like an amateur.

And then, a second glimpse. Curtains were drawn aside from an upstairs window, and Dag could see into a room with a circular wooden table set for breakfast. Kim stretched, arching her back like a cat, and found herself a seat facing away from the window. Her jet-black hair sucked at Dag's attention like a vacuum. Who was she, and what was she playing at?

Enough cloak-and-dagger antics. Enough mind games. Enough.

Dag sat back on his haunches, stuffing the blanket back into his pack. He was all too aware that if he lost momentum, he might very well lose his nerve. It had been the same on the speedboat racing back through an Arctic night. They had been going way too fast trying to evade their pursuers, but the grizzled security contractors were dispassionate, just another night's work. Lowell had laughed uproariously, frigid wind whipping his mirth away over the dark waves, totally consumed by the joy of the hunt even though they were the prey. Then, as now, Dag realized that sometimes the only path was forward.

Lifting a gloved finger, he pulled a branch back a few centimeters. The property was still deserted, low-hanging mist evaporating from the pasture in the morning sun. A flock of seagulls flapped over the boathouse. The branch sprang back into place as Dag stepped back, released the submachine gun from its magnetic clip, and hefted it, the weight reassuring in his hand, affirming the illusion of control.

Dag sucked in three quick breaths, pushing the air out between his teeth, and then moved around behind an oak, where his angle of approach would be hidden from the upstairs window. Then he was out into the open, moving at a controlled trot. The grass was soft and springy beneath his feet. The morning air tasted fresh. Time slowed, and his senses jacked up to maximum capacity, just as they had when the sicarios had come down on him and Federico.

Closing the distance to the house, Dag pressed his back to the wall immediately adjacent to the door Kim had retreated into. Trying to calm his hammering heart, he listened over the rush of blood in his ears for any indication that his presence had been detected. But there were no sounds except for the whisper of the surrounding forest and cries from the gulls overhead. Reaching over with his left hand, he tried the doorknob. It turned in his grip. Crouching in front of it, he pressed his eye up against the crack separating the door from the frame. The dead bolt wasn't engaged. Unless there was a third mechanism invisible from the outside, this door was unlocked just like the others had been.

Swinging the door open, he leaned out from the frame to peer in over the barrel of the gun. Inside was a mudroom full of boots and hanging coats. He stepped forward and quietly shut the door behind him. Beyond the mudroom, a hallway stretched away in front of him, a colorful runner covering the dark oak floor. He moved forward cautiously, swinging around every corner to cover adjoining rooms.

The house was enormous. A few dozen people could reside there comfortably. Thick wooden beams traversed the high ceilings. The kitchen was professional grade, enough space and high-end equipment for a team of chefs. It smelled of freshly ground coffee and waffles. Worn tables, chairs, and couches clustered across a wide hall that took up half of the ground floor and featured large windows looking out over the pasture and down to the sea, and a hearth nearly the size of Analog's. Everything looked lived-in and well cared for.

Black-and-white photographs decorated the whitewashed walls, ink printed directly on millimeter-thin sheets of steel. They varied in size and shape, but all were portraits. An old woman whose face was a labyrinth of wrinkles winked at the camera. A sprinter gasped for air after crossing the finish line, hands on his knees. A preschool class stared at their teacher in rapt attention as she read to them from a hardback copy of *Harold and the Purple Crayon*.

There. A staircase leading up to the second story. Dag was building a mental model of the house inside his head—the room Kim sat in was up and to his right, toward the back of the house. He ascended, testing every step for a creak until putting his full weight on it. The stairs deposited him in another hallway, this one circling the second floor of the house, with many doors leading off it.

Dag spun at a sudden sound to cover its source in his line of fire, but it was just the gurgle of a toilet flushing somewhere on the other side of the house. He could hear murmured voices and someone brushing their teeth. Pipes creaked as a shower was turned on. He twitched the gun this way and that, but none of the doors onto the hallway opened. The house was waking up. For a moment, he imagined how it might feel to step out wrapped in a towel and find yourself staring at a man in a camouflage jumpsuit holding a submachine gun. His time was running out. He needed to find her before they found him.

He needed answers.

Reviewing from memory the number of windows on the back side of the house, Dag arrived at the door behind which Kim must be sitting. A knot tightened in his stomach as he stared down at the brass doorknob. *May I join you?* The cicadas had been singing that night out on the La Condesa balcony. The tequila smooth and warm in the back of his throat. He had been surprised and immediately enthralled by the approach of the woman in the scarlet dress.

How easily she had snared him. His riposte might not be as carefully engineered or effortlessly executed, but it was finally at hand.

CHAPTER 13

Dag burst through the door, blood pounding in his ears. Gun raised, he pivoted right and left to survey the room. Kim was where he had last seen her, sitting at the table facing him, with her back to the window. Sitting next to her was a slim man with dark skin, hair, and eyes. He was dressed entirely in black leather and looked like he might have just stepped out of casting for a cyberpunk drama. The rest of the room was empty, save for bookshelves and artwork.

"Slowly now," said Dag, voice lined with razors, "raise those hands, palms open."

Keeping the gun trained on them with his right hand, Dag reached behind him with his left to shut and lock the door to the hallway. No sense in letting someone pop their head in and interrupt the interrogation. Then he took one long step forward to close some of the distance between him and the table. His soft-soled boots made almost no sound at all on the hardwood floor.

The dark-haired man raised his long-fingered hands, wide eyes looking back and forth between Dag and Kim. She offered Dag nothing but a bright smile.

"Dag," she said. "Welcome. I was hoping you would join us. It's been too long."

Adrenaline surged through Dag. Even after using the information Diana had dredged up to trace Kim through a barrage of straw men, even after seeing her collecting firewood this morning, he somehow believed he might walk in to find a look-alike or some other clever facade. But the inflection of her voice, the intensity of her gaze left no room for doubt. This was the woman from Room 412.

"I said," said Dag, trying not to let the gun tremble with his racing heart, "to raise your hands."

"Oh come on," she said, voice relaxed, even chiding. "No need for such nonsense. Javier's made us a fabulous breakfast, and it would be a crime of stupendous proportions to let it get cold. It's no small task to make fried chicken and waffles from scratch. But I know it's your favorite, and Javier insisted. It's just a little tradition we have here on the island when someone passes their final exam."

Her carefree manner was throwing him off. He was the one with the gun. He should be framing the conversation, not her. This was supposed to be an interrogation, not a friendly conversation. He was here for a reckoning. But he let his eyes flick down to the table for a moment. Mismatched plates and silverware on a plain white tablecloth. Two huge platters sat in the middle, one stacked high with thick waffles and the other supporting a mountain of golden-brown fried chicken. There was hot sauce and maple syrup, steaming coffee and fresh orange juice. And it was set for three.

Who was ambushing whom?

"Hands *up!*" He tried to bolster his confidence with an injection of righteous anger.

She sighed, exasperated. "Mr. Calhoun," she said, "we both know you're not going to shoot me right now. You simply don't have the temperament for it. Moreover, doing so would hamper your ability to answer the many burning questions you must be harboring at this very moment. You don't know Javier, and you might shoot him on the unfair and inaccurate assumption that you could pressure me to accede to your demands.

But that would be extremely rude, especially considering the trouble he went to on your behalf to prepare such a delicious meal. He slaughtered the chickens himself, just for you. However many times you've enjoyed fried chicken, I'm sure you've never tasted it this fresh. Your final option would be to shoot yourself. But while that would surely stanch the existential angst that is central to human experience, you might find yourself somewhat miffed in whatever afterlife awaits us, having done yourself in on the brink of discovery and gastronomic delight. I can only imagine the woeful expressions on the faces of your fellow shades."

He had scent masks to avoid expertly trained Rottweilers, enough ammunition to neutralize a cadre of bodyguards, and infiltration gear Navy SEALs would gawk at. But this was a contingency Dag was unprepared for.

Javier made a pained expression and shrugged, hands still raised. "I'm sorry, man," he said. "Emily's always like this."

Kim shot him a look. "And what is *that* supposed to mean, exactly?"

Javier just shrugged again and rolled his eyes at Dag.

"Who *are* you?" asked Dag, desperately trying to regain his handle on the situation.

"First things first." Kim rubbed her hands together. "In this case, that means a breakfast of champions." She pushed her oversize glasses up her nose and rolled up the sleeves of her flannel shirt. "Now, Dag, if it makes you feel better, you're welcome to keep your firearms. They're very nice, very posh, actually. That looks like a brand-spanking-new Tavor SAR Flattop B37, if I'm not mistaken. And with a P341 sidearm and a snazzy stealth jumpsuit, you're ready to face the apocalypse. But while Javier and I do have our vices, we are not the Four Horsemen. We are, aside from these butter knives, entirely unarmed. So even if you doubt the integrity of my promises regarding the incomparable quality of the waiting meal—wrong though you might be to do so—you can rest easy in the knowledge that if you do, despite my assurances, decide to in fact shoot us, we will have no convenient means to defend ourselves but sly wit and Grade A maple syrup."

CHAPTER 14

It was as if Dag was trying to make his feedless way out of a dark and unknown forest, following cairns left by previous explorers, only to discover impassable ravines, engorged rivers, and paths that petered out to nothing among thickets of bramble. All his training, all his careful planning, all his contingencies had been wiped out by a gourmet breakfast prepared by people he assumed to be his nemeses. Assumptions were dangerous but necessary. The important thing was to update them when the world changed, avoid cognitive lock-in. But how to make sense of what was happening on this remote island?

"This might be TMI," said Javier, glancing down at his feet, "but I hated my mom."

Dag was walking beside him around the perimeter of the grounds, Javier occasionally pointing out features that Dag might not have noticed. The sun was shining down from above Mount Baker, and Dag was woozy from a heavy meal on top of an empty stomach.

"My dad left when I was five, about a month after my sister, Rosa, was born," said Javier. "I don't remember his face or his voice. I don't remember anything from the time before he left. My mom was absent in every sense but physical. She was far more interested in her next fix than in either of us kids. She'd disappear for days at a time. I stole money from her purse to buy groceries at the liquor store. Living the American dream, right?"

Javier frowned, delicate eyebrows knitting above his long, expressive face.

Dag held his peace. Javier had something to say, and Dag needed all the explanations he could get.

"I hated my mom," said Javier, "but I loved Rosa. She was the most precious thing in the universe. Wide, innocent brown eyes, a head full of thick brown hair, skin the color of caramel—Rosa was the only thing in the world not tainted by disappointment, resentment, or corruption. She deserved better." Air hissed between his teeth. "That's why I never ran away. It would have been so easy, but I couldn't abandon her. I did my best to protect Rosa from my mom's string of junkie boyfriends. They provided exactly what you'd expect: verbal, physical, and sexual abuse. I called the cops and was beaten for it. I'm guessing you know the drill."

Dag nodded. Scenes from his various foster homes flickered before his mind's eye. His fingers twitched in sympathy as he remembered stringing rosary after rosary with blistered fingers, high on varnish. Every kid in the system had a story just like this. The system itself inflicted more stories like this on every kid.

As they walked, Javier shared his.

Numbers soared and hummed with underlying logic for Javier. Equations danced to a universal rhythm where there was always an answer, always a next step, always a new discovery to be made. When his mom pulled one of her disappearing acts and the siblings had to live on canned tuna for a week, he did proofs in his head while changing Rosa's diapers. His mom eventually returned, tears falling from eyes in which dilated pupils hung like harvest moons. Even when his mom was home, she wasn't really there. While Javier tried to keep the house in order, she would stay in bed for days, lost in an early incarnation of the feed, eschewing meatspace for the more tractable digital variety.

School might have been Javier's escape hatch, but he had few friends there, having little in common with his classmates. While they were hanging out and causing trouble, Javier was trying to raise his sister, protect her from his mother's lovers, and finish homework assignments in the middle of the night. Emily was Javier's only real friend growing up. She was a few years older, but he had skipped a few grades and they ended up in the same math class.

Dag thought of the closet in his DC condo filled with sketchbook upon sketchbook upon sketchbook. Whatever Javier had discovered in mathematics, Dag had found in illustration. He poured every ounce of energy onto the page, until whatever horrors the day had brought were drained of their emotional charge, neutralized by the ground wire of creativity.

Javier smiled. "Emily was the smartest person I had ever met. She understood people in the way I understood numbers. She could intuit what really mattered, people's hopes, fears, and dreams. She was the only person who understood me, even though I didn't tell her anything about what was happening at home. After she went off to a special charter high school for gifted kids, she pulled some strings and got me accepted as well. The first two months of my freshman year were the most magical of my entire life. I was eleven years old, and at home things were as bad as ever. But in the classroom, I was digging into advanced calculus, and Ms. Mendez told me I could go as fast as I wanted through the material. New horizons opened up in every direction. I started to believe that maybe life didn't have to be one extended panic attack."

Color abruptly rose into Javier's cheeks, and he rolled his eyes. "Sorry," he said. "I realize we hardly know each other. I just try not to think about this stuff most of the time, so . . ."

Dag shrugged. "Not a problem. 'One extended panic attack' is a more accurate summary of my own life than I'd like to admit."

Javier nodded and seemed to retreat into himself. They stopped by the spot where Dag had hopped the fence the night before. As they stared out across the pasture at the cows chewing placidly, Javier reached out and gripped the fence. His knuckles turned white as he squeezed the wood.

"Around that time was when Mom told us we were moving to Houston," continued Javier. "She was jubilant. Her latest boyfriend had an uncle with an apartment where we could crash. We wouldn't have to pay rent." Muscles worked along Javier's jaw. "I . . . exploded. I smashed up the kitchen, told my mom exactly how useless and pathetic she was until she screamed and raked her nails across my face. Then she started sobbing, and I stalked to the room that Rosa and I shared. Blood poured into my eyes as I packed my bag, but when Rosa peeked in around the doorjamb, I knew I couldn't run away. She was six years old."

Javier shook his head sharply and peeled his trembling hands away from the fence. They began walking again, back toward the buildings and the sea. "Houston was horrible. The apartment was a meth den crawling with junkies and vermin. I lifted spare change from unconscious addicts to buy food. I knew we were going to die there amid the miserable dregs of humanity. But then, two weeks after we'd arrived, Emily showed up."

He looked at Dag, and there was wonder in his eyes. "She walked right in as if she owned the place. A skeletal man covered in tattoos tried to challenge her, but Emily pulled off her big pink sunglasses and skewered him with a stare that had more wattage than a nuclear power plant. She was fifteen years old and half his height, but the guy stumbled back, mumbling incoherently. She went straight to our mom. 'Here's a week's worth,' she said, holding up a bag of crystals. 'It's yours if you sign these papers.' I had never seen my mom do anything so quickly." He shuddered. "There was this look, this *hunger*, on her face that I still dream about. Then Emily came over to where Rosa and I were huddling in a corner. 'You're coming with me,' she told us. 'We're going home.'"

A gust of wind carried a gale of laughter toward them. The kids were piling out of the main building onto the lawn. A Frisbee sliced through the air. A game of hide-and-seek commenced. The teenagers split off into cliques brimming with social intrigue.

"That's what we're building here on the island," said Javier, opening his hands. "A home for people like us. People like you, Dag."

"That's a touching story," said Dag. "But you don't invite people into your home by mindfucking them."

Javier's face hardened. "Oh, but this isn't just any family," he said. "It's not enough to construct a refuge. Dr. King was right. 'Injustice anywhere is a threat to justice everywhere.' We don't hide from the world—we change it."

CHAPTER 15

"What I want to know," said Dag, "is why I'm here."

Emily didn't bother to look up from where she was working in the garden. A murder of crows exploded from a distant copse of trees, screeching and wrestling as they pursued each other. The pungent smell of compost mixed with the sharp aroma of freshly cut grass.

"If we're going to chat," she said, "then you may as well get down here and help me."

Dag paused for a moment and then knelt in the dirt beside her. She handed him a dandelion weeder and then returned to pulling up various flora that had invaded the pumpkin patch. The earth was soft and cool beneath his fingers. He plunged the forked tool into the ground and tore up a flowering purple bull thistle, roots and all.

"What you have to understand about the Island," she said, punctuating her clauses by tossing clumps of bluegrass onto the pile of trimmings, "is that I didn't intend for it to turn out like this. I never meant to build an empire. I just wanted to help my friends. But favors are accretive. The more you do, the more you can do. People learn they can rely on you and come to you when they need something. If you help them, they are always eager to return the favor. Without you even realizing it, your bank of karma can grow Too Big to Fail."

"How about you stop trying to dodge my questions," said Dag, struggling to uproot another thistle. "It's as bad as talking to politicians."

"You're no fun at all. And I challenge you to name a politician half as droll as I," she said, with a flourish of dandelions. "Anyway, the beginning is the only place to start. Otherwise your questions will yield nothing but more questions."

He glared and she sighed.

"If you insist, we can attack from the flank," she said. "What do you want to know?"

"How did you get your hands on everything in Room 412?" His head spun remembering the empty bed surrounded by a kaleidoscope of intimate personal history.

"Oh, come now," said Emily. "I would have thought you'd long since figured that one out on your own. We pulled everything from your feed archive. Although I did the typographic cutouts myself. I was quite proud of that touch, very noir. Aha!" She yanked a particularly stubborn mass of roots from the damp earth. The sleeves of her flannel shirt were rolled up. She wore no gloves, and dirt smudged her smooth, pale skin.

"And you, dropping into my feed and then vanishing . . ." The wink, the air-kiss, slipping in and out of his digital world like a magician's coin.

"Yes, yes, yes," Emily clucked with disappointment. "If you're going to fit in here, you really must hurry up and think. The kayak, the waiting breakfast—we've known precisely where you've been and what you've been up to the whole time. It's simply a matter of tapping your feed."

"Tapping my feed." Dag's voice faded into disbelief. The feed was your personal lens through which to gaze into the digital abyss, the algorithmic curator that delivered what you needed when you needed it from the surfeit. It was the permeable membrane through which you experienced and participated in culture, the arbiter of what you found when you searched and what you discovered when you dipped into the roiling, throbbing cosmos of global conversation. Any individual voice or channel or vector was necessarily partisan. But the feed itself . . . The feed was infrastructure. Plumbing didn't know or care about a resident's sexual preferences any more than sidewalks pondered the daydreams of pedestrians. The feed was neutral. It was inviolable. It was sacred.

"Javier is *so* good with computers," she said. "Did you know he contributed to the original codebase for Commonwealth security architecture? It was obvious to me that he was a genius since the day we met in math class. Just like you and me, his home life was fucked up beyond belief. Stellar mind though, one of a kind. Rachel, bless her ambitious little heart, was lucky to have him. But you know how these things go. Pretty soon bureaucracy built up in Commonwealth like plaque in an artery. And there's nothing Javier hates more than a suit telling him what he should or shouldn't do. It's one of those classic corporate dilemmas: the people who make the best things resent the people whose job it is to look over their shoulder. Drives people like Rachel mad. She knows you can't build an organization and let everyone just run free. Anarchy ensues. She wakes up with cold sweats, worried her precious office park has turned into a drunken orgy complete with floggers and butt plugs. It offends her sense of scale, her faith in manifest destiny."

Emily caressed a plump orange pumpkin. "So Javier left, but not before installing a back door for himself. And you know hackers—the first thing they do with their back doors is build more back doors for redundancy. It's all very overwrought if you ask me, like preppers stocking for the apocalypse. If the world really does end, all that ammunition and gold bullion won't do anyone much good."

Dag remembered the poise with which Rachel carried herself in Analog, how the lamplight had played across the deep lines of her face, the scar that bisected her left eye. It took a special kind of determination to corral the world's tech back end and build it into something greater, to stitch together the feed, thread by binary thread.

Then the full implications of Emily's anecdote hit.

"You piggyback on Commonwealth?" He jabbed his weeder into the dirt for support. A frisson of personal violation overcame him. Tapping someone's feed was infinitely more intimate than breaking into their home. It was the cultural main line, the ever-present open connection between mind and net. Your feed was yours and yours alone, the system safeguarded by Commonwealth's unprecedented and famously resilient security. That was the sacred covenant of the digital world, trust's guarantor.

"Is this how you treat all potential clients?" she asked.

"What?" he managed, breathless.

"Are you happy, Dag? Like, really happy?"

"Excuse me?" Rubbing his forehead, he streaked dirt across half his face.

"Are you happy? It's a simple question."

"What does that have to do with anything?"

Emily unleashed the full ferocity of her stare from beneath the brim of her sun hat.

"You're here because I'd like to offer you a job," she said.

CHAPTER 16

"Shankar Vedantam wrote that those who travel with the current will always feel they are good swimmers, while those who swim against the current may never realize they are better swimmers than they imagine," said Emily as she washed the dirt off her hands in the enormous stainless-steel kitchen sink. "The Island is a moon that exerts gravitational pull on the currents of culture."

Dag snorted. "Through hacking and blackmail, you mean."

Emily winced and wiped her hands dry on a towel. "Absolutely not," she said. "We aren't binary butchers. We aren't gangsters. Coercion is no kind of victory. It depends on the maintenance of a delicate balance of power. It's a bet against change, the only constant. No"—she sliced the air with a hand—"here on the Island, we win hearts and minds."

"You're doing that politician thing again," said Dag, as he rinsed dirt off his forearms.

"Come," said Emily. "See for yourself."

He followed her out into the main hall that took up half the ground floor of the house. Just a few hours before, Tavor clutched in a sweaty grip, he had crept through this very room in search of Emily. Now there was a fire roaring in the hearth, and the vista beyond the wide windows was suffused with afternoon light. And there were people, about a dozen of them broken up into a few small groups. No kids here. This felt more like an operations center than a classroom. They huddled in conversation nooks, sipped steaming mugs of coffee, or gazed off into the digital infinite, mumbling subvocal commands and twitching their fingers. Javier sat in a wing chair by the window, swaying to music Dag could not hear. He laughed at something, then looked up to give Dag a little wave and a wan smile.

Emily escorted him to a man and a woman sitting at a coffee table in a corner.

"Dag," she said. "Meet Frances and Ferdinand. F and F, this is Dag."

"Aha! At last, the infamous Dag," said Ferdinand.

Frances's face lit up. "We could use some new blood around here. It can get quite claustrophobic, you know."

"We're twins," Ferdinand continued. "Fraternal, obviously."

"Pleasure to meet you," said Dag, extending a hand.

They shook enthusiastically.

"This is a special place," said Frances.

"A safe place," said Ferdinand. "Javier said to make you feel welcome. And the most welcome I ever felt was when I got here and discovered other people like me."

"Our father raped us," said Frances. "Until we killed him."

"Slowly," added Ferdinand. "But we were minors, so we got out right quick, and then we met Emily."

"Boys and girls," said Emily gently. "We may want to take it a little slower, let Dag get oriented."

"Oh," said Frances, taken aback. "Well then."

"No," said Dag, unsure how to react, "it's okay." He made eye contact with Frances. "When I was eleven, the boys in my foster home abused me too. They were supposed to be my brothers."

"See?" Frances rolled her eyes at Emily. "It's important to be honest with people."

Ferdinand waved a hand. "Let bygones be bygones," he said. "Dad's rotting in the ground, and we're making sure people like him can't hurt more kids."

Dag frowned. "How can you make sure of something like that?"

Ferdinand looked to Emily, who urged him on with a nod. He started ticking off fingers. "The updated and amended Justice for Victims of Trafficking Act, budget reallocations to expand social services, federal reform of foster care requirements, new bills passed in Washington, Mississippi, Minnesota, New York, and California, FBI partnerships and funding to local law enforcement in specific municipal hot spots."

Dag remembered the anti-human-trafficking legislation. It had won bipartisan support and surprised observers by flying through the House and Senate on the way to the president's desk, somehow managing to avoid the tangled mess of congressional horse trading.

"Plus," said Frances, "we've extended ongoing grants to various local nonprofits serving victims of abuse and to investigative journalists working to expose the various criminal organizations that profit off it and—"

Dag held up a hand. "Sorry to interrupt," he said, "but I don't understand how you're connected to any of these things."

Ferdinand's eyes lit up. "Behold!" he said and shared his feed.

Images, data files, maps, and chat windows blossomed in front of their collective mind's eye. Ferdinand called up an image of an older gentleman in a conservative blue suit.

"Senator Watkins," he said.

"I know him," said Dag. He was a curmudgeonly social conservative from West Virginia who owned a pair of Westies that he loved more than anything on the face of the earth.

"Of course," said Ferdinand, not missing a beat. "And we know him better," he giggled. "Much, much better." He began scrolling through photographs, videos, audio recordings, message chains, until the digital breadcrumbs that Senator Watkins left in his wake danced around them. It went by too fast for Dag to take in any specific details, but the bigger picture was clear as day.

"You tapped his feed too," said Dag.

"Oh yes," said Frances. "Of course."

Dag turned on Emily. "So much for not blackmailing people." Through whatever crack they had pried open to get root access to Commonwealth, they were fishing for sensitive information to use as leverage for the endgame they sought, however noble it might be. It was devious and almost alluring.

"Blackmail?" said Frances, aghast. "Heavens no. Tapping the good senator's feed is just the beginning." She highlighted a section of data tunnel from fifteen years before. "You see, Mr. Watkins didn't always support legislation like the Justice for Victims of Trafficking Act. In his view, it was just another example of federal overreach. Big proponent of small government, our Mr. Watkins. Believes that the local sheriff or maybe the state police should be able to handle such things—no need for Washington to get involved, with its taxes and its inefficiencies. But he's dead wrong on that one. When you're dealing with international organizations made up of professional criminals, local law enforcement has no chance in hell of actually busting a slave ring. But the stubborn senator was dead set on scuttling the bill. And we just couldn't have that, could we? His prissy ideology isn't worth people's lives, after all. So . . ." She raised a hand, palm up, as if offering a small delicacy to her brother.

"We helped Senator Watkins see the bigger picture." Ferdinand grinned.

"Both Frances and Ferdinand have PhDs in clinical psychology," said Emily, "as do many of our other core team members."

"You would not believe the crazies they sent us during our postdoc," said Frances. "I mean, you read about it in the textbooks, but when you see it in real life . . ." She shivered.

"So you can imagine," said Ferdinand, "that Watkins was small-fry to us. So transparent you almost wish he had more complex ulterior motives. But really all he cares about is holding his seat through reelection, grooming his two dogs, and not embarrassing himself in front of his wife, who's a real hard-ass. Oh, and for some reason he hates chocolate, really despises it."

"Unforgivable," muttered Frances with a scowl.

"So in his case," continued Ferdinand, "all we had to do was drop a few select documentaries into the media feed he shares with his wife. He's not a big documentary fan—always opts for rom-coms, if you can believe it. But his wife is a serious churchgoer, an old-fashioned God-fearing woman who believes you've got to look the devil in the eye. So when these heart-wrenching films about girls abducted from rural Thailand and smuggled into Idaho popped up, she demanded they watch them. Then she demanded the whole congregation watch them and organized a bake sale at the local high school with proceeds sent to relevant charities."

"And when the bill came up for a vote in committee," said Frances, "good old Senator Watkins *sponsored* the damn thing. Because he knew if he didn't, he'd never live it down."

"Had he tried to scuttle it, she probably would have taken the Westies into sole custody," said Ferdinand. "She's ruthless when riled, a real terror to behold."

"And now for the grand finale . . ." said Ferdinand. He pulled in graphs, crime statistics, news reports, government audits, trafficking busts, white papers, court cases, and cost/benefit analyses, aggregating them and overlaying the entire digital narrative onto a timeline anchored on the policy milestones he and his sister had orchestrated.

"We've had statistically significant improvements on every quantifiable metric," said Frances, zooming in and highlighting specific peaks and troughs. "There's been a twenty percent increase in successful human-trafficking prosecutions nationwide and a thirty-two percent decrease in estimated total throughput of the black market networks. The FBI has broken up the two largest rings operating out of Seattle, and they were major feeders to the rest of the country. Increased funding to local sex-crime and domestic-violence police units has financed better training and equipment to strengthen enforcement efforts. Audit procedures have been strengthened for the foster care system and juvenile reintegration programs, with additional dollars going to grassroots initiatives that show real results. Inner-city schools in eighteen states now have more capacity for after-school programs and counseling."

Emily put a hand on Frances's shoulder. "The project Frances and Ferdinand pioneered was our first program," she said. "It also inspired us to open the school right here on the Island. We do our best to find and serve the brightest students who slip through the cracks of the system. Even an improved system has too many cracks."

Ferdinand gave a tight-lipped smile. "There's always more to do," he said.

"That's a good segue," said Emily. "Thank you, both. Dag needs to see the other projects."

Emily showed him around, introducing him to a series of people and ideas that Dag began to understand were a cohesive effort of subversive, progressive political activism. They had pushed through the state and national tax reforms that had simplified the federal tax code, closed hundreds of loopholes, eliminated outdated subsidies that were jealously guarded by special interests, and reversed the megatrend of American median income decline and the cavernous wealth gap. The relaxed immigration and trade rules they had championed helped drag the country, and the global economy, out of the latest recession while simultaneously stimulating new business formation, scientific research, and cultural dynamism among immigrant populations. After years of struggle, they had reallocated public funding from private prisons to the education system. Dag was intimately familiar with many of the individual laws and regulations in question, having lobbied on behalf of both proponents and opponents at various times.

He remembered his morning walk in San Francisco contemplating the nation's evidence of progress—and his subsequent admission that so little of his day-to-day work had contributed to anything so high-minded. This oddball collection of castaways was shaping socioeconomic policy like a potter throwing clay.

CHAPTER 17

"This is a lot to take in," Dag said to Emily. "You're targeting influential individuals and manipulating their feeds in order to influence their worldview and decisions."

She nodded. They had stepped out onto the deck. The air was thick with the smell of honeysuckle. "I told you," she said, "hearts and minds. By adjusting the lens, we help leaders see what's really important and take appropriate action."

The scheme was nefarious and beautiful. Nudging decision makers in the right direction by having teams of psychologists personally curate their digital experiences. "And they don't even realize it's happening," he said, unable to keep a growing sense of wonder out of his voice.

Emily grinned. "There are two broad families of martial arts," she said. "Hard forms, like karate, use direct strikes and meet force with force. You might aim to break an opponent's arm with a block. Soft forms are all about using the minimum force possible to deflect an opponent's attack to their disadvantage. Instead of blocking, you might redirect a kick to throw your opponent off balance. In the fight over ideas, we use the softest of soft forms. We plant seeds and nurture them to maturity. We encourage potential opponents to take our side of their own volition."

"Incredible," said Dag. His professional success depended on his ability to persuade. This was a tool of unprecedented power. It gave Emily and her cohorts direct access to influencer mindshare. Not even the most experienced and well-resourced propagandists could accomplish a minuscule percentage of what was happening in the room behind them. "I . . . I don't know how to feel about it." His own candidness surprised him.

"That's a natural response," said Emily, tapping her chin. "It can take some getting used to, but ultimately it's no different than much of what you do. We simply use everything at our disposal to encourage the system to do what's right. In fact, the biggest difference is that we work on our own account."

"You're saying your power isn't for sale."

"Let's be real," she said. "Whether or not you admit it, you're getting tired of rationalizing everything. Cynicism can only carry you so far. You're too smart for it."

"Fuck you too. Maybe I want a yacht. Maybe I just don't care. You think of that?"

She arched an eyebrow. "We champion our own interests. There are gray areas in the middle of the bell curve. But down at the tails, there is right and there is wrong. We're not shy about what we believe in, and we do everything in our power to effect meaningful change."

They stood in silence for a moment, staring out over the pastoral scene.

"Why did you do that?" asked Dag. "Room 412, I mean. What was the point? If your plan was to confide in me, why didn't you simply invite me to the Island?"

"Every time we start a new project, we go bigger," she said. "Skirting the edge of failure is the only way to know we're being ambitious enough. We can't allow ourselves to get comfortable. These issues are too important. There's too much to do. So this time, we're going after the big kahuna, the high muckety-muck, the top dog." She leaned over the deck's railing, resting on her elbows. "I've always been obsessed by the tragedy of the commons, the open-access problem." She lifted her chin to indicate the cows in their paddock. "Unrestricted grazing on common lands was actually the original example used by the persnickety Victorian economist who coined the term. Funny how we are so good at dreaming up fancy tech but can't for the life of us figure out how to cooperate."

Dag thought back to the game theory thought experiments he and Gretchen had dreamed up in grad school. The tragedy of the commons—overexploitation of a shared but underregulated resource by individuals for selfish gain screwed over the community as a whole. What made matters worse was that the loss was widely distributed, diffusing political will, while those few who captured the gain fought tooth and nail to maintain their benefit as free riders.

"One of the many flaws in our nature," said Dag. "We can't trust each other enough to all just get along. Not much you can do about that."

"Maybe, maybe not." Emily plucked a honeysuckle blossom from the vine and slurped in its sweet nectar. "When you were in San Diego, did you ever try Baja-style fish tacos?"

"Once or twice," said Dag, remembering the sea lions.

"Mmmm-hmmmm." Emily licked her lips and tossed away the flower. "Squeezing a lime over grilled fish piled on a handmade tortilla—that might be my definition of happiness. Pure magic. Now San Diego is just another pile of ash in the SoCal blaze. Ocean acidification has pushed most of the fish species that used to grace taqueria grills to the point of extinction. For you, that might feel redemptive, given how shitty a time you had down there. Then there's the hurricane that leveled the Yucatán, the floods in Bangladesh, the drought up and down the West Coast—and that's not to mention the death of the Great Barrier Reef or the islands and coastal areas reclaimed by rising sea levels. But if there's one truism that's worsened the impact of every human misstep, it's that there's profit in tragedy."

"You insinuating something?"

"You tell me."

Her gaze was open and frank. After a moment, he looked away. "I've done some things I'm not proud of," he said. "But that's lobbying. We don't choose our clients. Our job is to help them get what they want."

She tossed another honeysuckle blossom out from the deck, and a breeze sent it spiraling toward the pumpkin patch. "Given what happened to your biological parents, it's only a matter of time before you start having second thoughts about aiding and abetting."

Dag's face hardened. "Fuck you for judging me. Fuck you for cracking my feed. And fuck you for bringing up my parents."

"Everyone has their line," she said, "even if years of making seemingly insignificant ethical compromises shifts integrity around like dunes on a desert. Would you represent the Ku Klux Klan?"

"No," he said sharply. "Of course not. Who do you think I am?"

Faster than he would have thought possible, her hand was at his throat. She squeezed, not hard enough to choke him but with enough pressure that he felt his carotid throb. He froze, and she leaned in until her face was inches away from his.

"Who *are* you?" she hissed, eyes wide and electric behind her oversize glasses.

Dag swallowed, his Adam's apple bobbing up and down beneath her hand.

Her eyes narrowed. "You came all this way," she said. "I thought you would have an answer to my question by now."

He could feel her hot breath on his lips.

"We need your help," she whispered. "There's no other way. I give people second chances, and this is yours."

"How?" His whisper was hoarse.

Releasing her grip on his throat, she shoved her open palm into his sternum, and he stumbled back against the railing.

"Lowell Harding," she said.

CHAPTER 18

A hand gently shook his shoulder, and Dag came awake, bleary and disoriented.

"What? What is it?" His tongue was chalky in his mouth, his eyes gummy as he blinked in the darkness.

"Come on," said Emily, sitting on the edge of the bed. "Put on a jacket. I want to show you something."

Rousing himself instantly, he shimmied away from her and sat ramrod straight against the headboard. His Tavor was in the closet and might as well be a thousand miles away. The commando camp instructors were haranguing him from the depths of memory. Stupid, stupid, stupid.

"What the hell?" he demanded. "It's the middle of the night."

"Calm down," she said with mild exasperation. "If I was here to kill you, you'd be dead already."

Okay, facts. He was on the Island, in the room they had assigned him. He had come to root out Emily, and she had turned the tables by attempting to recruit him to her cabal. The world was dark beyond the window. Dawn was hours away. Reason began to beat back the initial flash of dread. As the fear subsided, aphrodisia overcame him in a hot, unsettling rush, which he quickly suppressed. She wasn't here to seduce him.

"Why—"

"Just come," she said, cajoling. "I promise it'll be worth it."

Just when he thought things couldn't possibly get weirder. Fuck it. He grunted, threw off the covers, stumbled to the closet, and pulled on his jacket. As he stuffed his arms through the sleeves, he looked down at the guns leaning against the closet wall. Against his better judgment, he left them there. They hadn't proved useful so far, and he doubted she had roused him for a duel.

"Here," she said, holding something out to him. "This is for you."

He squinted in the darkness. A mug, steam billowing. He accepted it, sniffed. It was brimming with hot cocoa, tiny marshmallows bobbing on the surface.

"Lights?" he asked.

"Nah," she said. "They'd torch our night vision. We'll be okay."

He slipped on his shoes, and she led him out into the hall, treading lightly. There was just enough ambient light not to trip. The walls, the floor, the steps, the carpet were all gray on gray in the gloom. Neither of them said a word as they traversed the shadow world. An illicit thrill ran through Dag, the private bond of sharing a clandestine adventure.

They padded across the wide living room. The dying embers in the hearth painted the dimness in flickering blood-red hues. Emily fiddled with the French doors, and they opened with a rush of cool air that raised goose bumps on the backs of Dag's hands.

And then they stepped out into the night.

Dag had to focus to keep his cocoa from spilling as they descended the steps. At least it was a little easier to see out here. As soon as they reached the gravel path, Emily took them off it.

Setting off across the lawn, they moved away from the house, barn, and school. The land sloped up gently toward the woods, and they stopped just before reaching the dark forest.

"This should do it," said Emily, turning to face Dag and plopping down cross-legged on the ground, hands clutching her own mug of cocoa.

He looked at her uncertainly, and she patted the ground beside her.

He sat and took a sip of cocoa. The rich, creamy chocolate was fiery with cinnamon, cayenne, and rum, the perfect draft to fortify oneself in the early hours of a chilly morning. The drink sent fingers of warmth through every inch of Dag's body, reminding him of a tour through a client's chocolate factory taken many years before. Sean had assigned him the case to cut his lobbying teeth. The chocolate industry was a microcosm of the global political economy—supply chains extended all the way back into the shaded forests of Latin America, while marketing and distribution channels sought out the bourgeois oases of San Francisco, Taipei, and Toronto. He had to help the client navigate intersecting layers of endemic corruption and unravel a complex regulatory regime that spanned four continents. It sparked a sense of wonder in Dag, illustrating the immense complexity behind the simplest of pleasures.

Emily set her mug down beside her and flopped back onto the grass.

"This is why we came here," she said, pointing up.

Dag lay back and followed her finger with his gaze.

The sky was a brilliant dome of glittering stars, the Milky Way's fuzzy halo splashed across it, his feed tagging constellations. Dag remembered looking up on the long paddle over. How determined he'd been, how sure of himself, his goal. He'd found what he came for, but whatever he'd been expecting, this wasn't it. Instead, he was afloat in ambiguity and simultaneously at the brink of something invisible. He was on a roller coaster that had just reached the apex of its first ascent, stomach in his throat as he anticipated the plunge.

"I've always loved the stars," said Emily. "They're my outlet. I think it's because they're hopelessly beyond my control. They force me to take a step back, steady busy hands, all that. Nothing I can do about it, you know? My mom gave me a telescope when I was seven. Best present I ever got. Did Javier tell you his story?"

"Mm-hmm." Dag remembered his slender hands clenched into fists.

"Frances, Ferdinand, the rest of the team, the kids down in the school—every single one of them has a similar story. Even you, at least once you became a ward of the state. Me, though? My parents were great. Sure, we had our differences. The rest of our family was back in Seoul. They didn't have many friends in LA, so it was mostly just the three of us. They forced me to eat broccoli, but, well, they weren't like the monsters that folks here have had to contend with. But they were both hit by a bus while crossing the street to the farmers market one day, and that was that. Killed instantly."

"I'm—I'm so sorry," said Dag.

"The risks people run for kale, right? No, don't worry about it. Not your fault. I'm not fishing for sympathy. I've always been a control freak. I filed all my own paperwork at school and did the family finances as soon as I learned arithmetic. Weird, I know. The point is, when my parents died, I just . . . kept going. I arranged everything. The funeral. The will. The legal loopholes necessary for me to just keep doing my thing, going to school, living in my family's house, without a guardian or adult around. It was complicated, but I just never stopped. I went through all of high school that way, and whenever I came across another kid stuck in a downward spiral, like Javier, I looped them into the big algorithm in my head, made a space for them. I could just see how people worked, you know? How the system operates. How to make it do what I wanted. It's just this big mess, this huge mass of incentive structures with nobody in charge and everyone trying to do their best. Then we grew up. Some of the crew started to help. They had their own ideas, their own skills, their own tools. When Javier opened up the feed, gave us access to Commonwealth, that raised the stakes, but it was still the same game. Everything just got bigger and bigger and bigger."

They lay in silence for a few minutes, muting their feeds. The rush and pull of waves hitting the rocky shore lay just on the edge of hearing.

Dag could feel his heartbeat in every extremity. His thoughts circled like a merry-go-round.

"Looking up at the stars?" Emily's tone was different now, husky with emotion. "It gives me perspective. But it's also a reminder to always dream bigger. There's always more to be done."

An owl hooted from somewhere off in the forest.

Dag plucked a single blade of grass, crushed it between his fingers, and raised it to his nose. The scent was sharp and unmistakable, an olfactory snare drum.

"Have you ever heard of Château de Chambord?" asked Dag.

"Nope."

"It's a palace in the Loire Valley. King François the First built it in the early sixteenth century. It's this enormous mansion. Gray stone walls. Conical towers. But the most opulent part is the sprawling lawns. Hunter-gatherers, ancient Egyptians, Socrates—none of them tended patches of grass in front of their homes. Think about it. Lawns are worthless. They take acreage and labor to maintain yet produce nothing of value. Lawns were invented in the late Middle Ages by nobles who wanted to flaunt their wealth. Lawns are pure luxury. The bigger your lawn, the more land and peasants you needed to cultivate it. Lawns became a primary symbol of political power, so much so that upwardly mobile merchants and other nouveau riche couldn't wait to grow their own. The industrial and information revolutions birthed a middle class itching to spend their Sundays mowing the grass in front of their cookie-cutter suburban châteaux. And now, here we are, lying on yours."

"I never knew that," she said. Her laugh tinkled up into the night. "That's a really cool story."

"It's a clever piece of trivia," said Dag. "But the whole thing terrifies me. Everything we do, everything we believe, everything we are, we think it's ours to choose." His voice quickened, words rushing to get out. "But even something as inconsequential as wanting a lawn in front of our homes isn't a true choice. It's the product of a never-ending series of historical accidents. We take the world we're born into for granted. We imagine that we control our thoughts and dreams. We think we're free to be who we want to be. But there's this vast hidden architecture that shapes us, and we don't even know it. It's like we're actors in a play who don't realize we're working off a script."

Emily shifted on the grass next to him and let out a long exhale.

"Even actors have a choice," she said, serious again. "Once you know there's a script, you can choose your own inflections. You can learn to improvise. You can make the play better. Understanding how things came to be frees us to imagine new possibilities. That's part of what our whole effort here is all about."

"But even your desire to fight the system is the product of personal history and cultural memes." Dag waved a hand to encompass the Milky Way. "You said the stars are an outlet for you because they're hopelessly beyond your control." He patted the ground beside them. "What makes you so confident that anything down here is so different?"

"The twins told you about some of the results we've achieved so far," said Emily. "Seeing real changes happen, even if they're small, makes me believe more change is possible. We're building momentum." She paused. "But your question goes deeper than that."

There was a moment of contemplative silence. A meteor traced a brief fiery arc across the sky above them.

"Ultimately, the only power we have is to choose how we see the world," she continued. "We don't control what happens. But we do get to decide how to interpret what happens, how to synthesize it, what to do next."

She paused again, choosing her words carefully. "You're saying that there are reasons why the world is fucked up, and that's just the way it is. If you turn out to be right, all you're left with is the cold comfort of saying, 'I told you so.'"

She paused and her voice sharpened. "There's nothing I hate more than that phrase. It kills potential in the cradle. If I could erase it from the human psyche, I would. *But*"—her tone changed again, soft but insistent, as if issuing a challenge—"when you do what you think is right, you're building a foundation to do more. If you're optimistic and you turn out to be right, you've helped create a better world and you have leverage to improve it further. If there's one thing I believe, it's that optimism compounds better than cynicism. You can either complain about how some French noble predetermined your desire for a lawn, or laugh at how ridiculous life is and build yourself a rock garden. It all depends on your point of view. And at the end of the day, your point of view makes all the difference in the world."

CHAPTER 19

Dag's paddle sliced through the water, sending ripples out across the mirrorlike surface. He had declined the offer of a private plane, opting to return to Lummi Bay the way he'd come. It was strangely alien by day, as if he'd never been this way before. The ocean reflected the slate gray of the overcast sky. The San Juan Islands rose from the sea like the forested backs of breaching whales. Morning sun shone through a halo of fog that absorbed and distributed its light in a glow that seemed to emanate from all directions, casting no shadows.

It took an hour of paddling before Dag felt he was truly alone. Maps, recommended routes, and current overlays hung at the edge of consciousness in his feed. But he was also here, adrift on the Salish Sea, sweat cooling under his splash jacket and blisters rising on his palms. It was as if he were emerging from a strange and marvelous dream. A private island populated by political activists with a secret weapon. Emily had targeted him for recruitment, not blackmail. Indulging his curiosity had yielded questions instead of answers.

The pleasant soreness in his muscles was back, all numbness and lactic acid. The fog held him in its muffled pocket. Tiny droplets of cold spray sprinkled his face with every stroke.

In his first few months at Apex, Dag had wooed a congresswoman to change her tune on immigration reform. He knew he was getting to her, making progress. She waffled back and forth in their conversations, and he arranged a final lunch to seal the deal. Sean had attended, along with the congresswoman's chief of staff. The lunch started well, bouillabaisse and raunchy gossip from the Hill. After the second glass of wine, they got down to business. Dag delivered the final pitch with aplomb. When he finished, the congresswoman nodded thoughtfully. But then her chief of staff leaned over to murmur something in her ear. Panicked that a single whisper might undo months of patient persuasion, Dag jumped in with a stirring appeal and call to action. But his spiel softened her resolve, and the lunch yielded naught but small talk and a large bill. Afterward, Sean had taken him walking along the Mall. *You had her*, he said. *You just needed to let her decide it was her idea. Never sell past the close.*

Emily didn't sell past the close. Her strategy seemed to be overwhelming you with a barrage of new information until you reached the conclusion she deemed inevitable. Dag didn't feel won over so much as resurrected. No, that wasn't right. Resurrection could happen only after death, and he was still traversing Hades's realm. His descent had begun long before his visit to the Island, long before La Condesa. Whatever her ways and means, Emily was right that he was eating himself up inside. The act of lobbying required a certain sense of cynicism toward the democratic process. That cynicism had appeared cosmopolitan and sophisticated when Sean had initiated him into the lustrous K Street universe. Dag had successfully internalized the ground rules of power, but world-weariness came up short. What was capacity without conviction? Cynicism was as empty and fragile as shed snakeskin.

Idealism was a strange house to enter via a broken window. Room 412's gallery of Dag had revived Gretchen from the ashes of memory. All red hair and green eyes, she had regaled Dag in grad school with impassioned manifestos about the accelerating rate of species extinction, rapid growth in displaced-community populations, and the policies needed to effect change. He teased her for her naïveté, and she retorted with snide comments about the complicity of joining an unjust system. Maybe this was the natural way of things. Career nonprofit staff spiraled into cynicism as they faced the futility of so many failed social-impact projects while savvy lobbyists discovered idealism like divorcées falling back in love.

If this was a midlife crisis, he was already sick of it.

And yet he couldn't help but envy the staunch beliefs and pragmatic operations of the Island's residents. That they had so effectively compromised his feed proved their otherwise preposterous claims to digital omnipotence. That they had so efficiently dismantled his life demonstrated the intimate influence such power endowed. This must be the single biggest security exploit in Commonwealth history. The unassailable stability of their internet infrastructure was the secret sauce that had secured their global monopoly. Emily and Javier had stolen the keys to the kingdom. And unlike empires of old, this dominion had the global reach, granular personalization, and infinite scale of software.

He tried to focus on his breath, lose himself in the paddling. But he couldn't quite hit the right rhythm. Every pull was a fraction of a second too short, every twist of the hips a tiny bit off. Strokes were throwing spray instead of coming up clean. His form was inefficient, wasting power. He needed to get a grip if he was going to make his flight to DC.

A needle of pain pierced his left thumb. He held it to his mouth to suck the burst blister. He was on course, and his feed assured him there were no foul weather warnings. But despite it, he felt sure that there was a storm brewing just over the horizon. He could almost smell the pungent zing of ozone, sense the oncoming squall in the rising hairs on the nape of his neck.

Ahead, the mainland materialized out of the mist. His dark, massive destination.

CHAPTER 20

DC buzzed by beyond the windows of the coffee shop. Staffers power walked between meetings, issuing curt orders to distant peons. Interns scurried in their wake, trying to avoid stepping into muddy puddles that would ruin their one good pair of slacks. A mountain of news alerts and messages sat impatiently in his feed. At least Apex paid his premium to keep it ad-free. Dag sipped his espresso. Washington was a municipal Narcissus, a city obsessed with itself.

"How are you feeling?" Sean sat down opposite Dag with a cappuccino and a concerned expression. With his carrot-colored beard and sharp blue suit, he was the picture of a K Street silverback.

"Better," said Dag. "Much better." It was true. What he'd discovered over his monthlong leave of absence had transformed his paranoia into something approaching a sense of clarity. Maybe he needed to embark on life-threatening adventures more often.

Relief softened Sean's face. "That's really good." He tugged at his beard. "I've been trying to keep the other partners at bay. I mean, technically, you're well within your rights to take leave. Extenuating circumstances and all that. But you know how it is."

In the cutthroat world of high-stakes political lobbying, partners did not let life get in the way of work. Family, hobbies, R and R—these were luxuries for the dim-witted and unambitious. Leisure was the pawn's respite. Apex harbored no such lowlifes, and the only thing that had enabled Dag's exception was his narrow escape from death and Sean's endorsement. But even those ramparts had their limits when besieged by implacable internal politics. Dag looked directly into Sean's eyes. "Thank you," he said. "I deeply appreciate it. I needed it. And, well, I have something that I think may appease the horde."

"What's that?"

"A new client, a whale."

Sean raised his cappuccino to his lips. "Is that right?"

"They're a foundation based outside of Seattle," said Dag. "They've got a portfolio of issues they champion and want us to be their boots on the ground in the capital. Here's a breakdown of their position on current legislation." He added an overview to their shared feed. "And here's the best part." Dag raised a finger and grinned. "We have carte blanche on billable. They want results."

When you could fine-tune the personal microculture of any individual, gaming financial markets was child's play. Javier used Mozaik software protocols to identify specific institutional investors who were particularly bad actors. Some laundered black market cash via baroque schemes, while others followed the more prosaic path of leveraging superior processing power and legal gray areas to rig the market. The Island would take a position on a trade and cater the opposing fund manager's information diet to encourage them to overpay. Do it a few dozen times, and the results compounded into a hedge fund. Nobody was the wiser, and the losers deserved the hits they took. The whole setup meant that, in effect, Emily was infinitely resourced. Writing a blank check to Dag's firm for cover was a drop in the bucket.

"I see," said Sean, leaning back.

"We're to get started immediately," said Dag. "I'm already lining up meetings. We've even got a slot on Markoff's calendar—you know how tough he is to nail down."

"I'm sure the partnership will be impressed," said Sean, but there was something off in his tone, a subtle distance.

"It'll bump our Q3 numbers, and given the breadth of their interest areas, it'll give us a reliable baseline for next year." Dag injected extra enthusiasm into his voice to mask his lack of surety.

"Kudos." Again, that faint coolness.

Dag frowned. "What's wrong? I thought you'd be happy to hear this."

"Oh, nothing," said Sean, sitting forward and raising his cup. "We should be celebrating over a single malt, but this coffee will have to do for now." He smiled. Did it reach his eyes? "Seriously, this is a big deal. It'll cement your well-deserved reputation as the firm's rising star. It's good timing too. You don't want to be the guy who slacks off after they make partner. This isn't a job where you can ride the coattails of tenure. So, well done."

"Thanks," said Dag. "That means a lot coming from you." He searched Sean's face for any hint of irregularity but came up dry. Enthusiasm and pride were written across his features. Dag must be overreacting, reading too much into things after spending a month pulling back the curtains on a conspiracy.

This was DC. Home turf. No submachine guns required.

A toddler trundled over to their table and grabbed a handful of Sean's trousers, looking up at him with beseeching blue eyes. She wore a polka-dot dress and bright-red shoes.

"Whoops," he said, smiling as he bent over, scooped her up, and deposited her on his lap. "Looks like somebody went exploring."

A harried middle-aged man hurried over to their table, wincing apologetically.

"I'm so sorry," he said. "She's just at that age, you know? Wilma, come on, let's leave these nice men be."

"It's a pleasure to meet you, Wilma," said Sean, poking her nose and instigating a bout of giggling. "Now be a good girl and do what your daddy says."

"Thanks," said the man, and he picked up his daughter while balancing his coffee. "She's got spunk. She gets it from her mother."

Dag and Sean stared after them as the café door swung shut.

"Do you ever think . . ." Dag trailed off. Sean didn't talk about his divorce, and kids were a perilously related topic.

"I've got nieces and nephews aplenty," said Sean, as if letting something go. "Between them, Mr. Snufflebunch, and Apex, I have more children than I can handle."

"Boardrooms have more immature brats than preschools?"

"Precisely," said Sean. "Which brings us back to your new client."

"A lucky break," said Dag.

"Speaking of lucky breaks," said Sean, "someone's been asking about you."

"Oh?"

"Looks like you may be harpooning two whales in one go."

"What do you mean?" Dag's pulse accelerated.

Sean tugged at his beard and said, "Harding."

Dag suppressed a shiver. Somehow, he hadn't quite believed it would work. Despite the overwhelming evidence on the Island, a part of him had written it off as some kind of parallel universe existing only in the mist-shrouded Pacific Northwest. But here it was. The invitation. All according to plan. It was eerie.

Sean peered at him closely. "Look," he said, "I know you're probably not excited to hear this. We reassigned you to Commonwealth for a reason. But, well, he's asking for you."

Dag remembered late nights soaked in rum and debauchery. Swimming around a yacht in shark-infested waters after losing a hand of slapjack. Placing higher-stakes bets on the ascension of a certain warlord and the downfall of a particular executive. A parade of women with fire to match their curves. Living at full throttle with eyes for nothing but the win.

"That's the thing about this business," said Sean with a sad shrug. "At the end of the day, it's all about the client. And the client sent Masterson packing with a string of expletives I won't repeat here. You know how Lowell is. And you know what that means."

For a split second, Dag considered confessing everything to Sean right then and there. His mentor's earlier discomfort finally made sense. Dag would explain that Sean needn't worry, that although Dag had once pulled every string at his disposal to escape Harding's orbit, this new development was actually part of a larger plan. He would bare his heart and, in doing so, invite Sean into the inner circle of his trust just as Sean had done for Dag years before. With an ally at his side, surely Dag could strike faster and surer.

But the vision passed almost as soon as it appeared. Such a tack would invite nothing but disaster. Sean would be more likely to institutionalize Dag than abet his cause. The only thing more insane than this plan was how it would sound to the uninitiated over lukewarm espresso.

"I understand." Dag was careful to couch his voice in apprehension. It wasn't hard. His misgivings were real, even if they stemmed from a different source than Sean might assume.

"Look, it doesn't have to be for long," said Sean, doing his best to sound encouraging. "Harding claims Masterson is failing at executing a milk run, and he wants you to drop in and fix it. We'll have you on a new account in no time. Plus, you have the new client to contend with." His tone gave the lie to the confidence in his words, but that wasn't what worried Dag. "This isn't the way I wanted to welcome you back. But on the other hand, you're in demand. That goes a long way with the partners."

Dag drained his espresso, the dregs as thick and strong as diesel.

"Don't worry," he told Sean. "I'll handle it."

If only he could be so sure.

"Oh, and one other thing," said Sean with a sympathetic wince. "Don't forget to pack a parka."

CHAPTER 21

Wintry light shone from the distant sun skimming the edge of the horizon like a child's pebble skipping over the surface of a pond. Dag jerked against the restraints as wind buffeted the chopper. He pushed away the outside temperature notification in his feed. Knowing precisely how freezing it was going to be wouldn't lessen the sting. Beyond the glass bubble of the cockpit, a leaden sky hung over an ocean the color of charcoal that stretched as far as the eye could see, interrupted only by occasional tufts of crumbling foam at the peaks of breaking swell and dirty chunks of ice bobbing along tenacious currents. Turbulent columns of Arctic sea smoke spiraled over the chop, steamlike ghosts forming where frigid air met warmer water.

It had been years since Dag was above the Arctic Circle, and the accelerating pace of change was tangible in a way that no mere report could communicate. The vast expanse of perennial sea ice had been in dramatic retreat even when Dag was a child. Polar bears had been consigned to live on only as the tragic heroes of nature documentaries. Even so, when he was last here, there had still been microcontinents of sea ice choking the Arctic Ocean. But every annual increase in global temperature calved great chunks off those massive bergs. Every time that happened, there was less ice to reflect the sun's radiation, which further accelerated temperature increases. It was a self-reinforcing loop, a runaway process that had doomed an ecosystem, threatened a biosphere, and made Lowell Harding billions.

"Isn't it beautiful?" A rapturous smile lit up Lowell's baby face. He was strapped into the seat next to Dag, rakish gray streaks along the temples of his shaggy mop of light-brown hair.

Ahead of them, an oil platform rose from the churning waves. Massive pillars plunged down to the seabed, and pedestal cranes towered over the main deck in a forest of steel lattice. Flares puffed up from the exhaust stack like matches struck in a blizzard. Pumping stations, power generators, control centers, barracks, and storage tanks formed a miniature city on the deck, everything painted in garish shades of yellow, red, and black. Dag looked up from the platform to see its many siblings stretching out to the horizon like an archipelago of industrial islands on a dark and hostile sea. Running lights blinked off drones and helicopters swooping and hovering among the array of platforms. Tankers, icebreakers, and support vessels plied the waves between them.

"What happened with Masterson?" asked Dag. "Sean said your reprimand was . . . colorful."

A shadow flickered across Lowell's face, but his smile returned almost immediately. "Do you know why we're not at the Ranch, Dag?"

The Ranch. Dag had killed his first stag in the acres of wilderness surrounding Lowell's estate. He remembered the thick smell of blood, how the beast's eyes had glazed over after shuddering out its last breath. It had taken all his willpower not to vomit as they quartered the animal and carried it through miles of backcountry. That had been the longest shower Dag had ever taken, scrubbing at his steaming skin long after the muck had washed away. Later in the evening, he had been happy to partake in the Ranch's unparalleled bourbon collection. If he couldn't rinse the feeling from his body, perhaps he could drown it. The alcohol had fortified him to stomach the rich venison, swimming in butter and garnished with rosemary.

The chopper came down for a low pass over the platform. At this distance, pipes, wiring, and pumping units were visible. A spider drone was repainting the side of the bridge. Antennae whipped back and forth in the frigid wind like prairie grass in a tornado. A worker in a heavy parka making his way along a gangway turned and waved at them as they roared past, his face hidden behind a mask and goggles.

Dag was pressed back into his seat as they accelerated up and away from the deck. He turned his head over his shoulder and caught Lowell's sparkling green eyes.

"You wanted to show off your empire," said Dag, "not just invite me to the throne room."

The corner of Lowell's mouth turned up. "Ahh," he said. "I can already see I made the right decision."

Dag arched an eyebrow.

"Masterson," said Lowell with a hopeless shake of his head, "committed the ultimate sin. I had no choice but to throw him out. A pathetic little man."

"He failed you, then."

"Oh, he certainly did, but not in the way you mean," said Lowell. "He was a competent lobbyist, not a natural talent like yourself. But failure was not his failing." He gave Dag a confessional look. "You know me better than that, surely."

Dag snorted. "He bored you."

Lowell's hands shot out fast as a snake and pinched Dag's cheeks like a doting grandmother.

"Aha!" he said. "It's good to have you back at my side."

Dag rolled his eyes. "You're a cruel old man."

"Is that why you deserted me after delivering this frozen kingdom?" Lowell swept his arm across the cockpit to take in the stormy vista beyond the glass.

"It's not as frozen as it once was."

Lowell nodded sagely. "And that brings us to the heart of the matter, does it not? The thaw unlocked the world's last oil frontier from its frozen vault. You wrangled the Arctic Council to win me concessions for the entire Lomonosov Ridge. Extracting its hidden treasures further expedited the thaw—a scheme profitable enough to make Rockefeller blush." He sighed. "And upon our victory, you sidled off to coddle some other client."

"Apex is a partnership," said Dag. "They needed my attention elsewhere."

"Hmm, and such a promising young don couldn't get a bunch of stodgy old louts to change their minds?"

Dag had known this was coming. It was critical that he pass the test. The Island had tapped Lowell's feed two years prior in preparation for this initiative. Once Dag signed on, Emily showed him the occasional searches Lowell made to keep an eye on his former aide. While Dag was traveling back to Washington to meet with Sean, Javier had dropped subtle reminders of Dag's competence and Masterson's lack thereof into Lowell's feed. The results spoke for themselves.

Dag shrugged and looked directly at Lowell. "I asked to be reassigned away from you," he said. "The partnership was opposed. I had to pull strings to get transitioned out."

"Now why would you go and do a thing like that? After all I've done for you?" Lowell hid the intensity of his curiosity behind a sad-puppy expression.

Dag let a few seconds pass as the weight of their shared history came to bear.

"Because," he said at last. "I don't dawdle on quicksand."

Now it was Lowell's turn to let a long moment of silence slip by. Dag's stomach proceeded to tie itself in knots. It might be over before it had even begun. But then Lowell barked out a harsh laugh, and the tension drained from the cockpit.

"Yes," he said. "Yes, yes, yes." His voice increased in volume with each word, and he shook his hands in the air, fingers splayed. "By all the gods of compound interest, welcome home, my boy."

CHAPTER 22

The helicopter swung in for a landing on Lowell's flagship, a monumental icebreaker that towered above the rolling seas. Running lights glowed in the Arctic dimness and the deck was abuzz with activity. The rotors kicked up spray as they settled gently onto the helipad.

"It'll make me sound old, but I still remember when you needed a human pilot," said Lowell as they pulled up the hoods of their parkas. "And let me tell you, the landings weren't half as smooth."

They unclipped their restraints, opened the doors, and dropped onto the deck. Dag caught his breath as frigid wind razored across his face, instantly numbing his nose and forming ice crystals on his eyelashes. No matter how many times he visited, the intense humidity in these latitudes always shocked him. The helicopter's engine whirred to rest behind them, and the invisible blur above their heads slowed until they could differentiate the individual rotors. It smelled of salt, grease, and raw fish. The thrum of the great marine-diesel engine in the belly of the ship reverberated up through their feet.

"It's as cold as an ice queen's twat," said Lowell, hunching against the wind. "Let's get inside before my face falls off."

They descended diamond-grip steel stairs from the helipad and hurried across the main deck to the five-story bridge superstructure. This class of ship was now rarely used except to accompany container vessels through the Transpolar Passage, which ran directly through the high seas at the center of the Arctic Ocean. Melting ice had already made the previously restricted Northeast and Northwest Passages accessible in summer, establishing new connections between the Atlantic and Pacific. Yet another second-order effect of climate change that Dag had helped Lowell profit from. The Arctic Council deal had secured trade as well as drilling concessions. The specialized infrastructure and technology required to operate here made his group the natural leader and established a high barrier to entry to fend off potential contenders.

The wide superstructure door hissed open in front of them, and they stumbled inside.

"Welcome back, sir," said a striking, tall blonde woman with a Danish accent. She wore a conservative suit that set her apart from the other crew members in coveralls, who milled about farther down the wide hallway. "I trust you had a good flight."

"You remember Dag," said Lowell with a wink. "Our political wunderkind."

"Good to see you, Freja," said Dag. "Ready to have someone to argue with again?"

"As long as you're ready to lose." She gave him a cool look. Freja had no official title within Lowell's corporate behemoth but played a role somewhere at the intersection of assistant, confidante, and consigliere. She was the engine that realized her boss's ambitions, and woe betide the fool who stood in her way. She set off down the hallway, heels muffled on the rubberized floor, and they hurried to catch up. Grizzled crewmen twice her size got out of her path like animals fleeing a forest fire.

"It's not about who wins or loses," said Dag in a playful tone he knew drove her crazy. "It's about which strategy is best."

"Speaking of strategy," she said, "we have a problem. The delegations from Vietnam, Turkey, and Switzerland have indicated support for the proposal. Rachel Leibovitz just published a sympathetic op-ed."

"Where does that put the current tally?" asked Lowell.

"Over the top," she said, anger seething beneath her words. She dropped a series of infographics into their shared feed. Polling statistics hovered in color-coded groups connected by treaty, financial, and trade affiliations, all backlinked to individual delegate profiles and cross-referenced with specific terms in the agreement itself. "I still can't believe this. Five years ago, we sank an identical initiative before it even left committee. Now we're firing on all cylinders and *losing*."

"We're not losing," Lowell growled as he hit the elevator call button. "We just haven't won yet."

"I'm ever so buoyed by your confidence in the face of facts," said Freja, manipulating and highlighting the data to illustrate how various statistical models all projected the initiative to pass by a slim margin. "A global carbon tax would castrate us. It would fundamentally undermine the value of half our assets and slash the IRR on the remaining half."

Their triumvirate stewed in awkward silence as the elevator rose. Dag couldn't help mentally cataloging which players had reached their own conclusions and to whom the Island was applying covert pressure. Javier had shown him the dossiers and social graphs. Dag had met Trần Thị Mai Loan, the Vietnamese delegate's chief of staff, at a few diplomatic cocktail parties over the years. Fifty-four months of carefully timed drip from the Island had altered her media engagement patterns to reflect a clear shift in priorities toward advancing climate talks. She was the primary gatekeeper protecting her boss's time and attention, and his policy platform had absorbed her new perspective as if by osmosis.

When the doors opened, they stepped out into an identical hallway, minus any officers or crew members. Pipes and brightly colored bundles of wire formed a canopy above their heads. Their footsteps echoed off white walls that were interrupted only by the occasional control panel and fire extinguisher.

"It's been a long day of travel," said Lowell. "Time to rest. We'll reconvene in the morning and get to work." He dismissed the shared feed, and the superimposed data vanished. "With the three of us working together, those bastards won't know what hit them."

Freja snorted and then gestured to a door in the corridor's wall. "Your quarters, Mr. Calhoun," she said. "See you bright and early." Then she stalked off down the hall.

Dag ducked away as Lowell ruffled his hair.

"What the hell?" said Dag, batting away his hand. Freja was the only person he'd ever seen who was able to maintain composure in Lowell's presence.

The older man twitched his eyebrows, eyes bright.

"Let no one call me an ungrateful patron," he said.

"What's that supposed to mean?"

But Lowell had already spun away, whistling as he walked down the corridor.

Suppressing a yawn, Dag turned back to the door as it sensed his presence and slid open. He stepped through and into another world. Dark wood paneling and shelves of paper books gave the living room the atmosphere of a colonial-era study. Leather chairs sat around a mahogany coffee table upon which rested a box of Cuban cigars and a crystal decanter of scotch. Filaments glowed in antique light bulbs. It smelled of rosewood and tobacco. A porthole in the outside walls looked out over the darkening churn of the Arctic Ocean, which seemed a world away. To the right, one door led into a study dominated by a wide desk covered in classical accoutrements, and behind another was a bathroom equipped with a full Jacuzzi. Dag ran a hand through his hair—only Lowell would commission apartments like this on a working vessel where space was the hottest of commodities.

Now that he was finally alone, the full weight of Dag's jet lag hit him like a sledgehammer. Lowell had always been exhausting to handle—the man loved to keep those around him off balance. But the plan Dag had hatched with Emily brought a whole new level of anxiety to every interaction. The final month leading up to the vote would be a delicate game of cat and mouse. If he hoped to pull it off, he needed to take every chance at shut-eye he could get.

Walking back across the living room, he pushed open the double doors that led into the bedroom and froze. His heart leapt into his throat, and his hands closed into fists. Was this some kind of cruel joke? Had Lowell seen through the facade already and brought him here only to have him executed in a vicious nightmare worthy of a James Bond villain? A thousand prayers and regrets flitted through Dag's mind.

A king-size four-poster bed dominated the bedroom, maroon curtains tied back discreetly. His shoes sank into thick carpet. But there, facing away from him, standing upright on its back two legs, was a polar bear. Even as he tried to make sense of what was in front of him, some part of his brain realized things weren't quite right. The beast's fur was sleek and creamy, but its skin hung too loosely on its body. It had less bulk than even the starving bears Dag had glimpsed years before, desperately hunting for seals as their habitat melted away beneath their feet.

The monster began to turn, and Dag belatedly realized he had taken two paces back and raised his hands. He ran down a mental list of what he might use as a weapon but couldn't come up with anything deadlier than an anachronistic encyclopedia. He yearned for the guns and tactical gear he'd left behind in his new room on the Island.

But then the creature completed its turn, and Dag's jaw dropped. It wasn't a polar bear. It was a woman.

Wide dark eyes stared out at Dag for an infinite moment. Then she shook the bear's taxidermy head off her own and spread her arms wide, letting the pelt pile on the floor around her naked body. She gazed at him evenly. Dark locks tumbled across tan shoulders. Small areolae highlighted her full breasts. A thin line of trimmed pubic hair called the eye to her sex. She was a wild goddess, an erotic vision born of ice and fire.

"They say there are only hundreds left." Her voice was a low growl with a Korean lilt. "Haunting the northernmost villages of the Arctic nations like angry ghosts. There's something romantic about that, the tragedy of living out the last days of your entire species. But what do I say? I say, whistle while the world burns, Mr. Calhoun."

She held out a hand. "Will you help me fuck the pain away?"

CHAPTER 23

She called herself Hannah, and she was another test. A gorgeous lady of negotiable virtue didn't just wander into your berth to assay your sexual mettle. Neither did a savvy captain of industry hand out such favors without an ulterior motive. As soon as the pelt settled to the floor around Hannah's shapely legs, the message was clear. If Dag was to rejoin Lowell's inner circle, he must first consummate his loyalty.

Lowell, a shit-eating grin plastered across his face as he peered at Dag over the brim of his steaming coffee mug, never passed up the opportunity for another game.

"Sleep well?" Lowell could barely contain himself.

As tests went, spending a night with Hannah was hard to complain about. Dag's chosen profession didn't leave much time for romantic relationships and he never paid for sex, which in combination meant that he didn't have much of it. On the whole, that wasn't such a bad thing, considering how uncomfortable he was with the prospect of coitus. Sensing Dag's shyness, Lowell had teased him about it over the years, finding ways to insert seductresses into Dag's path who turned out to be on company payroll. Dag had been steadfast in politely declining their advances, resulting in ever more teasing.

Knowing that this time he had no choice but to win back Lowell's trust, Dag had pushed down a sense of unaccountable guilt and finally surrendered to Hannah's charms. Dag could feel the tips of his ears turning scarlet. He tried to wipe away fresh memories of flesh, broken taboos, and unmentionable transgressions. Half his body ached, and the other half smarted from fingernail scratches. They had done things to each other he'd never even known to fantasize about.

Seeing Dag flush, Lowell broke out into raucous laughter.

"Attaboy," he said, slapping the table between them. "Did you hear that, Freja? We've finally made a man of him."

Freja gave Dag an unreadable look and said, "I'm happy to hear you're settling in."

"You've always been obsessed with Korean women," said Lowell, tapping his temple. "I don't forget things like that. Sexual predilection is a window into the soul."

"Let's get to work," said Dag, turning away to pour himself a coffee. "From what Freja said last night, we're about as bulletproof as a high-thread-count duvet."

Lowell slid his chair back, scooped up his mug, and stepped over to the wide window.

"This is our domain," he said, pressing a hand against the glass. In the Arctic half-light beyond, drilling platforms stood out on the marine horizon like industrial Christmas trees. "The three of us in this room—we won it, we secured it. Freja, you took an idea and turned it into a well-oiled machine. Dag, remember the look on Lisa's face when the votes were counted?"

Dag couldn't suppress a smile. Lisa Burke was the most vocal opponent to the Arctic Council deal. They had circled each other for the three years it took to ratify the agreement, often running into each other on the way to or from meetings with staffers and appointees. The expression on her face when the council's decision proved she had been outmaneuvered was a thing of tragic beauty. Lowell sent her a gift basket filled with BDSM toys and a note suggesting she find new ways to vent her frustration.

"It seems inevitable in retrospect, but do you remember what the so-called experts were saying up until the eve of our victory? They said it was impossible." Lowell took a sip of coffee. "It was impossible technically—the conditions were too extreme. It was impossible commercially—the logistics and economies of scale were too complicated. It was impossible politically—to wrangle concessions from countries with competing claims that were ready to go to war over the North."

He peeled his hand off the glass, its shape outlined in condensation. "And now, now that we have rendered their armchair criticisms moot through old-fashioned execution, they seek to steal our hard-earned spoils. And both of you know the extent of what's at stake. Not just this godforsaken wasteland, but the bets we've made around the world." He spun and looked at Dag and Freja in turn. "A strictly enforced global carbon tax would undermine our central investment thesis and eat away at the very foundation of our business. But we have a secret advantage, a trump card they simply can't compete with."

His expression softened, and a genial smile lit up his face. "Us." He held out a hand with a finger pointed at each of them. "We built this. We will rebuild it if need be. And in the meantime, we will pull out all the stops and sink this motherfucking initiative before it cements the hits we're already taking on market cap."

Setting his mug down on the table, he clapped his hands three times. "So," he said in a let's-get-down-to-business voice, "what do we do?"

Dag looked at Freja. She waved him on with a manicured hand. "Please," she said. "Enlighten us. You're supposed to be the political wunderkind, aren't you?"

Turning back to Lowell, Dag considered the man he had agreed to betray. Lowell lived for the win and would do whatever was necessary to take what he wanted. He saw opportunity in disaster and viewed laws as tools rather than ethical guidelines. He could be a total asshole and had serious boundary issues. But at the same time, Dag couldn't deny that a certain kind of friendship had grown between them.

It had started with a simple mutual respect for the other's efficacy. Whatever people might say about his values, nobody could deny Lowell's credentials as a world-class capitalist. He had a meritocratic bent that had inspired him to choose to work with Dag instead of a more experienced senior partner. Lowell was the client who had guaranteed Dag's professional trajectory at Apex. Over the years they'd worked together, Dag had come to see this strange, charismatic man as a kind of older brother.

Lowell grew up penniless in a Texas ghost town. Surrounded by hangers-on from a forgotten generation, he would retreat into the ruins of a long-abandoned Walmart and dream of escaping the shabby world into which he'd been born. He had emerged with a chip on his shoulder and an unquenchable thirst for more. On the basis of a boldness many would call madness, he'd amassed a fortune. Dag respected that. It was real. Beyond that, they shared a carefully cultivated cynicism, a sense that they owed nothing to a fucked-up world. Dag now saw that as profound entitlement, but Lowell was still a friend, even if he was an insane megalomaniac.

"If the deck is indeed stacked the way that Freja's polls suggest," said Dag, "then we're going to have to throw a Hail Mary. We need to cut a deal with Eddie Hsu. He'll be able to strong-arm the Chinese to lean on their vassals, and we'll have our numbers."

Freja snorted, and Lowell's face darkened.

"You know what I think of Hsu," he said.

Dag shrugged. "I thought you said you wanted to win."

They both stared daggers, and Dag squirmed in his suit. The scratches on his lower back chafed. Despite the trappings of wish fulfillment and the pleasures of experimentation, the previous night's carnal spree had left him disgusted with himself.

It clarified just how negotiable his own virtue really was.

CHAPTER 24

"The Estevez clan fell through." Sean's voice was tight. "That bastard Carlos told me he'd back the bill in the Senado. But when it came down to it, he voted the other way."

A chilly breeze gusted over them, and Dag pulled up the collar on his charcoal wool jacket. At least this wasn't the Arctic. There had been just enough time after wheels down for him to shower and change at his condo before this meeting. The wind ruffled the reflection of the Washington Monument in the pond at the center of Constitution Gardens. Dag's gaze traveled up from the rippling water to the thing itself. Thrusting up from the National Mall like a patriotic phallus, the monument was the tallest obelisk on the planet and its tallest stone structure. From this distance, Dag could barely make out the line a third of the way up that showed where construction was halted and later resumed with a different shade of marble. Twenty-three years the delays had lasted. Twenty-three years of insufficient funding, infighting over control of the commissioning society, and of course, the chaos resulting from the Civil War. It was Dag's favorite symbol of America, a country that always fumbled but never quit trying to outdo the rest of the world.

"Carlos and his clique are climbers," said Dag. "But they've never had enough conviction to take real risk. That's why they've stayed at the middle of the pack for so many cycles."

"We'll need new blood."

"Try Francisco Vasquez. His family doesn't have the highbrow connections, but with their media footprint, he should be able to put some real pressure on the fence-sitters. Plus, Francisco needs to impress his auntie if he ever wants to lead the family. Give him the opportunity to prove his worth. Combine that with a push from the World Bank over distressed debt, and you've got a strong enough hand."

Sean sighed. "That'll add at least another nine months."

"Nine months of billable hours."

In the silence that followed, the crunch of their feet on the gravel path seemed unnaturally loud. A huge weeping willow trailed leaves into the pond. A flock of mud-brown sparrows flitted past. No other pedestrians were nearby—it was an unseasonably cold morning, and Washingtonians were cradling cups of steaming coffee and blessing the miracle of central heating.

Dag glanced sidelong at Sean. His face was unreadable behind his bushy red beard. It would have been better to ease into this, but there wasn't time. The carbon tax vote was coming up next week in Taipei, and they needed at least a few days of grace in order for the proposition to have a chance of succeeding. Lowell knew that, and Dag needed to maintain the appearance of pursuing his best interest with haste and efficacy. Until the crucial moment, it was of paramount importance that Dag act the part. Lowell must never know that the game was rigged against him.

"I need to talk to Eddie Hsu," said Dag.

Sean stuffed his hands into his jacket pockets. They continued along the meandering path, the water to their left. The sky was a vast dome of gray above their heads, draining the city of color and lending it noir overtones. Ghostly memories of Gretchen slipped into Dag's mind, her hair as red as Sean's beard. In between hotly contested debates, they'd imagined futures of whispered conversations fraught with geopolitical consequence. Though they differed in their outlook, they shared the urge to become players in the great game. The reality of it was shabby compared to the grandeur of their dreams.

"That's quite a request," said Sean at last.

"I know," said Dag. "It's for Harding."

"Even so."

"There's no way around it—we need to call it in."

"I see."

Dag kicked at a loose pebble, and it bounced along the path in front of them. "Look," he said, "I'll ping Francisco, set up a meeting with you, inject him with a sense of urgency. I can also get you an invite to Donya's art auction in February. That shindig is packed with enough La Condesa posh to give you a whole cast of new supporters. It won't just be good for this deal, it'll be good for the firm over the long run, cement our relationships in Mexico. It'll prove useful for your Pemex work too."

Sean gave him a long look, and Dag struggled to hold his gaze. Once fraternal, their rapport had grown brittle. But Dag couldn't quite diagnose where the phase change might have begun.

"You do realize what you're asking," said Sean. "Multiple senior partners will have to call in favors to arrange this."

Dag nodded solemnly. Hsu had orchestrated Taiwan's ascendance, made it the crux balancing East and West, moved the UN headquarters to Taipei. "If Apex wants me to represent Harding, they have to assign the resources he's paying us to deploy. It's as simple as that."

The path deposited them at the Reflecting Pool. The wind had died, and the Washington Monument faced off against the Lincoln Memorial across water as still as glass, a tribute erected to the man who had ended the Civil War and allowed for the great obelisk to be completed after so many years lying fallow.

At length, Sean sighed. "I'll see what I can do," he said.

CHAPTER 25

Dag stared down through the window of the jet. The Rockies, bald except for a few snowy peaks, rose up from the dry expanse of the Great Plains. A sense of manifest destiny had inspired American settlers to venture out across their newly claimed continent. Verdant wilderness and untold fortunes awaited them, along with infection, violence, and disaster. They had pressed ahead into the unknown, hoping to escape the lives they left behind and forge something new and wild and beautiful with whatever they could pack in their wagons or tuck away in their souls.

Now he could zip across the country and around the world in a matter of hours, sheltered from the elements in an aerodynamic cocoon where the greatest risk was boredom. What might those early pioneers make of such technological wizardry? In their eyes, would his magical accoutrement offset his inability to shoe a horse or trap a rabbit? Transported to the present, would they be disappointed that humanity used its surfeit scientific mastery to play ancient games honed to perfection in the backrooms of Renaissance Venice, Ming Beijing, and Pharaonic Egypt?

His ultimate destination was across the Pacific. Taiwan, an island that Eddie Hsu had elevated from pawn to queen. Dag would have to be extraordinarily delicate dealing with such an adept. Winning someone to your cause was one thing. Bringing them to exactly one hair's breadth of switching sides without actually succeeding was something entirely more nuanced. His chest tightened when he imagined the inevitable fallout with Sean and Apex. When the partners stuck their necks out on your behalf, you damn well didn't come home empty-handed. But having made a deal with the devil so many years before, he could hardly expect to renege unscathed.

Memories scrolled by along with the landscape below. Driving out over county roads to buy up thousands of acres of unincorporated land with heavy rainfall and unassailable water rights. Petitioning federal officials to send the National Guard to the edge of the great blaze instead of its smoldering heart, condemning Southern California to the flames. Vast construction projects rubber-stamped by desperate politicians, providing shelter to millions of refugees and lining Lowell's pockets in one fell swoop. Given how many people lamented the inevitability of climate change, it was surprising how few actually bet on it. But just like any other addiction, convincing yourself that you were smarter than everyone else was ultimately self-destructive.

He remembered the cows grazing on the Island's idyllic paddock. *I've always been obsessed by the tragedy of the commons, the open-access problem.* Emily was right, and the intensity of her gaze was tangible even in memory. We might have invented chocolate and sent a woman to Mars, but humans still couldn't figure out how to collaborate on fundamental things, like making sure our own planet would support future generations. Science had cut away technical problems like a hot scalpel through butter, but social problems persisted because there was no perfect solution, only the messy ongoing processes of commerce and politics.

Wrestling with those questions had brought him and Gretchen together in the beginning and driven them apart at the end. At first, they enjoyed whiskey-fueled debates charged with grad student enthusiasm. Eventually, the arguments became circular and ideology corroded affection. There hadn't been a fight or a dramatic falling-out. Instead, they succumbed to the creeping obsolescence of a relationship gone stale. They tried sex. But copulation couldn't replace conversation and resulted only in an awkward morning after. As they lost hope of changing the other's worldview, they faded from each other's lives. At the time, it had been the natural thing to do. Now, it seemed a damn shame. If you couldn't come to terms with those across the aisle, you lost your claim on the common good.

Will you help me fuck the pain away? A popular approach to suffering injustice and the burden of collective stupidity. Unbidden, the pelt fell away from Hannah's shoulders and she stood there, naked and luminous. Dag's heart skipped a beat, and he reached out to touch the window in front of him, plexiglass cool against his fingertips. A shiver rippled through him. Curling tendrils of suspicion crept into his heart like an acrid fog. He didn't want to fully acknowledge it lest his attention lend it credence. *You've always been obsessed with Korean women. I don't forget things like that. Sexual predilection is a window into the soul.*

Lowell might be wiser than he knew. If true, it was outrageous, a violation far deeper than the revelations plastered across Room 412. But at the same time, it was so very perfect, as beautiful and deadly as nightshade.

Pulling up his feed, he checked the flight path and reviewed the itinerary. Then he leaned back in his chair and ran his hands through his hair. It might not bear thinking about, but it couldn't be dismissed. Opening his eyes, he rerouted the plane to San Francisco.

The view shifted as the jet banked onto its new course. The early settlers who braved countless dangers to traverse the mountains thousands of meters below hadn't laid claim to virgin territory. They paid the blood price for their bounty, the natives unprepared for the dual onslaught of disease and deadly new technology.

History could seem irrelevant to the present's unrelenting pace of change. What insights could a medieval text bring to bear when science had transformed the human experience so completely? But history had been Dag's favorite topic during his graduate studies. At Georgetown, he'd always tried to sneak extra courses into his schedule and transfer the credit to his degree program. Gretchen had teased him about it. Many of his fellow enthusiasts mined the *Iliad* for mythological archetypes, anthropological clues, or fodder for academic debate. They assumed the actual story was largely fanciful, a pretty tale wrapped around a historical battle. But Dag, soaked in sordid reports of actual Washington dealmaking, had found the plot entirely believable, or at least as credible as the dissolution of the European Union or the genesis of World War I. Analysts liked to generalize geopolitics into abstract trend lines, explaining wars with complex economic reasoning. But in the real world, the human beings in charge often made momentous decisions for far more obscure, far more personal reasons. Helen wasn't a metaphor—she was flesh and blood.

A face really could launch a thousand ships.

CHAPTER 26

Dag had thought he was prepared. He had tried to calm his mind as he stepped through the thick oak doors, still his racing heart as the red satin curtains parted. But even though he knew it would come, the silence ambushed him completely. The sixth sense of the world's information highway roaring around him vanished along with the latent awareness of so many small but crucial details. He could no longer refer to the time it would take for the plane to refuel, the ETA to his final destination, or his weighted stream of messages. It was like losing a limb.

Nell's hand touched his arm, and he was unusually aware of its warmth, its smooth dryness, the color of her slender umber fingers against his olive skin. The sense of sudden isolation heightened every sense, pulling him bodily into the present moment.

"It gets easier," she said with smiling gray eyes. "But it takes time. A few more visits and you won't give it a second thought."

Dag let out a slow, controlled breath. "I'm okay," he said. "It's just so . . . quiet."

"Don't tell Dylan that"—she shrugged in the direction of the solo saxophonist performing by the giant hearth—"or he'll demand a drummer."

Dag smiled weakly and let her guide him through tables packed with Silicon Valley royalty. A stooped bartender laughed uproariously as he shook a cocktail. An adolescent girl checkmated her opponent in a game of chess and smacked the timer with a triumphant grin. Feedless, an engineer sketched out a concept for a friend on an actual paper napkin.

"Here we are, Mr. Calhoun. Enjoy your time with us," said Nell, tucking a lock of hair behind her ear before returning to the reception area.

Dag slid into the booth and stared into the fire. The dancing flames helped calm the existential panic of disconnection. With each breath, he could feel his heart rate slow. Unlike the other patrons, he wasn't just here for recreational reasons or to shirk the burden of celebrity. This was perhaps the only location where he could allay his suspicions without fear of direct reprisal. Yes, this was the right move. Otherwise, the battery acid of uncertainty would eat away at his sanity.

"Hello, hello." Dag jerked forward as lips brushed his ear, the whisper dripping with innuendo.

Diana appeared from the booth behind and slid in across the table from Dag. She winked, tongue darting out of her mouth to lick her lips suggestively.

"Does it have to be *every* time?" asked Dag, trying to regain his composure.

"Only until you catch me. But I think you like it."

"I don't," he said. "You can take my word for it."

"Some men like to be hunted," she said. "Did you know that bears have the most scent receptors of any terrestrial mammal? They're my spirit animal. I can smell it even if you don't know it yourself yet."

"Thanks, but I don't want to be anyone's prey."

"Aha." She raised a finger. "But that's the thing—prey doesn't get to choose. You can run, but you can't stop being prey."

"I'm pretty sure it doesn't count as tracking me down when I told you exactly where and when to meet."

"But the fact that you keep inviting me to these clandestine inter-ludes suggests you're finally falling for my feminine charms. I mean, I'm not at all surprised. I am, after all, totally irresistible."

"No wonder you were fired from the CIA. Do you treat all your clients this way?"

She harrumphed and tossed her curly brown hair. "Like they could have fired me. Those bureaucratic dimwits had their heads so far up their asses they could self-diagnose colon cancer. And as for my other clients, none of them are as cute as you, sweetie." She blew him a kiss. "Are you going to hold a grudge just because I've got a crush?"

Dag couldn't help but crack a grin. "I pity the fool who tries to stand in your way."

"Now *that*"—she clapped her hands—"is a sentiment I can get behind. You're learning. Slowly, to be sure, but you can only ask so much of the duller sex." She ran her fingers along the wood grain of the table, and her tone turned pensive. "Damn, it's been forever since I was off-grid. Such an odd feeling, reminds me of learning to swim when I was little. My dad was right there with me in the pool. One minute I was giggling nervously at his assurances, and the next my head dunked under and I was alone." She mimicked ducking her head beneath the surface. "That was the scary part. Not just not being able to breathe, but not being able to hear or speak."

"At the end of the day, humans are social animals," said Dag. "Maybe communication is just as life-affirming as a breath of fresh air."

She squinted at him for a moment. "Dag Calhoun," she said, "you've got a philosopher hidden beneath all that spit and polish."

He shrugged. "It only comes out when I disconnect."

"Speaking of," she said, looking around Analog, "I didn't expect you to be an unplugger. You're too grown-up to be an experimental trust fund baby and not famous enough to need refuge from the suffocating attention of the masses. So is this your version of kink? You wanted to get me truly alone so you could share your most intimate secrets and lure me into your bed once and for all?"

Thoughts churned in Dag's head as he stared across at her. Nine thousand meters over the Rockies, this had seemed like a good idea, a hedge. But here, sitting across from Diana, looking into her brown eyes, struggling to keep up with her banter, he had to confront the magnitude of the trust this plan required. Their professional relationship had been productive and reliable since day one. But even though intercourse wasn't the endgame, securing her help required Dag to offer himself to her on a level far more intimate than sex. He wasn't ready to be that vulnerable. By the same token, he couldn't leave this stone unturned. The saxophone was too loud, the fire oppressing, the tapestried walls claustrophobic.

"Okay, dude," said Diana. "Talk to me. You're starting to creep me out."

"Look, I—" He faltered. "It's—sorry, but this is hard for me to say. I need your help with something. You're the only person with the statistical and computer science chops to do it. Plus, well . . ." He felt color rising into his cheeks. "You're the only person I can trust with something like this. I hope I can, anyway."

She frowned. "You can trust me," she said.

"Yes, well . . ." He faltered again.

"Look," she said, "if you're hiring me for another job, why are we here? Why not meet, like, anywhere else, where you can just shoot me a data dump with background? It'd be a hell of a lot easier than a full verbal briefing. Want to just step outside? I promise I'll join you for a fancy cocktail afterward."

He shook his head. "No, we can't. Hopefully, this is nothing more than a wild-goose chase, in which case I'm just being paranoid. But if I'm right, then I can't risk having this conversation accessible by feed."

"Then just mark it private."

"That won't work—there are people who can circumvent Commonwealth settings."

"That's—" Her nostrils flared. "That's ludicrous. Look, I know there are loads of conspiracy theories out there. Lord knows, enough of them are true—I saw it from the inside at all the three-letter acronyms. But feed infrastructure is airtight. That's how the whole damn system works. That's why Commonwealth is more powerful than any national government. Without it, everything would fall apart. You need me for my expertise, and my expert opinion is that you should chill the fuck out."

"I've seen it happen," said Dag. "I've seen them do it."

Her expression vacillated between fear and pity. "Does this have something to do with your new girlfriend? Sheesh, I knew I shouldn't have helped you track her down. Now she's got your head tied up in a thousand knots, hasn't she?"

"I'm giving you root access to my feed and entire archive," he said, and a burden seemed to lift from his shoulders with this irrevocable leap of faith. "You'll see the invite as soon as we leave Analog. You'll need it to execute the analysis."

Diana's mouth dropped open. Even as his mind reeled over what he'd just committed to, Dag couldn't help but relish the fact that he had, for once, ambushed her.

CHAPTER 27

Every visit to Taiwan cast a lurid fluorescent light into Dag's soul. As the geopolitical hub of the Pacific Rim, it was a frequent destination for him. But there were too many dark memories buried here, too much he wanted to forget. So as the car whisked him away from the high-speed rail station, he was grateful to lose himself in the briefing.

"It hasn't been easy because Hsu's never held an official position," said Javier, live video of him and Emily streaming at the corner of Dag's visual field. "But we've teased out correlations among those closest to him on the social graph and corroborated that with semantic analysis of his communications archive as well as financial contributions from groups he's affiliated with. Then we built it up into a model of his track record along various policy vectors, which you can see here."

The digital geography of Hsu's life spread out across the shared feed. Algorithms structured individual data points into matrices that piled up into ridges associated with specific policy-issue areas. The topography evolved over time, shaped by the erosion of changing opinion, network effects, and outside variables. Ridges grew and shrank relative to one another as the news cycle adjusted and different topics took center stage. A previously cohesive heuristic would split into smaller tributaries as new public interests emerged and Hsu's priorities, competitors, and collaborators changed. The information landscape morphed in real time as the leading edge of the present introduced new data.

Beyond the feed, Dag's car navigated smoothly through the narrow streets. Skyscrapers rose on all sides, sheer cliffs of graphene festooned with glowing characters. Autonomous cars zipped around each other in a cloud-choreographed dance, and drones buzzed through the airspace between the buildings. Street vendors hawked stinky tofu, oyster pancakes, and fried dumplings. The sidewalks were bustling with pedestrians in every manner of stylish cut. Enormous abstract sculptures rose from the center of every intersection, the city's modernist menagerie.

Focusing his attention inward, Dag tightened the parameters. Tracts of data sloughed away until a single mountain range dominated the view—every scrap of Hsu's digital debris associated with international climate change accords. This ridge had grown in every dimension over the past few years and in the preceding six months had expanded dramatically as the United Nations Climate Change Conference in Taipei grew steadily closer. Now that there was only a week left before the convention, the data blossomed as it intersected Hsu's live feed, sucking up every last detail. Zooming in, the moraines and outcrops resolved into discrete messages, video clips, parsed financial transactions, search histories, content-consumption metrics, metadata statistics, stress tests, scheduling blocks, and influence charts. If the feed was a digital mirror, they were looking at the sum total of Hsu's reflection.

Dag suppressed a shiver. It was from precisely this kind of surgical invasion of his own feed that Emily had handpicked the montage for Room 412. Now he was complicit in playing voyeur. But as distasteful as it was, he couldn't deny its utility in service of their current mission. The ends would have to justify the means.

"Where have you made adjustments?" asked Dag, as the car pulled onto the highway. They were leaving the downtown core, and the buildings got progressively smaller as they spiraled out from the city center.

"This is our first international initiative," said Emily, "so we haven't been working on Mr. Hsu for very long."

She layered on yellow scaffolding that highlighted every tweak the Island had made to Hsu's feed over time. They were curating his media to emphasize analyses favoring the global carbon tax legislation, prioritizing communications from colleagues who had already pledged their support for the initiative, amplifying any climate-friendly Hsu posts while muting his more ambiguous opinions to create a feedback loop, and injecting thematic entertainment featuring protagonists who succeeded by finally deciding to take a stand. Taken as a whole, the yellow scaffolds buttressed certain sections of the overall ridge while undermining others. Over time, they were beginning to subtly shift the shape and direction of its formation, not unlike Olympic curlers sweeping ice to hone the trajectory of their stone.

"As you can see, his head isn't where we'd like it yet," she said. "Our tools are powerful but only really effective over the long term. The convention represents a hard stop."

"Why not throttle up?" asked Dag.

"Our power stems from nuance," she said. "We can't risk overdoing it. If Hsu suspects something or tunes out, we lose our advantage."

"And that's where I come in," said Dag. His attention migrated outside the feed, to the countryside flying by on either side. The city was now a smudge on the horizon behind him, and the highway wove through startlingly green rice paddies, the terraced fields rippling under the kiss of a breeze. "I'm your closer."

"Remember what I told you here on the Island?" asked Javier, jaw muscles bunching. "When my sister and I were at our most desperate, Emily stood up for us. She didn't have to. She had more to lose than to gain. But she decided that she couldn't live with herself if she didn't take action. The risks we take define who we become."

"Countless people have sacrificed far more for far less," said Emily. She marshaled the considerable power of her stare, snapped her fingers, and then pointed at Dag. "You're the person who is going to pull the emergency brake on climate change."

Dag stared directly into her dark eyes, noticing for the first time that her irises were flecked with gray. This enigmatic woman had so deftly plucked him away from his once stable, if disaffecting, life to dub him a player in her great game. In return, she offered that most ephemeral of grails—the opportunity to contribute to something larger than himself.

"What do the shrinks say?" he asked.

"We *heard* that." Another video feed popped up with Frances and Ferdinand. "Just because understanding feelings is our profession doesn't mean we don't have any ourselves."

"Ahh," said Dag.

Ferdinand turned to Frances. "I'm telling you," he said, "it's not fair. Why don't *we* get to go to Taiwan? I mean, the *xiaolongbao* there . . ." He raised a hand, mimed an exploding firecracker with his fingers, and smacked his lips. "That's true magic, that is. Pure, savory, steamed dumpling joy. I would demand you bring some back for us, but they're only good when they're hot enough to burn the roof of your mouth."

"A miracle wasted on our uncouth salesman," said Frances. "A man with no respect for the delicate sciences beyond the grasp of his crude intellect. It is the curse of the wise to suffer the petty degradations of the ignorant."

Dag chuckled. "If you can indulge my unprofessionalism for a moment, perhaps you can share with me the fruits of your enlightened perspective."

"Don't try to ply us with your empty praise," said Frances. "Your compliments will get you nowhere."

"I dunno," said Ferdinand. "I like the sound of *enlightened*. It has a certain ring to it."

"F and F," said Emily, "I hate to spoil your fun, but Dag is en route to his meeting with dear old Eddie. Can we save the idle chitchat for later?"

"Idle, schmidle," grumbled Frances. "Fine."

Ferdinand dropped a series of files into the feed. There were extensive notes dissecting Hsu's microexpressions, picking apart his writing for keyword preferences and emotional undertone, and linking various policy positions to relevant episodes in his personal history.

"We made the calibrations to his feed based on these assays," said Ferdinand.

"I want to start with your endpoint," said Dag. "What's the bottom line?"

Frances tugged at her double chin. "Hsu's a pragmatist. We've used a two-prong approach, nudging him toward realizing the moral imperative of the agreement and emphasizing the practical benefits of its passage." She wiggled her head from side to side in a noncommittal gesture. "But my professional opinion is that we haven't been able to affect his sentiment to predictive depth. Hsu isn't committed to an opposing ideal—he's partisan only to his own interests, which involve Taiwanese primacy. But with regards to the carbon tax, he's still on the fence."

"A pragmatist, I can handle," said Dag. "Thank you, I need to brush up on these files. Time to stack the deck."

"Dag," said Javier, palms pressed together and long forefingers brushing his lips. "Thank you. And good luck."

"Can you give us a minute?" Emily directed this to Javier and the twins.

They saluted, and their video streams blinked out.

"Hey," she said to Dag, and her voice dropped an octave. "I know we're asking a lot of you. There's so much to take in."

"Oh, you know, it's not so bad," said Dag. "You're only turning my world upside down."

The ghost of a smile graced Emily's lips, fervent and somehow sad.

"I just want you to know that we believe in you," she said. "*I* believe in you."

They signed off, and Dag was alone with his feed.

Pushing it to the periphery, he surveyed the foothills the road was winding into. Tea plantations stretched off into the distance, the squat little trees a darker shade of green than the flamboyant rice paddies. The car crested a hill, and the earth fell away as they shot over a bridge. A small river surged below, carving boulders from the sides of the narrow valley through which it flowed. The white water swirled in bubbling eddies that spiraled away downstream in the violent current.

For a long time after they cut the connection, Dag could still feel the weight of Emily's gaze.

CHAPTER 28

Dag had been expecting a palace. It might be a confection of frosted glass or a sophisticated reimagining of traditional Chinese architecture, but surely the man who had transformed Taiwan from an awkward footnote into the jewel of the Pacific Rim would take offices commensurate with his station. However, when the car finally pulled off the two-lane country highway, gravel crunched beneath the tires as it parked in front of a modest single-story house backed up against a forested hill.

Stepping out of the car, Dag stretched and felt his neck crack. He had been traveling for too long, mind absorbed in his feed even as his body grew stiff from inactivity. Bracing fresh air sharpened his senses, and he surveyed the surrounding terrain. They were far from even the smallest of villages, and the house commanded a view over a wide swath of countryside. It might be humble, but perhaps Hsu preferred privacy to opulence. If that was the case, then the files in Dag's possession were that much more valuable.

"Mr. Calhoun?" The voice from behind him was soft, with the odd inflection of a Mandarin speaker who'd learned English from a South African.

"That's me." Dag turned. A young man in a charcoal suit was walking across the gravel toward him. Not Hsu—Dag matched his face with the records—a staffer.

"I am Zhou Baihan, Mr. Hsu's personal assistant." He extended a hand, and they shook. "Welcome to Taiwan. I trust your journey wasn't too unpleasant."

"Far from it," said Dag. "Smooth sailing."

Baihan gave a tight-lipped smile. "Come in, come in. We need to make the most of the afternoon."

Dag followed him up the steps and into the plain brick house. They removed their shoes in the narrow anteroom and proceeded into the living room. The furnishings were sparse—the only exception was an enormous tank that ran the entire length and height of one wall. Brightly colored fish of all shapes and sizes darted through live coral, seaweed oscillated languidly, and a cluster of pink sea anemones wiggled their tentacles. The tank was large enough that it gave Dag the impression of looking through a window into a tropical reef. As he stepped forward to peer through the glass, light scintillated off the scales of a school of a dozen tiny fish that changed direction as quickly as a distracted mind.

"Beautiful, isn't it?" asked Baihan. "It's one of Mr. Hsu's small indulgences. He says it reminds him of his youth. He was an enthusiastic diver."

An eel slithered out from under a fan of purple coral with sinewy grace. In his feed, Dag cycled through pictures of Hsu, decades younger, seawater dripping from his hair as he pulled off a scuba mask. Another piece of the puzzle that was this man's identity.

"I've never had the courage to try it," said Dag.

Baihan laughed. "Me neither. It seems to me like tempting fate, pushing our bodies to explore places where we don't belong. I like to keep my feet planted firmly on the ground."

As Dag followed Baihan up a hallway, he tried to quell the anxiety taking root in his gut. Until now, everything had been an abstraction, a thought experiment where the cleverest scheme would take the day. With the Island's tools at his disposal, he could thread the eye of the needle, narrowly failing to win Hsu to Lowell's cause without tipping his own hand to either. But now, as they walked past a well-stocked kitchen that smelled of garlic and pepper, the canny brightness of plans well laid collapsed into prosaic reality. He was in a man's home, a man whose life Dag had merrily riffled through. There were so many vectors for potential fallout to consider. If Dag took one misstep, they would lose their best chance to secure a global carbon tax. Even if he performed par excellence, he would still need to calm a raging Lowell and avoid the guillotine the firm reserved for big bets taken and lost.

They stopped in front of what must have been the door to Hsu's office. Dag was aware of the feeling of the ash floor beneath his feet, the restraint of the unadorned white walls, the smell of a lived-in home. Then Baihan opened the door and led Dag inside.

But Hsu wasn't waiting for Dag with an enigmatic smile behind a mahogany desk. It was a bedroom, not an office, as sparingly decorated as the rest of the house. There was a small bed, sheets tucked in neatly on all sides, and a window that looked out over the road Dag had driven in on.

"Go ahead and get changed," said Baihan, gesturing to a stack of clothing on the edge of the bed. "The more sunlight we have, the easier it'll be."

Dag looked from the clothes to Baihan and back again. "The easier what will be?" he asked.

Baihan raised his eyebrows, and Dag noticed a small scar on his temple. "I was under the impression that you were here to meet Mr. Hsu," he said.

CHAPTER 29

The clothes were a perfect fit. Dag pulled on wool socks, skintight synthetic base layers, quick-dry pants, and a thin fleece sweater. Everything was expedition-grade and smelled brand-new. Hanging his suit on a rack in the closet, he paused to consider the uncanny anticlimax of this reception. Like so many in Dag's circle, Hsu apparently liked to keep aspirants on their toes.

When he emerged from the bedroom, Baihan, who had changed into similar attire, showed Dag to the back door, handed him a pair of hiking boots, and pointed to a forty-liter backpack leaning in a corner. "That's for you," he said and began to lace up his own boots.

Dag joined him, sitting on a low wooden stool as he cinched the laces tight. Dag was jittery. Whatever this was, it wasn't what he'd planned for. Doubt cast shadows across his carefully calibrated pitch. The worst part was that Dag was all too aware that it was a ploy, but it was working anyway.

They shouldered their packs, and Dag tried to gauge its contents. Heavy, but not overly so. Following Baihan's lead, he clipped the strap around his waist so that his hips could bear the weight. Then they set out through the back door.

Vegetables grew in sturdy raised beds that reminded him of kneeling beside Emily, pulling thistles out by the root. *Are you happy, Dag?*

Like, really happy? The earth had been moist and dark, gritty under his fingernails. What was happiness, anyway? The fleeting pleasure Hsu might relish at the sight of his flourishing fish tank? The imperial anticipation Lowell might enjoy at the prospect of a new conquest? The moment when the first splash of Talisker 18 hit Sean's tongue, his eyes half closing as he inhaled the aromatics? Happiness seemed a losing proposition to Dag. The fish would die. The victory would prove Pyrrhic. The tumbler would soon empty. Joy was nothing but a cursory peak on the sine wave of life.

Opening a wooden gate, Baihan led Dag from the garden and onto a narrow trail that ran straight up the hill behind the house. Before plunging into the undergrowth, Dag looked up at the dark forest that went on for as far as the eye could see. Then he hooked his thumbs under the straps of the backpack and set off before Baihan disappeared around the first bend.

The path was spongy under his feet, and he had to dance around patches of mud that turned it into soggy muck. Sunlight fell through the canopy of oaks and laurels, their broad leaves throwing distinctive shadow patterns on the ferns that carpeted the forest floor. The rich, loamy smell filled Dag's nostrils. Baihan hiked quickly up a series of switchbacks, and Dag was soon short of breath trying to keep up.

"How far are we going?" Dag gasped when they reached the crest of the first ridge.

Baihan was careful not to smile. "Don't worry," he said. "Clichés aside, in this case the destination is really the destination. Here, have some water. We need to stay hydrated." He handed over a bottle, and Dag took a swig. It was fresh but sharp with minerals.

They continued, and it soon became apparent that the initial hill had been nothing but a foreshadowing of things to come. They ascended steep ridges and then dropped into narrow valleys, often fording engorged creeks. Dag was grateful for his boots, which were waterproof and came halfway to his knee. After just such a crossing, Baihan threw a hand back to touch Dag's chest.

"Look," he said, voice laced with wonder. "Blue tigers."

Dag looked up from the rocky bank where he had just managed to land. He twitched in surprise. Just a meter over their heads fluttered thousands upon thousands of butterflies, migrating up the valley. Their wings were black with elongated blue spots that shone whenever they passed through one of the rays of sunlight that penetrated the leaves above. Almost as soon as they appeared, they were gone again, vanishing into the shadows upstream.

Baihan nudged Dag with an elbow. "That's not something you'd see if we were at a luxury hotel in Taipei."

"I've never seen anything like it," said Dag with genuine fervor. "But I'm surprised Mr. Hsu doesn't want to be in Taipei himself for the run-up to this historic vote." Dag himself felt painfully out of the mix. The last days before such a conference were always a fevered string of meeting after meeting after meeting, running from predawn coffees to extended nightcaps in the early hours of the morning. It was a whirlpool of influence, currents pulling everyone in every direction at once. Despite the verdant beauty, he would have felt a lot more comfortable in the mad pressure chamber of political maneuvering before the impending deadline.

Baihan shrugged. "Mr. Hsu prefers to play by his own rules. For isn't doing so the best way to gain advantage?"

We're going to have to throw a Hail Mary. The global carbon tax would hamstring Lowell, and Eddie Hsu was the only person with enough leverage to have a chance of averting disaster. Lowell and Freja had seen the truth in that, and now Dag had to reassure himself that the place where the vote would be determined wasn't the conference center packed with delegates negotiating in hushed tones, but wherever Hsu was.

Baihan's pace never waned, and Dag noticed the forest changing as they climbed. It reminded Dag of forced marches through Namibian badlands and Alaskan excursions through the muck left behind by melting permafrost. Now, they were surrounded by ancient cypresses whose red-brown trunks rose in vertically fissured pillars more than thirty meters tall and whose branches were heavy with scaly dark-green sprays of foliage. They walked among giants, cocooned in a cathedral hush. The trees gave off a spicy coniferous scent that reminded Dag of the winter he'd spent selling Christmas trees from a parking lot outside Denver.

The forest floor ended abruptly in a rocky ledge, and the path led over a narrow cable bridge suspended between two cliffs. Baihan continued without pause, resting a hand lightly on the cables to either side and absorbing the sway of the structure into his gait. Dag's stomach turned as he considered the crossing, but he couldn't afford to let his guide get too far ahead. Why exactly couldn't they have this conversation in a conference room? Why did power brokers demand theatrics? Wasn't ruling enough? Clenching his teeth, he placed sweaty palms on either side and edged out onto the bridge.

A hundred meters below, white water roared through the chasm. For a moment, he was in the back of the county van navigating through the San Diego suburbs, anticipation and fear wrestling for command of his psyche. The certain knowledge of how bad it might get tainted the burgeoning hope that this time might be different. Clutching his backpack to his chest, he had followed the social worker to the door of the dilapidated double-wide, heart beating even faster than it was right now. The thin wooden slats beneath his feet seemed far too thin, the bridge far too unstable to deliver him to safety.

He inched along and tried to tear his eyes away from the maelstrom below. Forcing himself to focus on Baihan's outline at the far end of the bridge, Dag tried not to get sucked away by the undertow of memory. He could have grown up a happy middle-class kid in Culver City. He would have made friends for fun instead of survival, learned to play soccer, and grown up with parents who loved him instead of used him.

But this damn island had stolen it away from him, and he had spent the rest of his life skirting the edge of the abyss.

There was a sudden movement on the trail beyond Baihan. Dag squinted, trying to see through the fine mist. Someone—no, some*thing* stood high on the path behind his guide. It was the size of a large dog with thick tan fur and faint yellow markings. Did they have wolves in these mountains? Dag hurried forward as fast as he could, sucking in a breath to call out a warning to Baihan. But then the beast raised its head and looked directly at Dag. The cables bit into his palms as he fought to parse the sight. It had brown eyes and a black muzzle. Large pointed ears rose from the back of its head, twitching back and forth like an antenna searching for signal. But what froze Dag's shout in his throat were its horns. Curved and conical, they swept back from its head and completed the picture of some kind of demonic deer. Sensing Dag's agitation, Baihan looked over his shoulder. Reacting to his movement, the creature sprang away, disappearing into the underbrush.

Dag stumbled off the other side of the bridge and onto solid ground. Baihan patted him on the shoulder and handed him an energy bar.

"You're lucky," said the younger man. "Serows are quite shy. It's rare they come this near humans."

Now that he wasn't dangling over a crevasse, Dag's initial fear of the animal seemed silly. He took a bite and did his best to rally. As soon as the dense, chalky bar touched his tongue, he realized how hungry he was. "I thought it was a wolf," he said sheepishly.

"Nothing so sinister," said Baihan. "Don't worry, they're vegetarian."

Dag grunted around a mouthful of bar and stuffed the sticky wrapper into his pocket. Downstream, the sun was setting over the range of foothills they'd climbed through. It was a reddish-purple semicircle above the horizon, and Dag shivered as its fading rays made him aware of just how chilly the shadows were. His sweat had cooled as soon as they paused for this break, and his body was losing heat fast.

This had to work.

Dag would play Hsu's little game. He would do whatever Baihan asked of him. If he veered off course, if he wasn't perfect, this would end in disaster. With delusions as their only comfort, world leaders would continue the suicidal trajectory toward unchecked global warming. Having helped build a profitable but broken system, Dag knew how difficult downward spirals were to avert.

Expectations bore down on him from all sides. Emily's impassioned manifestos. Lowell's elaborate schemes. Sean's paternal advice. Dag had so many conflicts of interest, they were hard to keep straight.

This absolutely had to work.

Dag hefted his backpack. "So," he said, "where are we setting up camp?"

"No camp," said Baihan, rummaging around in his pack. "Onward and upward."

He donned a headlamp, lit it, and handed Dag one of his own. They both pulled down jackets from their respective packs, and Dag felt the chill begin to recede. And then they were off again, following the rocky trail up and into the night.

Hours crept by at a glacial pace. As the last glow of dusk faded, stars emerged in the sky above, their brilliance occluded only by dark patches of cloud chased across the heavens by gusts of chilly wind. The acidic burn in Dag's thighs and calves compounded into pain and then dissolved into distant numbness. Blisters formed on his heels, and he began to feel like Atlas under the weight of the pack. The world shrank into the tight cone of his headlamp, a universe of rock and mud illuminated in sharp contrast.

What conversation they'd shared faded into reflective silence. There was nothing but the next step. Nothing but exhaled puffs of condensation. Nothing but that strange kernel of being that became apparent only in the absence of its trappings. The narrow path joined a marginally wider one and curved up the slopes of hills that became cliffs. They trudged on. The temperature plummeted to a point where Dag could hardly believe he was on a subtropical island. They pulled on hats and gloves, layered windproof shells over their down jackets. A narrow wooden platform appeared out of the darkness on their left, followed by a series of low wooden huts that his feed tagged as a trekker basecamp. Baihan didn't pause, and Dag dared not stop lest he lose the momentum that was the only thing keeping him going. They gulped down water and chewed through energy bars at regular intervals. The forest turned from soaring cypress to scruffy fir, and then the trees disappeared entirely, the landscape a barren expanse broken only by alpine scrub. Time melted into an extended singularity. The air thinned, and Dag found himself chronically short of breath and took pains not to hyperventilate. His muscles begged for fuel, his thinking became fuzzy, and a mild sense of nausea suffused his body.

Dag ran into something and stumbled. It was Baihan's backpack.

"Almost there," said Baihan, putting a steadying hand on Dag's shoulder. "But this is where we part ways. From here on out, it's your journey."

Dag looked up at him through eyes glazed with exhaustion. This political-staffer-cum-alpinist superman seemed unfazed by the climb. Between jet lag and altitude, Dag was ready to keel over.

"Follow this to the top." Baihan gestured, and a thick chain glinted under Dag's headlamp. "Good luck."

As if in a trance, Dag gripped the chain and forced his feet to march upward. The coldness of the steel leached through his gloves, and soon he couldn't feel his fingers. Nevertheless, he was grateful that it was bolted to the rocks—the path had long since faded into bald granite that pitched up at such a steep angle that Dag was happy his headlight lacked the power to illuminate whatever terrifying heights he now traversed. The chain was his literal lifeline, his connection to a world unhinged. Hand by hand, step-by-step, he confronted the godforsaken hoop Hsu demanded he jump through.

CHAPTER 30

The climb seemed to go on forever. After what felt like hours, the chain finally terminated at an enormous boulder. Prying free his deadened fingers, Dag dropped to his aching knees. Above him and outside the cone of his headlamp, a rocky crag materialized in shades of gray. He retched but came up dry, then crawled up the last section of path to the summit.

Rounding a final turn, he sprawled out on a narrow wedge of flat granite, his cheek flush with the frozen stone. Rolling his hips, he twisted his body into a sitting position, resting the backpack against a large pile of rocks behind him. He sucked in a few deep breaths and felt his last reservoirs of energy run dry. His stomach heaved again but nothing came up. He closed his eyes to still his spinning head. When he opened them again, the dizziness had calmed ever so slightly, and he realized that the gray luminescence he'd noted earlier was in fact impending dawn. Reaching up, he clicked off his headlamp and raised his gaze to see where he was bound to die, because there was no way he was walking off this damn rock.

With a tangerine flare, the lip of the sun burst over the horizon like a Broadway debut. It rose over a vast white ocean whose pillowy expanse was broken only by a few jagged alpine islands. And then the sea of clouds danced. Faces, castles, landscapes, dragons, poems, lovers, cabarets, spacecraft, and monsters formed and dissipated faster than Dag's imagination could catalog them. The twirling celestial metamorphosis was shot through with every shade of amber, saffron, crimson, rose, and azure. Sheer splendor stole away whatever breath altitude had deigned to forgo.

"Niitakayama nobore," said a reverent voice.

Lacking the energy to startle, Dag craned his neck and saw a slender old man sitting atop a boulder above and behind him. Hsu wore a simple wool jacket over canvas pants. His short-cropped gray hair framed a long face etched by wrinkles and sun exposure. Where Dag felt himself to be at death's door, Hsu appeared entirely comfortable, with a walking stick balanced over his knees. Perhaps this was nothing but a morning stroll for him.

"Our humble island has seen many masters." Though he spoke to Dag, Hsu's eyes followed the otherworldly carnival splayed out before them. "The Polynesians, Han, Verenigde Oostindische Compagnie, Qing, Japanese, British, Americans, Chinese Nationalists, Communists, pirates under every manner of flag—all of them have sought to bend Taiwan to their will. Some have succeeded, selling our women into sexual slavery and reaping the fields we sowed. But none have held sway for long. We are a fierce people, difficult to cow."

Hsu patted the rock on which he sat. "Niitakayama," he said. "That's what the Japanese dubbed this mountain at the turn of the twentieth century. Its literal translation is New High Mountain, which was accurate if entirely unimaginative. To find a higher peak in the western Pacific, you have to venture as far north as Kamchatka. Mount Fuji is nearly two hundred meters shorter. No matter how that fact may have frustrated Japanese exceptionalists, they had no compunctions appropriating it. 'Niitakayama nobore'—'climb the New High Mountain'—was the secret code the Japanese Imperial Navy used to order the attack on Pearl Harbor."

He gestured out across the roiling skyscape. "More than two thousand Americans were killed, and over a thousand more injured. Do you know how many Japanese soldiers died that day? Sixty-four. The date may live in infamy, but what the Japanese gave, the Americans reciprocated with prejudice. Two atomic bombs. A scientific feat that ushered in a new era of warfare." He smiled thinly. "I like to think that though it bided its time, this mountain took its revenge. Whatever their claim on New High Mountain, the Japanese failed to climb it."

Hsu descended to sit beside Dag.

"Now," said the older man, "we call it Yushan, Jade Mountain, for the gem it resembles when sunlight gleams off the snow-covered peak in winter. I harbor a vain hope that such a name is more fitting, for it speaks to the mountain itself without comparison to some other distant crag. You have done what the Japanese Empire couldn't and scaled Yushan. We can only hope your ambition does not overreach as theirs did. I am just an old man, Mr. Calhoun, but I wonder what grand design calls you here from distant shores. To what end do you hope to compel Taiwan?"

Dag marshaled his scant mental resources. Whatever advantage access to Hsu's feed may have lent him, exhaustion was clawing back. "I'm here representing Lowell Harding," he said.

"Ah yes," said Hsu. "America's infamous playboy billionaire."

"Mr. Harding may have a reputation as a bon vivant," said Dag, "but he takes his business seriously."

"And what business, pray tell, does Mr. Harding have here?"

Most important negotiations hinged on a single decision based on no more than a few minutes of discussion. One way or the other, everything else was just execution. Staffers could work out the details. "Mr. Harding is extremely concerned about sustainability and the impacts of climate change," said Dag, falling back on his talking points. "But he is equally concerned with promoting the economic growth on which so many millions of jobs depend. There is no doubt that we must aggressively reform our planet's energy system, but we must do so in a way that doesn't endanger the commercial infrastructure that powers the world. Jet fuel got me to Taiwan." He pinched the collar of his jacket. "Many of the synthetics in this fabric are petroleum-based. The rice paddies and tea plantations I passed through on the way to your home use oil-derived fertilizers. Mr. Harding supports the high-minded principles behind this week's summit in Taipei, but a few of the specific provisions in the version of the proposal that is up for debate would hamstring the global economy and put millions out of work. We must find a way to advance the cause of environmental sustainability without threatening the sustainability of our very way of life."

"Of course, Mr. Harding controls much of the commercial infrastructure whose fate you lament."

Dag nodded, and his head swam as he tried to channel and synthesize what he'd learned about this man's background. To his surprise, the Commonwealth connection was still strong enough on this remote peak to overlay his feed on the dancing clouds. *Hsu's a pragmatist.* He had dealt with the devil on numerous occasions, always managing to extract valuable concessions for any sacrifices on his part. A pragmatist would be open to collaborating with Lowell, for the right price.

"Mr. Hsu," said Dag, "I'm sure you are under no illusions about my partisanship. I am paid well to represent Mr. Harding's interests. But my personal bias does not undermine my argument. Yes, a global carbon tax would hurt Mr. Harding. I'll be blunt, it would hurt him badly. But it would also hurt many firms across the industrial sector and increase the cost of living for many hardworking middle-class people who can't afford and don't deserve such an injury to their pocketbooks. Climate change is a dire problem. We need an aggressive, innovative solution. This is not it."

This was a tried-and-true argument, the thrust of which he'd relied upon for years. But using it now, he had to suppress a shudder. At heart, it was self-reinforcing logic that did nothing but further the status quo.

Although it was certainly true that much of the economy was powered by fossil fuels, men like Lowell had bet on the viability of excuses and against the very change to which they paid lip service, turning what used to be a respectable thesis into a brittle husk invigorated only by short-term profit.

The truth was that while a global carbon tax wasn't perfect, any independent economist would attest it to be the strongest mechanism by which to create meaningful behavioral change. For so many decades, the international community had neglected to pass one precisely because of its efficacy—and because Lowell and his allies fought tooth and nail to paint it unreasonable. The emptiness of the argument hadn't initially bothered Dag. In Sean's words, *A good lobbyist uses all the tools at his disposal.* But Emily had forced Dag to acknowledge something he already knew about himself. That, despite his credentials, he *wasn't* a good lobbyist.

Cynicism can only carry you so far. You're too smart for it. The moral flexibility that made men like Sean so good at representative jujitsu had robbed Dag of the thrill that had inspired his career in politics. Room 412 had been plastered with professional achievements Dag would rather forget, knowing as he did what actually went on behind the scenes.

I give people second chances, and this is yours. Dag knew he didn't deserve one, but maybe just once, he would try to do the right thing. To ensure the passage of the carbon tax, he had to believably attempt to win Hsu over on Lowell's behalf, but ultimately fail. That meant offering a price that appeared reasonable but that Hsu would refuse.

Hsu nudged Dag's boot with his walking stick. "But Mr. Harding didn't climb Yushan—*you* did." He tapped his knee for emphasis. "Your associates pulled quite a few strings to arrange this meeting on such short notice. Needless to say, I had you vetted. And some fascinating things came to light. You are a *most* intriguing character, Mr. Calhoun."

Dag kept his poker face carefully in place.

"I had heard of your firm, of course, but I did not know its young hero by name. You've served Mr. Harding admirably through the years. One might even say you've been instrumental in helping him amass his fortune. Wrangling natural resource *and* trade concessions from the Arctic Council all in one go? My, my, Mr. Calhoun. On such foundations empires are built. But dramatic ascendancy casts dark shadows. I am an old man and not easily surprised. However, Baihan can attest that when we autopsied the skeletons in your particular closet, I raised not one but two eyebrows. Ask him, he'll confirm it."

A cold sense of dread spread from Dag's gut to his fingertips, but there was nothing to do but listen.

"On the surface, I can see why you and Mr. Harding get along. Tough childhood, pulling yourself up by your bootstraps, the American dream incarnate. Congratulations on making partner, by the way—I hear that's quite a big deal. But go just a little further back, ask what cruel twist of fate condemned you to such a difficult upbringing, and it sheds quite a different light on your subsequent accomplishments."

Nausea reared its ugly head again. He was back in La Condesa, hands slipping on the puke-covered duvet, staring up at the photo plastered above the headboard. "Look—"

"*Here*, Mr. Calhoun." Hsu slammed his walking stick onto the granite with a sharp *crack*. "They died here on this island. The Japanese couldn't escape its orbit, and I'm beginning to suspect that you haven't been able to either. Baihan interviewed the director in charge of investigating the disaster. He's long since retired, another old man, but he still remembers standing by as the rescue crews dug bodies from the wreckage. The mudslide took out the entire city block, including the boutique hotel where your parents were weathering the storm. Bad luck upon bad luck. Their first real holiday as young parents, child left under the care of their only living family member, an ailing aunt who was so affected by her sister's death and the burden of caring for her bereaved nephew that she suffered a stroke a year later and was permanently hospitalized.

Young Dag, suddenly alone and on the brink of second grade, fell into the vast maw of the state-ward meat grinder."

As the sun advanced above the horizon, the dancing clouds slowed and collapsed in on themselves. Then the entire layer began to sink, revealing the mountain range hidden beneath its blanket. Avalanches of mist sluiced across passes and down valleys, siphoning away like bathwater down a drain. Dag couldn't keep his hands from shaking.

"Quite a story," said Hsu. "But your parents were not the only victims of Typhoon Razif. It took 719 lives. There was a preschool on the same block as your parents' hotel. The Storm of the Century, they called it. But Typhoon Aoki supplanted its primacy only two months later. A dozen more over the next five years stole the title until the moniker began to lose its luster. But we are a nation accustomed to natural disaster. We rebuild again and again. You yourself demonstrated such resiliency, overcoming hurdle after hurdle to escape your lot and claim opportunities most Americans take for granted. Although, once claimed, you catapulted ever upward to pursue ends that seem at odds with your origins. Southern California, your childhood home, burned to the ground in an unprecedented wildfire while you helped Lowell Harding seize real estate assets that the flames would render valuable. You opened the Arctic for a drilling operation whose externalities accelerate the grand tragedy that hijacked your childhood. The debate over anthropogenic climate change ended decades ago, and we're living through the effects of my own generation's shortsightedness. So"—Hsu pressed his hands together and touched his lips with the tips of his forefingers—"you must forgive my curiosity about what's going on inside the soul of a man who returns to the country of his parents' passing to petition on behalf of the very cause that contributed to their demise."

"A soul is a man's own," said Dag, voice taut and trembling. "I am here to forge an alliance, not to excavate personal history."

"Ahh," said Hsu, disappointed. He reached into a small shoulder satchel and produced a shiny orange and a knife. Flipping out the blade from the handle of the knife, he proceeded to peel a single helical ribbon of skin until the fruit sat naked in his palm. Wiping the blade on his pants, he returned the knife to the bag. Then he pulled apart the orange into equal halves and offered one to Dag. Dag waved it away, but Hsu insisted. "Don't be ridiculous," he said. "You need the blood sugar."

Accepting the fruit, Dag bit into a section, and juice dribbled down his chin. The sharp combination of sweetness and acid woke something inside him, and he remembered how drained he really was. The pungent scent of citrus was reinvigorating.

"Baihan tells me you are a student of history," said Hsu. "Did you know that oranges come from southern China? Their seeds soon spread to Taiwan, and from here to Japan and Southeast Asia and westward to reach Europe and the farthest shores of Africa. Columbus himself brought the first orange seeds to the New World." He swallowed the last piece with obvious relish. "What have you brought to barter for the alliance you seek?"

"Mr. Harding will guarantee Taiwan exclusive most-favored-nation pricing and terms on all supply contracts," said Dag. "He will also grant Arctic concessions to the state-owned CPC Corporation, to be developed jointly with shared royalties."

Hsu met this proposition with silence.

"That is all I am prepared to offer," said Dag.

"I see," said Hsu, and somehow Dag knew that it was true, that the veteran patrician intuited, or at least suspected, the impulse behind the overtly reasonable but insufficient bid. The old man tossed the fragrant globe of orange peel off the front of the peak, and the ribbon of skin distended as it plunged into the abyss. Then he touched Dag's shoulder lightly.

"Niitakayama nobore," he said.

CHAPTER 31

The day of the vote had arrived, but Dag did not join the throngs of delegates, press, and staff flocking to the conference center. Instead, he found himself wandering the streets, sipping on iced milk tea, and dodging scooters and pedestrians. As Taiwan's geopolitical star rose, Taipei had grown into a megacity. It was now the keystone of the Pacific Rim, the hub that served as a clearinghouse between East and West. The crowds through which Dag roamed were filled with people in that special category of borderless professional, the post-nation-state elite who flitted between Manhattan boardrooms, San Francisco hacker dens, and Delhi art galleries with equal ease.

Votes were mere theater. The real decisions were made in advance and behind the scenes. That's what his misadventure up Yushan had been all about. But theater was compelling. Drama, ritual, tradition. Politics was show business. The only difference was that blockbuster success yielded more than mere celebrity. It was entertainment with teeth. Dag didn't want to be anywhere near the conference center, but curiosity set his thoughts racing nevertheless. Anticipatory tension made his insides itch, his hands fidget, and his stomach clench. Stepping around a vendor selling fresh mochi sprinkled with ground peanuts, Dag summoned his feed.

The conference exerted a gravitational pull on world attention. Overlong and fastidiously researched essays picked apart every possible angle that every single delegate might bring to the convention. Analysts trawled data pools in search of statistically significant insights. Pundits waxed lyrical on everything from domestic political events in participating countries to delegates' wardrobe choices. Debates raged over the choice of venue, projected impacts on various industries, and jurisdiction. Cheerleaders claimed the proposal was a panacea certain to save the planet, while skeptics decried it as a blunt instrument sure to crush economic growth.

But all that was background noise. The real action was in the live feeds around which commentary bucked and bellowed like a mad bull. Delegates were filing into the enormous circular hall where the vote would take place. Cameras recorded them from every angle as they shook hands, traded compliments, and made their way to their seats. Every gesture, expression, and comment was analyzed sixteen different ways with speculation fanning out across the global network until the next bit of action snatched the spotlight. Details might be crucial or nonsensical, but they were all dissected with unreasonable scrutiny. It was exhilarating and exhausting. After a few minutes quenching his curiosity, Dag needed a respite.

Acting on a whim, he ducked into what turned out to be a bookstore. Every book faced cover-out from the dense forest of shelves, and Dag was immediately absorbed in scanning the thousands of titles on offer. Most of the books were in Mandarin or English, with some Spanish and Arabic thrown in for good measure. As he grazed, Dag occasionally picked up a book and flipped through it, only to replace it on the shelf. *Books are sharks*, he remembered reading somewhere once. *There were sharks before there were dinosaurs, and the reason sharks are still in the ocean is that nothing is better at being a shark than a shark.* As antique media went, books were still far more popular even than vinyl, surprising analysts who predicted time and again that the feed would render them obsolete. Perhaps being outside the feed was in fact part of the appeal, offering readers something similar to what Analog patrons sought. Of course, that line about sharks must have been from a twentieth-century source, for the metaphor broke down now that the marine predators were all but extinct. With luck, today's vote would shift civilization's direction onto a path that might allow for such species to return in a distant, happier future.

For all that Lowell's business operations might threaten biodiversity, he reveled in the natural world. The shark analogy reminded Dag of the searing, unadulterated fear that coursed through his system when he threw down what he thought would be the winning slapjack hand, only to be trumped by Lowell, who hadn't been bluffing after all. The roar of inebriated laughter that followed chilled him to the core. The entire group had climbed to the deck of the thirty-meter catamaran, regaling Dag with shoulder punches and gallows humor. The Galápagos were one of the last places on the planet where apex predators still roamed the deep. A triple shot of *rhum agricole* and a sharp push sent him plunging into the heaving water. He had never swum so fast in his life. He pumped his arms and legs as fast as he could while trying not to look like a flailing seal. The others had turned on the submarine lights on the bottom of the two hulls. Lungs bursting, eyes burning in the brine, Dag watched with sick fascination as the ghostly shadows of hammerheads circled below. This was how it was going to end, torn to shreds in a foreign sea because he had lost a card game. What would Darwin think? But then, somehow, he was back at the stairs on the stern, spluttering for air as his half dozen compatriots pulled him from the water, pounded on him on the back, chanted his name, poured liquor down his throat, dried him off, and dealt another hand. Freja lost this time, and Dag had cheered her on with the rest as she completed her circuit with a lazy backstroke.

Emerging from the end of a corridor of shelves, Dag discovered a section devoted to calligraphy notebooks. There were options in all shapes, sizes, and formats, with pages of every imaginable thickness and texture. Remembering Nell's guest list in the Analog anteroom, he selected a pad of creamy 100gsm cartridge paper and a graphite 2B from the adjacent rack of pens, pencils, and brushes. Approving the purchase via feed, he rejoined the cosmopolitan multitudes and dipped back into the conference coverage.

An imposing woman was delivering a statement in the measured cadence of a professional politician sticking to the speechwriter's notes. Dutiful applause filled the circular hall at regular intervals. More than two billion viewers were watching the feed and following the ancillary coverage with rabid curiosity. Those in the hall tried to smile at the cameras, even though the cameras were everywhere. The procedural gears turned. New speakers took the podium, relishing the anticipation of the vote and riding the wave of attention like long-winded uncles at a wedding reception. Progress slowed as the tension mounted, and Dag had to escape the circus before it drove him crazy.

Superimposing a map of the city on the bustling crowd, Dag followed busy thoroughfares and redolent alleys, traversed soaring overpasses and verdant parks. He kept his consciousness light, like the fingers of a mother barely caressing the cheek of a sleeping child. If the shadows became too distinct, he'd flee them as frantically as those cast by the silent hammerheads. Instead, he focused on the giggling groups of college students, the humid thickness of the air, and the melodic jingle that issued from passing garbage trucks.

As his feet carried him across Taipei, Dag couldn't keep his thoughts from returning to Lowell. Lobbyists might not have their version of the Hippocratic oath, but advising clients and advocating their causes was not a responsibility Dag had ever taken lightly. It was a craft built on trust. Dag had made many professional blunders before, giving clients poor guidance or screwing up a certain negotiation. But he had never, ever intentionally misrepresented someone or undercut the mission they'd engaged him to execute.

It had all seemed so elegant and justifiable in the abstract. Seeking atonement for the sins of his past, Dag would leverage his history with Lowell to win the work but throw the fight, cementing the Island's carbon tax campaign. But up on that mountain, getting browbeaten by Hsu, knowing he was sinking the deal by underselling it, was so very different. *A global carbon tax would castrate us.* No matter how much he might have grown to despise his own role in Lowell's success, betrayal was much more difficult in practice than in theory.

And then, Dag was there.

It looked . . . entirely unassuming. There was a brightly lit convenience store on the corner, a tea shop halfway up the block, apartment buildings rising into the sky above. Of course, everything was new construction. Nothing looked the same. Calling up pre-Razif images, he layered what the neighborhood *used* to look like over its present reality. There was the small wooden temple perched between two condo towers. There was the fresh-juice vendor with their street stall. There was the cute little hotel his parents had stayed at on their way to explore this mysterious island that had attracted the fascination of tourists as it rose to unexpected political prominence.

Fingernails biting into his palms, Dag let the tide of Razif imagery rise. Weather reporters dissected the burgeoning spiral. Government officials issued dire warnings. Residents posted videos of wind ripping branches from trees, rain whipped into cascading sheets. Missives passed between his parents and his aunt, at turns worried and reassuring. And then the deluge. Audio clips of screams cut short. Security camera footage evaporating into a haze of static. An orgy of liquefaction transforming an entire hill into a mudslide that demolished the block in seconds. Increasingly desperate messages from his aunt, never to receive replies. Finally, the official call from the embassy. Dag remembered hearing her wail and then try to quiet herself so as not to scare him while he played with Legos in the next room.

Unclenching his jaw, Dag pushed his feed to the periphery and pulled out the pencil and pad. He sat on the curb, stared up at the buildings erected atop his parents' grave, and drew. Tears fell onto the page, forming salmon droplets where they mixed with blood from his nail-punctured palms. He drew for the fraught friendship with Lowell that he'd just forsaken. He drew for the unsatisfying fruit of ambition rewarded. He drew for the pain he'd repressed—and that Room 412 had so viscerally liberated. He drew for the parents he'd lost to force majeure and the aunt who hadn't been able to cope with the consequences. He drew for the other frightened foster children who'd taken out their pain on him. He drew for the broken system and the undying hope for change. He drew for the little boy that could have been. From where he sat in the eye of the storm, he reached for something sane, something simple, something *normal*.

The pencil clattered to the ground as his feed flashed with an urgent call notification.

Lowell.

Immersed in reverie, Dag had forgotten all about the vote. He recovered the pencil, steeled himself, and accepted.

"Congratulations," Lowell roared, raising an overflowing champagne flute over the video link. "We won. I knew I could rely on you to bring a motherfucker like Hsu into the fold. This'll put the damn issue to rest so we can get on with business. We've got a mandate." He beamed. "Now get your ass to Mexico City. Alejandro at Pemex is throwing us a party to celebrate. I promise you tequila flowing like Arctic oil, a harem of Hannahs, and billable hours beyond your wildest dreams."

CHAPTER 32

"I don't understand," said Dag as he cinched the bow tie into place.

"How did the actual conversation with Hsu go?" asked Emily.

"This is why I said we should never resort to meatspace work." Javier sat next to Emily as they beamed into Dag's feed from the Island.

"It went just as planned," said Dag. "There's no way he accepted the bid. He didn't even bargain."

Emily frowned. "What specifically did you offer him?"

Dag's view shifted beyond the feed. Staring through his hotel window at the sprawling urban monster that was Mexico City, he remembered how the clouds had danced around Yushan's summit. "A CPC royalty share on some concessions," he said. "Preferential national pricing and supply contracts. That's all. It's nowhere near enough, and Hsu knew it. Plus, if he were to have accepted, Baihan would have roped me in to coordinate details, which he didn't. But Hsu's delegates switched sides to defeat the initiative. There's no way that's a coincidence. I spent the entire flight banging my head into a brick wall—it just doesn't make sense."

"Hold on," said Javier, looking away from the camera. "Something just got flagged. Give me a minute."

Sitting on the edge of the bed, Dag pulled on socks and laced his shoes. Then he stood and faced the mirror. It was a decent fit and a good tuxedo, given the short notice. The Mexican elite threw very formal parties, and this was sure to be a stunner. He could pick up a fresh boutonniere en route to the event.

"Well," said Javier. "Isn't this interesting. Taiwan's Ministry of Finance just quietly announced the establishment of a new sovereign wealth fund, and I can see from Hsu's feed that the national account is being funded via transfers from various trusts and operating companies associated with him. I must say, the timing is quite convenient."

Emily narrowed her eyes. "So *someone* bought off the old man."

"I should be able to tunnel back through the transactions," said Javier, lines creasing his forehead. "But it'll take time."

There was a knock at Dag's door. He summoned a video stream of the hallway.

"Shit, it's Harding," said Dag. "I gotta go." Then, pitching his voice to carry, "Give me a minute."

Emily leaned forward, intent. "I won't deny that this is a giant setback," she said, "but the important thing is that we have the tools to fight back, no matter how long it takes."

Dag ended the call as he opened the door.

"There he is," said Lowell, pulling Dag into a crushing hug. "The man of the hour. I thought we could take a stroll before heading down to dinner, sneak in a little tête-à-tête before things get really out of control. You know how Alejandro is. I'll be disappointed if the festivities don't include an orgiastic human sacrifice at Teotihuacán followed by a whipped-cream slide down a pyramid. Remember the shale deal in Tamaulipas? I mean, *shit*."

"He has quite an imagination," Dag allowed. "Just let me grab my jacket."

The two tuxedoed men took the elevator to the lobby and walked out onto streets lined with brightly colored art deco buildings. Gnarled trees planted along both sidewalks and the median created a green canopy overhead that the late afternoon sun set aglow. It smelled of cumin and frying tortillas.

"We've been through a lot together," said Lowell. "I still remember when Sean introduced us the first time. You were straight out of Georgetown, all bright-eyed and bushy-tailed. He'd already tried to send a few associates my way. They said all the right things, but I could tell they just didn't get it." He shook his head. "Blue blood can get you an Ivy League education, but always having a trust fund to fall back on robs life of its vigor and young people of their chutzpah. I knew that when I put their feet to the fire, they'd ask for arnica. But you? You're fucked-up. Just like me. I don't trust anyone who isn't, and few enough who are."

"I remember that first conversation," said Dag. Whatever Javier might turn up, and whatever their next move might be, it was imperative that Dag keep up the act with Lowell. And the best way to do that was to pretend that the gambit had succeeded, that their old working relationship was back in place, that Dag had somehow won over Hsu. "I like Sean, and I owe him a huge debt for bringing me into the firm. But looking back, I had a serious case of impostor syndrome at Georgetown. I could play chameleon, and nobody would be the wiser. Even so, I knew I hadn't crawled around the Oval Office as a toddler or been to the right boarding school. Apex was the same way. You should have seen the on-boarding process, talk about privilege. You were the first person I met since high school who saw the world for what it really was—and acted on it."

"Well," said Lowell, "aren't we just two foxes in a motherfucking henhouse."

Dag snorted.

Lowell grinned. "Now look at us. Conquering the whole damn planet, leaving the trust fund babies to fight over the scraps. The way I see it, that's putting things right. When you've always had something to lose, you don't know what true desperation feels like. Nobody fights like a rat in a corner."

"The rats will inherit the earth."

"Now that's what I'm talking about." Lowell touched a graying temple. "I mean it when I say I owe you much of my success. This is as much a partnership as anything else. Without the Arctic, we wouldn't have the income to make all our other investments, which themselves rely on the accelerating impacts of the oil we're pumping. Against all odds, you made that happen. You grabbed the system by the balls and won us our concessions."

Dag waved away the praise. "Come on, Lowell. I was in the right place at the right time. And it was hardly my idea."

Lowell squeezed Dag's shoulder. "You don't get to where I am without giving credit where it's due." His tone darkened. "But you don't stay where I am without second-guessing everything—and everyone."

Dag's pulse jacked up. "Sound counsel. Is there something we need to worry about?"

They crossed a busy street and entered a semicircular park where paved paths meandered through a veritable forest. As soon as they entered, the sounds of traffic seemed hushed and distant. The silence only exaggerated the rush of Dag's pulse in his ears.

"The Arctic deal established our domain," said Lowell, "and this vote secured it. You were right that Hsu was the keystone, the point of leverage around which everything else orbited. To be frank, I'm amazed that the international community ever built the momentum to get something this dramatic to the brink of passage. Now that the initiative has failed, it'll take decades for them to consider any similar piece of legislation. That means our business model is still intact and that we have years of relative free rein ahead. It's a miraculous outcome, and one I wish I could thank you for."

Sweat dripped down Dag's sides.

"You know as well as I do that there are . . . nuances to our business," Lowell continued. "We do what we must, even if it's sometimes ugly. You worked on the Pemex partnership, so you shouldn't have any illusions about their history or associates. When the narcos control the territory where your best shale fields are, you only have two options, total war or partnership. Despite how it might play in the media, the latter is far more humanitarian than the former."

Dag's eyeballs were itching. There was something very wrong here, and it wasn't just what Lowell was saying. But their surroundings were idyllic. Birds chirped. Pedestrians walked by with well-groomed hounds. Someone elsewhere in the park was playing folk songs on an accordion.

"Sit with me," said Lowell, reclining on a park bench and patting the seat beside him.

Dag sat, his thoughts a distorted medley.

"The partner of your partner is . . . your partner. So imagine my surprise when I heard through the grapevine that my former lobbyist was trying to open Mexico up for Commonwealth."

A tight knot formed in Dag's stomach as a sudden suspicion turned to certainty. He looked up through the trees and across the road that circled the park. He tasted the bitter earthiness of espresso, felt the jitter of overcaffeination, saw the bubble of blood burst.

Cálmate, amigo. Estás en México. Relájate.

There, on the opposing corner, was the café where Federico had been gunned down.

"I asked that they spare you," said Lowell with a hint of sadness. "As a personal favor to me. You served me with honor and distinction. Nothing would blemish that, even if we'd decided to go our separate ways. But the cartels weren't about to let Rachel Leibovitz replace their monopoly on bandwidth. Federico had crosshairs on his back since the day he decided to treat with Commonwealth. And I hated to see you waste your talents on them. That's when I started giving Masterson hell. I wanted an excuse to rope you back in, and less than two months later, there you were." Lowell loosened his cravat. "You'll forgive me for not immediately welcoming you back with open arms. I needed to make sure the renewed loyalty you professed was genuine. That's where Hannah came in."

They say there are only hundreds left . . . There's something romantic about that, the tragedy of living out the last days of your entire species. But what do I say? I say, whistle while the world burns, Mr. Calhoun. Dag had known she was a test, but hadn't he passed with flying colors? *We've finally made a man of him.*

"Back when we started working together, strippers made you blush." Lowell chortled. "It was cute, really. A full-grown man. I mean, the look on your face. It was just like when you took your first stag out at the Ranch." He shook his head, as if relishing the memory. Then his gaze turned steely. "At one time, you would have declined Hannah's advances, no matter how enticing. So when you succumbed to her charms, I knew something had changed."

Dag's stomach roiled. He had miscalculated, certain that giving in to Lowell's honeypot would cement the man's trust, prove Dag's loyalty.

"After that, I had to assume you were a new man, perhaps with new priorities. So Freja followed you. And almost right away, you went off script, sneaking away for an unreported meeting in San Francisco." He raised a finger. "Tsk, tsk. What might that have been about, I wonder? Regardless, with our empire at stake, I couldn't very well leave you to your own devices with Hsu. I needed an insurance policy. So Freja arranged a separate meeting with him after you'd gotten your ass off that mountain." He screwed up his face. "To my everlasting disappointment, he confirmed my worst suspicions. You offered him a bum deal and gave up with barely a fight. I can't stand the man, and he drives a hard bargain. We had to set forty-five percent of our assets in escrow for his damn sovereign wealth fund in order to get him to bite. Now he can afford to buy himself a whole damn country. But it's better to save half your chips than lose them all. Which leaves me with only one puzzle. You're too experienced to have failed in the way you did. This was intentional. Why on earth would you do such a thing? Just don't tell me it was an attack of conscience."

Dag's mouth was dry as chalk. His eyes skittered left and right, searching for the sicarios whom Lowell had doubtless called back to finish the job.

Lowell sighed. "Don't piss yourself, kid," he said. "You don't want to ruin a decent suit. I didn't bring you here to have you killed. I'm more sad than angry. We had something, you and I. That's over, but I don't hold it against you. You made your play, and you lost. It'd be kicking a man on the ground to shoot you. I prefer opponents who have more to lose—and offer more of a challenge."

Lowell stood. He reached out a hand and gripped Dag's chin, forcing his gaze up so their eyes met.

"Don't fuck with me," he said. "And maybe you'll live long enough to accrue a few chips yourself."

Lowell spun on his heel and set off to attend his victory celebration. Dag watched him disappear around a curve in the path, hardly able to comprehend what had just happened. He sat there, hyperventilating, for what could have been minutes or decades. Not only had they failed to ensure the passage of the carbon tax, Lowell had seen through the trap before it sprung. Dag had managed to betray a friend, lose a client, tank his career, and botch his chance at redemption all in one go.

His only option now was to run back to the Island and regroup, develop a contingency with Javier and Emily.

Emily.

They had met in a hotel not far from this park. He remembered the sweet burn of the Casa Dragones, the exotic promise of a one-night stand, the trap into which libido led. Emily was an enigma, but he couldn't deny the strange fascination and affection with which he now regarded her. Against all odds, something was burgeoning between them, a feeling foreign to Dag. Something that might just be trust.

Darkness fell. Reaching inside his tuxedo jacket, Dag removed a piece of paper. Carefully unfolding it, he stared down at his handiwork under the glow of the streetlight next to the bench. No, he wouldn't go to the Island. Not yet. Just as Lowell had, Dag needed to vet his allies even more deeply than his enemies.

This far into the maze, who could tell the difference?

CHAPTER 33

"Boo."

Dag's interrupted yawn turned into a surprised hiccup. Diana must have slid into the booth during the half second during which his eyes had squeezed shut.

"Aww, that was precious," she said, biting her lower lip. "I'm not even sure what that was, but it was adorable."

Dag knuckled his temples, trying to recover whatever composure he had left after the red-eye from Mexico City.

"Look," he said, "I know we've got this thing where we do a bunch of clever back-and-forth before getting to the point, but I don't think I have the energy for it right now."

Diana rolled her eyes. "You say things like that *every* time," she said with exaggerated frustration. "It's like your back-and-forth go-to. Come on, man, branch out, expand your horizons, use that pretty little noggin of yours." She rapped knuckles against her own head to illustrate. "It's time to up your small-talk game. Find your inner creative. Unlock the magic within. After all"—she wrapped her arms around her torso and shivered—"I shudder to imagine a world without banter. How dreadfully *boring*. Do you really want to live out the social equivalent of brutalist architecture?"

"Concrete apartment blocks have a certain elegance to them."

"Gwaaah." She screwed up her button nose. "That's just gross. Be careful, or you'll start to sound like the twerps in Langley. All function and no form makes Jack a dull boy."

"I thought hackers worshipped the minimalist aesthetic," said Dag. "Renovated warehouses, exposed brick, tight code, unrestrained productivity, a Zen garden of the mind."

"Hey, hey, hey," said Diana. "Stereotype alert! By that logic, I'd assume you were a Hill brat leveraging Daddy's contacts to swing easy lobbying money. But ho! We're tight now, me and you, two peas in a pod." She frowned. "Or maybe I'm a pea in your pod. Or . . . I'm fucking up the metaphor, forget it. Anyway, your feed says otherwise, señor." She raised a finger. "Now I can finally understand why you wanted to meet here." Her finger spun in a neat circle to indicate Analog's roaring hearth, extensive bar, and chattering patrons. "Overkill, from what I can tell of their capabilities, and there are certainly less ostentatious ways to unplug. But it's classy opsec. I'll give you that."

"If I might interrupt." Nell appeared in a breathtaking turquoise dress, balancing a tray. "Two Caesars." She deposited an enormous glass in front of each of them. The liquid was a deep red, and the drinks featured a cornucopia of garnishes. "We have house-distilled, cucumber-infused gin, Clamato, muddled basil, a touch of passion fruit, Sardinian olives, and pickled green beans, topped with celery, rosemary fried chicken, and locally raised bacon."

Diana pressed her hands together as if in prayer. "You are a goddess, the source of all manna from heaven. These look *ravishing*."

"I'll leave you to it," Nell said with a bright smile.

"You do that," said Diana, rubbing her belly, "because I'm about to go Brutus on this Caesar."

Nell departed, and Diana turned back to Dag. "When you mention Canada, everyone thinks of maple syrup, or maybe poutine. But this," she said around a mouthful of bacon, "is the greatest gastronomic invention of our friendly northern neighbors. It puts the Bloody Mary to shame. And you, sir, need it. You look like you're about to fall off the edge of the known world."

"If we can get back to the question at hand," said Dag, trying to recover from the detour.

"I'm not saying a damn thing until you take a sip," she said. "It's a travesty not to enjoy such a work of genius."

Pushing the garnishes to one side, Dag tried the drink. It tasted of late-summer tomatoes, umami, brine, and Worcestershire sauce. The spiciness took a moment to hit and then traced a sizzling arc through his sinuses.

"See? The color's already returning to your face."

"It's a shellfish's worst nightmare," said Dag. His eyes smarted, but he couldn't deny the savory combination of food and alcohol was welcome.

"*There* we go." She clapped. "Up and at 'em. This'll do you good. Breakfast of champions. And"—she bit into a piece of celery with a loud crunch—"let me tell you, we are dealing with champions here. I mean, daaamn, son. These bitches are for real. I've never seen anything like it, and I've seen more than my fair share."

Despite his exhaustion, Dag's focus became laser sharp, taking in every detail with the combined clarity of an absent feed and a heavy dose of paranoia. This moment would confirm or deny the suspicion he hadn't wanted to admit to himself but had no option except to investigate. It would clarify just how much of his life was a lie. It would delineate just whom he could trust—and where he could run.

"What did you find?"

Diana raised a finger. "One," she said, "I confirmed your crazy story. They *do* have a back door into Commonwealth. There's no other way they could gain access to your feed in the way they did. That by itself is off the hook. Can you imagine what would happen if that came out? I mean, the whole global economy is built on their infrastructure. I'm tempted to post it just to see what happens." She saw the horrified look on Dag's face. "I said I'm tempted, not that I'm actually going to. Come on. Unless, of course, you want me to leak it . . ."

"No," said Dag immediately. "Absolutely not."

She raised another finger. "Two," she said, "I see you like Korean girls. I mean you *really* like Korean girls. They're the only ethnicity in your porn feed, and I've gotta say, I can see the appeal—some of them were smokin'."

Dag flushed. "Look," he said, "that's not—"

She raised a final finger. "Three," she interrupted, "I discovered *why* you like Korean girls. This is where things get weird. I had to rope in a statistician friend and his pure-math hubby, but don't worry"—she rolled her eyes—"I anonymized the data. They don't know any personal identifying information, and much more importantly, they don't know the system we're dealing with." She popped an olive into her mouth. "Your search results for any, ah, sensual queries yielded results heavily weighted toward Korean women with a specific kind of facial structure. They also popped up in your algorithmic feeds over the course of years with regularity many standard deviations above Commonwealth norms. Which, naturally, got me thinking, 'cause, let me just say, these ladies of perpetual indulgence resembled a certain enigmatic love interest I'd already helped you locate. And *boom*—was I right or was I right?"

Dag swallowed. He remembered Lowell's leer. *Sexual predilection is a window into the soul.* In this case, it wasn't so much a window as a vector. The polar bear pelt fell to reveal Hannah, the embodiment of an implanted aesthetic. The gin was going straight to his head.

"I was right," Diana confirmed. "Pure-math hombre tells me that Emily Kim's face is the 'absolute center of the possibility space.' That means, apparently, that whatever algorithm they had scraping for Koreans to populate your feed used her face as the model, essentially priming your sexual platonic ideal. No wonder you were so obsessed with her. I can get possessive with lovers sometimes, you know? But this girl? She takes it to a whole new level. Olympic gold for stalkers, no contest."

May I join you? It's beautiful out here on the balcony. And I believe I've exhausted the bartender's supply of small talk. Cicadas chirped. Tequila dulled the edge of Federico's assassination. Raven-dark hair framed a heart-shaped face that ignited prefabricated obsession without even having to try. The sly glimpses injected into his feed had fanned the flames until he abandoned everything he knew to chase her down. She winked, blew him a kiss—all unattributed snippets precisely calibrated to urge him on. The Caesar reminded him of the gasoline taste of homemade gin in the Berkeley alley where he'd purchased that sketchbook, the hotel he'd holed up in to sketch the face that haunted his dreams. How easily those lines and textures had found their way onto the page, how faithfully he'd reconstructed the digital apparition. Emily was Dag's flesh-and-blood Helen, carefully engineered and manufactured in his mind by Island hackers and psychologists.

Unperturbed, Diana bit into a piece of fried chicken. "But that's not even the most interesting part. These cowboys redefine the term *mindfuck*. I was super impressed by the whole bespoke fetish thing, but it turns out that infatuation was just a side project for them, or you, or I don't even know." Her expression turned pensive. "I think we'll need new vocabulary for this sort of thing." She swallowed the last of the chicken. "Regardless, they're using similar techniques on *every* part of your feed, from the news you read to the music you listen to. For example, over the last few years, they've been serving you media about self-actualization and environmental activism with progressively increasing intensity. Whenever you hadn't eaten in the morning, they slipped in top-notch fried chicken and waffle recommendations. They also exaggerated reactions to anything you engage with. For example, you shared a *National Geographic* story a year or so ago, and they ensured it was reshared many times over. Whereas when you posted professional advice for new lobbyists, they muffled the response. My statistician friend says they're harnessing the power of social validation to reinforce a certain worldview. It's like gardening, only they're cultivating ideology. Clever as fuck, if you ask me."

Diana hoisted a black attaché case onto the table and pushed it across to Dag. "We did everything in a sandbox, no networked processors. Here's what we found, complete with notes, diagrams, code, and analysis, all printed on honest-to-God dead trees. Your infosec is now, literally, in your hands." She drained the dregs from her glass and slammed it onto the table.

"Veni, vidi, vici," she said, and burped.

Dag's hands were shaking so badly that he spilled the cocktail. Thick red liquid oozed across the polished wood, garnishes stranded like beached whales on a tide of blood. He swore and attacked the mess with his napkin as the cocktail pooled around the black leather edge of the attaché case. Diana's hand pinned his down softly but firmly. He looked up, and her expression melted from detached professional enthusiasm to genuine horror.

"I'm sorry, Dag," she said. "Someone crawled into your poor little head like a goddamn stomach worm. I got so absorbed in figuring out how they did it that I didn't really think about how that must feel for you."

"How long?" he asked in a hoarse whisper.

She winced.

"Ten years," she said. "At least."

CHAPTER 34

Dag stepped off one of the plane's twin floats and onto the dock. Fog blanketed the Island, which was nothing but a dark shape shrouded in mist, echoing the black kernel lodged in his soul. The air was heavy and moist on his face, and his shoes squeaked on damp wood as he strode up the dock. Waves lapped against the pilings, and a gull squawked in the distance, its disembodied call haunting. It wasn't peaceful so much as hushed, like a tennis stadium where the crowd watches with bated breath as the player tosses the ball in the air for the match-point serve.

"Dag?"

It was her. Within a few steps, the indistinct shape waiting where the dock reached the shore resolved into Emily. She wore a turquoise knit cap pulled down over her ears and a dark-gray fleece jacket over jeans and suede boots. Steam wafted up from the mugs she held in either hand. Seeing her face, high cheekbones beneath thick-framed glasses, pink lips perked up into a slight smile, the direct intensity of her gaze, Dag felt something fall into place like the last piece of a puzzle. Was he reacting to the unending stream of psychological programming she had funneled into him year after year after year? Or was his new self-awareness what lent her visage this outsize impact? He couldn't help but stare for a moment, seeing her in this new and decidedly harsher light. Talk about making a first impression. This woman had reached straight into his mind to push and pull every emotional lever she could get her hands on, and that was long before he'd even set eyes on her. If only the frankness of her gaze made her own mind as transparent, but its purity was that of a mirror, reflecting only what stood before it.

"You okay?" she asked. "Sea landings can be a little harrowing, especially if you haven't flown in a floatplane before. Here." She held out a mug. "Medium-roast Sumatra beans, earthy and delicious."

He accepted the coffee, and the heat from the mug bled into his palms. It was obvious in retrospect. Emily had toured him through the entire facility, introduced him to the team. Ferdinand bragged about every detail of how they'd executed their anti-human-trafficking campaign. Years before, Sean had invited Dag along to golf with a few heavy hitters. Augusta had been brisk and windy, and Dag remembered the hard look on Senator Watkins's face as he held court for his underlings between holes. Dag had met Watkins on another occasion, visiting the man's office to discuss some now-forgotten piece of legislation. The senator from West Virginia hadn't budged an inch over the course of their conversation, but the photo of the Westies prominently featured on his desk undercut the brusque facade. The bill he'd sponsored had undoubtedly improved federal policy on what amounted to modern slavery, but did that justify invading his mind?

Her eyes narrowed, and she touched his shoulder. "You sure you're okay? You look like you've seen a ghost."

Saying nothing, he took a sip.

"Look, setbacks are painful," she said, wincing. "We haven't come up against a stumbling block this bad in a few years, and spirits are low. We invested a lot in cultivating the carbon tax deal, and we fumbled it. I'm going to have a lot of questions for you about that in the debriefing." She scrunched up her nose to readjust her glasses. "But this is a delay, not a defeat. It just means we have to dust off a contingency, and we never initiate a program without having plenty of those prepped and ready to go. Lowell may have won himself and his industry regulatory air cover, but he also spent a lot of political and financial capital to get it. Now it's time to attack from a completely new direction. I can't wait to show you the operating plan we've drawn up. We need your input on prioritizing different aspects of it, and you'll be getting back on that plane. We have to strike before they have time to regroup. You'll head out to DC tomorrow."

Her words pinged off Dag like raindrops off a corrugated steel roof, echoing hollowly in the strange emptiness inflating within him. He felt that if a breeze were to catch him from the right direction, he might simply float away into the fog. Unable to follow what she was saying, he focused instead on the thousands of tiny details. The spot under the right knee of her jeans that was starting to wear through. The thick yarn and rough weave of her knit cap. The precise angle at which she held her head. The almost imperceptible dimple in her left cheek. The number of centimeters her fleece was unzipped. The faint grassy smell of her.

"Come on," she said. "Let's get up to the house. No fried chicken and waffles this time, but we've got homemade yogurt and a literal truckload of blackberries."

She began walking up the gravel path. But Dag didn't follow. He stayed there, rooted to the spot, standing on the last plank of dock. The emptiness inside him had reached its limit. Having no more room to expand, it tried to find an escape. But with no release valve, the vacuum began to thicken and swirl, curdling into an emotion he finally recognized.

Rage.

"What the fuck?" he asked, voice low and cold.

She stopped short, boots crunching on gravel. Slowly swiveling her hips, she turned to face him. There was a hardness in her expression, a new rigidity in her posture.

"Is there a problem?" she asked.

He imagined throwing the steaming coffee into her face to see if second-degree burns would diminish her hauteur. She wasn't the principled leader of a quiet revolution. She was a chronic infection that had reduced him to nothing but a marionette.

"I know what you did," he said. She had obviously harbored no qualms about tapping Dag's feed and ambushing him with an intimate montage, so why had he assumed that the rest of her toolbox had remained closed? Why had he believed that she wouldn't use every technique at her disposal for recruitment as well as lobbying? And what right did he have to be unhappy about falling victim to tactics that he had condoned by agreeing to work with the Island?

"I've done a great many things," she said, warmth draining from her voice. "Some I regret, some I take pride in—but none I would change."

"It must be nice," he said. "To enjoy such a sense of agency."

Her head cocked to the side. "Agency?"

"It's beautiful," he said. "Like a Chihuly. Only instead of blowing glass, you mold people's lives."

"We don't take that responsibility lightly," she said. "And we only act where it's absolutely necessary."

"Really? And who gets to decide what's necessary?"

She sipped her coffee. "What's going on, Dag? You know what we do here. You're one of us." Her voice was cool, steady.

"One of you?" he said. "Oh, that's rich. This little conspiracy you've assembled." He gestured up the hill with his chin. "I'm not your guest. Not your comrade in arms." He spat off the side of the dock. "I'm your *target*."

For a long moment, she just stared at him.

"You didn't just crack my feed," he said, tone infused with self-disgust. "You've been manipulating it for a decade. You've been playing me just as surely as the marks you recruited me to woo. You engineered everything I saw, everything I engaged with. It's . . ." He shook his head, at a loss for words. "I'm not a person to you, I'm just some kind of blank canvas for you to scribble on."

Emily sighed.

"Javier went through a vegan phase," she said. "He was as enthralled by straightforward idealism as only a nineteen-year-old can be. Naturally, I was the first person he hoped to convert. But, what can I say?" She shrugged. "I like pork. I wasn't about to change what I ate based on his rant. But I did realize one thing. I wasn't facing up to what it meant to be a carnivore. I'm a city girl. I buy meat at the grocery store like everyone else. So I found a forum for wild-boar enthusiasts, and the following weekend they took me hunting. That was the first time I killed an animal. The first time I skinned and gutted and butchered an animal. It was bloody work, but they sent me home with a side of bacon. I fried it up the next morning. And you know what? It tasted fucking amazing. It took three years, but Javier came around. Now he slaughters his own chickens."

Dag recalled the nauseating smell he couldn't seem to shake after killing that stag on the Ranch.

"I know it's hard," she said. "But you know the stakes. Four thousand people died in the Yucatán just this year. Bangladesh is a failed state. Southern California is a wasteland. Fishing isn't even an industry anymore. Droughts and floods and wildfires and every other kind of extreme local weather pattern are out of control. We've gone so far that even if we're able to change course now, we'll be lucky if things normalize for our grandchildren's grandchildren's grandchildren. There's a line, and we crossed it decades ago." She shook her head sadly. "I wish that changing people's minds was as simple as making a rational argument. Our species would have averted so many disasters if clear-headed analysis won the day. Generating the greatest net benefit to society is so far removed from the institutional realities of policy-making. Entrenched interests. Bureaucracy. Corruption. Personal grudges and favors. Politics is the gap between what is and what should be."

"Playing politics is one thing," said Dag. "But why burrow into my life?"

She barked a harsh, humorless laugh. "Oh, come on. You were happy to have our help with Hsu. But when it comes to dear little Dag, all bets are off? That's the exact kind of hypocrisy Javier's dietary proselytizing revealed in me. Kill a pig. Bring home the bacon. Grow up."

And then a thought appeared in Dag's mind as if from nowhere, sparking and fizzing with righteous anger. His mouth twisted into a snarl. "If everyone is as enlightened as you," he said, "then I'm sure they won't mind me pointing out that they're your puppets too."

Her cheek twitched, telling him everything he needed to know.

CHAPTER 35

Sidestepping around Emily, Dag dashed up the path.

"No, wait!" she called after him.

Blood pounded in his ears as he sprinted past the school. A pair of young girls walking between classes stopped to stare at him blankly. He could hear Emily's footsteps behind him, but he was faster. *Here on the Island, we win hearts and minds.* The only thing Emily had neglected to mention was that Dag's had been taken as spoils years before.

"Don't do this!" she yelled, breathless.

And then he was at the house, leaping up the steps three at a time, bursting through the glass doors and into the large open living area. A fire glowed in the hearth. The team was grouped unevenly around tables and in conversation nooks. They were hard at work, absorbed in their feeds except for a few murmured discussions.

But when Dag crashed into the room, they all looked up. A dozen sets of eyes stared at him in surprise. For a fleeting moment, an unexpected stage fright overtook him. The abruptness and intensity of the attention threw him off balance. But the sound of Emily charging up the steps impelled him to speak. Truth was the only balm that would salve his fury.

"I know some of you better than others"—he raised his voice— "none of you well. But I do know some things about all of us." He made eye contact with Frances, Ferdinand, and Javier in turn. "We've all suffered. We've all sinned. And we've all decided to put ourselves on the line for what we believe in. That's what won me over during my first visit here last month. But there's something you need to know." Dag paused to push a data packet of Diana's findings to their feeds but realized nothing was archived because the revelations had come to light at Analog. He'd have to do this the old-fashioned way. "What if we didn't choose this path? What if we ourselves are the targets of psychological conditioning just like the leaders we seek to influence? What if our free will has been hijacked?"

"What are you talking about?" asked Frances. "Dag, why don't you calm down, have a glass of water, and we can all sit down and chat?"

Dag shook his head. "You don't understand," he said. "I've uncovered incontrovertible evidence that Emily has manipulated my own feed for more than a decade. She crafted my digital world and layered herself into it, making it easier to recruit and control me."

"You don't mean . . ." Ferdinand's face registered a sense of growing horror.

"That's right," said Dag. "I'm not the only one. She's done the same thing to every one of you. We're her pawns, remade in whatever image she downloaded into us."

Disturbed faces stared back at him in confusion.

"No, it can't be," said Ferdinand. "We're a family."

"She would never—" said Frances.

"You have the tools," said Dag, suddenly spent. "You know better than anyone how to prove the truth of this. Check your feeds, and for once, make your own decisions as to what to do about it."

Javier stood. "I think that's quite enough," he said.

Dag was about to retort, but then he noticed Javier's comment was directed at the group.

"Oh, you're no fun at all," said Frances with a dismissive wave.

"Thirty-seven days," said Javier firmly.

"That makes him . . . fifth!" said Ferdinand, punching his sister's shoulder. "He beat you, dummy."

Dag flinched as loud dance music suddenly filled the room, pulsing beats and trumpet crescendos. Everyone leapt to their feet, transformed from fearful to festive. Champagne was retrieved from the kitchen, and overflowing flutes handed out. Every single person filed past, hugging and congratulating Dag. A full-fledged party materialized out of nowhere.

Dag, mute with consternation, didn't know how to react. He hadn't known how the group would take the news. Maybe they'd revolt against Emily's iron rule. Maybe they'd refuse to acknowledge it and throw him out. Maybe they'd retreat into shock.

Frances grasped his upper arm. "I should be jealous," she said, smiling generously. "But I'm really just proud of you. Fifth is nothing to sneeze at, though my ranking will be demoted forever. I mean, you don't even have a computer science background."

"Thirty-seven days, baby!" yelled Ferdinand and poured champagne over Dag's head.

Dag tried to dodge out of the way, swiping the sparkling wine from his eyes and spluttering. "What is this?" he gasped. "What the hell is going on?"

Javier offered him a hand towel, and Dag wiped himself off.

"It's your graduation ceremony," said Frances. "We don't get too many opportunities to celebrate, and this is an important one."

Javier accepted the damp towel back, folded it neatly over his forearm, and stepped in close. "Remember your first visit?" he asked. "The breakfast I made you?"

Dag thought back to that morning. The satisfaction of finally locating Emily. The frisson of fear and excitement as he trespassed into the mysterious house. The smell of fresh waffles and fried chicken. The ultimate sense of dislocation wasn't that different from how he felt right now.

"You might have forgotten all about it," said Javier, "but Emily mentioned that the breakfast was a tradition."

"Something coy about a final exam?"

Javier nodded. "There are two steps to full admittance into our little clique," he said. "The first is following the trail of clues to find the Island. The second—"

"Is working out that we've been mindfucked," finished Dag. His anger, his entire emotional palette, had been snuffed out. "So all of you know already. And you're still here."

Javier's smile was pained. "It's a hard truth," he said. "And can take some getting used to."

Dag considered the gaping chasm that was his sense of self.

"That's one way to put it," he said.

"How can we justify using these techniques on others if we haven't experienced them ourselves?" asked Javier.

Suddenly, this place, these people, were far too much to handle.

"I need some space," said Dag.

Javier reached out a long-fingered hand to squeeze Dag's.

"Go up to your room," he said. "I'll make sure no one bothers you."

As Dag crossed the room to the stairs, he glimpsed Emily out of the corner of his eye. She was still standing near the doors he'd burst in through, behind where he'd made his appeal. Her face was composed, but her eyes were smiling.

Before he could glance away, she winked.

CHAPTER 36

They had assigned Dag a room during his previous stay. It was modest but contained a neatly made queen bed and a small private bathroom. The walls were white and unadorned. A window looked out over the forest that surrounded the compound. He could just see the copse of trees from which he'd spied on the building.

Closing the door behind him, he walked to the window and pressed his face against the glass. It was cold against his smooshed nose, and his breath immediately fogged up the surface, blurring the view. His life was a shattered mess. A major client had fired him, and surely the partners wouldn't wait long before following suit. He had no family to speak of and few friends. He had invested so much of his identity into the job, and now he would amount to nothing but a failed lobbyist. Sure, he could line up a position at a second-tier outfit, but could he really bring himself to represent the petty interests of people he didn't even respect?

Stepping back from the window, he moved to the closet. He'd left most of his gear here after his last visit rather than carrying it back with him in the kayak. Unzipping the backpack, he rifled through the energy bars, gels, and equipment. Emily had ransacked his life just as easily. Dag had risked his career by following her bread crumbs to this cursed island. At her behest, he'd wagered his career to assuage his conscience.

Now he'd lost the bet and himself along with it. He had no choice but to second-guess every belief he held dear, every opinion that appeared self-evident, his very perspective on the world.

The closet smelled faintly of cedar. His jumpsuit hung limply from a hanger, alone on the rack. Were his thoughts really his own, or just the output of a carefully constructed and intentionally warped digital-fun-house version of reality? He found what he was looking for and retreated to sit on the edge of the bed.

The Tavor was heavy on his lap. He ran his finger lightly over the teeth of the full-length top rail, along the matte-black steel of the chrome-lined barrel, and then down the reinforced-polymer handle. It was a compact, functional rifle. That's what happened when you designed a weapon in collaboration with the Israeli military. Pure function. They needed it to work. Every time.

It wasn't enough to flee the celebration below. He wanted to escape his own head.

Rising to his feet, he stalked to the bathroom and stared into the mirror over the sink. His reflection stared back from the depths of the uncanny valley. Revulsion curdled in his gut. He wasn't a person. He was a weapon just like the Tavor.

Forged for a single purpose.

He raised the rifle, sighted along the rail, and aimed it straight at the mirror. His finger rested on the trigger. Staring down the barrel of the gun into his own dilating pupil, Dag's thoughts finally started to decelerate.

"Bang," he whispered. "Bang, bang, bang."

A sudden violent mirage enveloped his mind's eye. Emptying the magazine into the smug partiers downstairs, the string of abusive foster families, the man who had called his aunt with the news of his parents' death, Freja with her icy aloofness, Lowell with his patronizing manipulations, the sicarios who had gunned down Federico, the partners who had withheld his promotion, every last person who had done him wrong. His imagination churned at a fever pitch, soaked in blood and gore and desperation. No need to reload. A single endless clip.

Then Dag lowered the gun, arms trembling, and stumbled back to sit on the bed. He remembered Javier recounting his rescue from the Houston drug den, Frances and Ferdinand's good-natured bickering, and all the incredible things these people had accomplished. He thought of the victories shared with Lowell and Freja, and the tiny slivers of hope he'd experienced even as a child of the system. The world wasn't etched in black and white. And whatever Dag's crimes, he wasn't a killer.

There was a soft knock on the door.

Dag didn't respond, but after a minute, it opened anyway.

Emily slipped inside and closed the door behind her.

She knelt in front of him and placed her hands on his. They were as warm on the back of his hands as the Tavor was cool beneath his palms. But she didn't look down at the rifle, not even a glance. Instead, she removed her glasses and looked straight into Dag's eyes. As with anyone who normally wears glasses, it was disconcerting to see her without them. She appeared more vulnerable. Naked in some ephemeral but significant way. It forced him to see her face anew.

They stayed that way for an eternal instant.

Then, slowly, Emily lifted the gun from his knees, checked the safety, and laid it gently down on the floor. Rising to her full height, she stretched like a cat, back curved and arms extended. She twirled lazily on pointed toes. As soon as she finished one full rotation, she sprang into action.

Suddenly she was sitting on Dag's lap, wrapping her legs around his torso, running her hands up the back of his neck and through his hair. She leaned in so their noses touched, her eyes wide and bright. She bit her lip.

"If you're obsessed with me," she said, "imagine how I must feel about *you*." Her breath was hot on his cheek. A lock of hair fell across her forehead. Dag remembered the scarlet dress, could almost hear the cicadas. "I've been inside you for years. It's time you returned the favor."

CHAPTER 37

The dead bolt released with a click as Dag approached. Taking a deep breath, he opened the door and stepped into his Meridian Hill condo. Inside, the air was stale and stuffy. Dag had always traveled a lot for work, but these past few months had been unusual even for him. He felt like a guest in his own home.

Moving to the kitchen, he filled a glass of water in the sink. Flying always left him parched. After turning off the faucet, he watched a single drop distend into a globule until gravity overcame surface tension and it fell to splatter on the bottom of the basin. He took a sip. The water tasted stale. He had bought this place for the view. There was a lot of glass, and all the windows looked out over DC. The city spread out before him, designed by a Parisian architect and trapped within the serpentine coil of the Beltway, protected by levies, dams, hubris, and the expertise of Dutch hydrologists. Taxation without representation. That was a sentiment he could identify with right now.

A soul is a man's own. How fragile Dag's pride had been on the summit of Yushan. How his hands had trembled as he parried Hsu's thrust even as exhaustion and altitude wreaked havoc on Dag's body. Emily had given the lie to that truism.

Pillow talk to change the course of history. There had been a plan. Of course there had. Afterward, tangled in sweaty sheets, consciousness tentatively returning from oblivion, she had laid it all out. The global carbon tax initiative might have failed, but they could attack from the flank. Instead of a top-down international agreement, they would dismember the fossil fuel juggernaut one limb at a time.

They would start right here in Washington. Lowell's industry had thrived for nearly two centuries, not just on the strength of its product but on the largess of taxpayers. Operators drilled on federal lands leased for cheap. Massive subsidies supported their balance sheets like pylons. Thousands of tax loopholes guaranteed they needn't contribute to the system they profited from. Meanwhile, their lobbyists ensured that such benefits were protected but prevented their extension to competing energy sources, slowing commercialization and adoption of renewables. If Dag and the Island could sever these benefits, it would cripple the industry. A global carbon tax would have priced in environmental externalities directly. This would accomplish the same thing by removing public support from companies that had long since betrayed the public trust.

Dag may have fumbled his second chance, but Emily had offered him a third.

Gulping down the last of the water, Dag left the glass in the sink. He trailed his fingers along the granite countertop as he exited the kitchen. He had been so sure that his dramatic revelation would undermine the entire Island operation. But the team's reaction had transformed the violation he'd felt upon hearing Diana's report into a bizarre hazing ritual. Adversity was the surest bond. But was this newfound kinship something he really wanted or something he had been engineered to desire?

The Island exerted an all-consuming gravity. However, the farther he veered from its orbit, the more tenuous its pull. Back in his condo, he wondered whether he might be experiencing something akin to Stockholm syndrome. Was Emily his closest ally or his nemesis or something else entirely? Narrative was so much easier to follow when you weren't living it.

He found himself in front of the hallway closet. He opened the door to reveal stacks and stacks of cardboard boxes. The musty smell of old paper washed over him. Choosing one pile at random, he knelt and dragged the entire teetering tower out into the living room. Then he took the boxes down one at a time, placed them in a circle on the floor, and sat cross-legged in the middle.

Pulling the closest box forward, he undid the intersecting cardboard flaps and coughed as dust puffed up like pollen. Swallowing away the chalky dryness, he reached inside and pulled out the first sketchbook that came to hand. He opened it to a random page and spread it across his knees. The paper was stiff and brittle under his fingertips, but the penciled illustration had survived the test of time.

An underwater kingdom came to life before him. A bait ball of thousands of sardines seethed in a flickering school. Sea lions herded the fish like marine ballerinas, darting in to snatch the occasional mouthful. They were sketched in extraordinary detail, muscles visible under their skin, unique patterns of fur, expressive whiskers, flippers guiding them through the tumult. A shaft of sunlight sliced down from the roiling surface above, shattering into crystalline shards as it struck the scaly mass of sardines. Down on the seafloor, an eel stuck its head out from an outcropping of rocky reef. A few jellyfish pulsed along with the gentle current, which was rendered in shading that gave the impression of movement.

A casual observer would have missed the key detail. Hidden away in a far corner and obscured by shadow, the face of a small boy peered out from the depths of the kelp forest, eyes directed not at the wondrous sight above him but out toward the viewer. Dag pulled away from the drawing, but the boy's eyes followed him until he snapped the sketchbook shut.

Dag's pulse quickened unaccountably. That was enough reminiscence for one day. His memory lane required skulking, not skipping. It wasn't until the boxes were shut back in the closet that he was able to calm his rapid breathing.

There was work to do.

Returning to the kitchen, Dag refilled the glass and opened the fridge. A plastic container of strawberries furry with mold. A gallon of milk long past its expiry date. A half-empty jar of olives that might have been from the previous century. He sighed.

After tossing the spoiled food, he took a seat at the kitchen table. Calling up his feed, he placed a delivery order for lamb vindaloo, garlic naan, and a mango lassi. Then he summoned the data dump from Emily and her team.

The multipronged counterattack required them to control one very specific variable. The Island hackers and psychologists could work their magic on the Hill as long as Lowell and his allies didn't catch the scent. If the industry suspected that the various initiatives were coordinated, the major oil companies would immediately overcome their vicious internal competition in order to bring the collective threat to a halt. And there was one man who the industry relied on more than anyone else for such high-level political insight and guidance.

Feeling at once piqued and guilty, Dag opened the entire archive of Sean's feed.

CHAPTER 38

Afternoon light filtered through the leaves of the large dogwood trees surrounding Sean's McLean estate. They were seated out on the back patio. Behind them, the expertly maintained colonial was a photogenic two stories of whitewashed brick. Mr. Snufflebunch, Sean's aging Irish wolfhound, snored beneath the table.

Sean opened the cooler and cracked a beer for each of them. He was wearing a hoodie with HARVARD LAW stenciled across the front and sweatpants to match. Out of his tailored suit, the big man looked more like a rugby player than a K Street striver.

"Remember that assignment you gave me for Congresswoman Devon during my first few months at Apex?" Mining Sean's archive was the voyeur's ultimate thrill. It contained everything. Every scrap that Commonwealth had sucked up over the years. Elementary school report cards. Stats from his brief tenure playing college basketball. Entreaties from the divorce that Sean refused to talk about. Receipts showing that Sean was a major philanthropist, something that Dag had never heard him mention over ten years of working together. A calendar as complex and colorful as a handmade quilt. Terse exchanges with his nemesis within the partnership. An oncologist's report from last week passing along test results showing positive for early-stage colon cancer.

Dag had finally pushed the files aside. It had left him thinking about the past—and feeling ill.

Sean squinted up at the deep-blue sky. "I think so," he said slowly. "We needed to slip her a note from the second-in-command of the teachers' union."

"Right," said Dag. "Only it wasn't as simple as an email. They wanted us to deliver the handmade card."

"Great job for a new associate." Sean grinned.

"Sure," said Dag. "But the issue was they needed to get it to her before the amendment vote, and she was locked up in her home with her chief of staff. No press, no visitors."

Sean guffawed. "*Now* I remember," he said. "You had a delivery boy smuggle in the note."

Dag grinned at the memory. "She was a pizza fiend," he said. "Eating it reminded her of being a campaign volunteer in Chicago, tasted like her receding youth. Whenever the two of them were together, they always ordered in. So I waited for the delivery guy and slipped him a hundred bucks to let me drop an envelope in the bag with the pepper flakes and Parmesan."

"Our man at the union wasn't pleased when he heard about it."

"But he got his amendment."

"He got his amendment," Sean echoed. "And if I remember correctly, I told you off for that ridiculous stunt and then gave you a raise."

"That's when I knew Apex was the firm for me," said Dag.

They took hits off the bottles, savoring the smooth ale and cool air.

"It's been a while since I've been out here," said Dag. "It's looking good. I love the smell of honeysuckle."

Sean shrugged. "I wish I could take credit," he said. "But really it's the gardeners and maid who handle everything. I just show up to sleep here most nights. You know how it is."

"Yeah, you should have seen my fridge when I got home from the airport yesterday. Strawberries, milk, and olives. All gone bad. I didn't even know olives *could* go bad. Is that sad? We work to acquire all this stuff and then don't spend any time actually enjoying it."

Sean sipped his beer and considered. "It's funny. I used to have a few friends who lived in the neighborhood. Their kids played soccer, and they dragged me to a few games. I liked the kids, real rough-and-tumble tykes. There were always parents at the matches, but one time I counted the number of people who had to step away for a call or dash off to an emergency meeting. Half. On average, one person from whatever support crew the kid had at the game disengaged by the time the final whistle blew. There are a lot of life coaches who would blow a gasket over stuff like that. But who moves to McLean? For the most part, it's DC players who want a backyard or have kids on the way. None of the lower-level staffers can afford it, so we're in a town of power brokers. What do you expect the soccer games are going to look like? Sara may have just scored her first goal, but fighting is escalating in Kashmir, you know?"

He waved his beer bottle around to indicate the house and grounds. "But to answer your question, if we worked in order to acquire this stuff and then failed to enjoy it, yeah, that'd be sad. But that misses the point. I don't work in order to buy a house like this. I work because it's the best game on the planet, and I'm fucking good at it. This stuff is just a side effect. So, in conclusion, don't overthink your empty fridge. You've got better things to do than shop for groceries."

"The Indian takeout tasted better than anything I could possibly cook anyway."

"That's the spirit," said Sean. "Where would we be without specialization of labor? That's why we dubbed you the ninja."

"That's why I have you manning the grill." Dag grinned. "The only thing I know how to cook is pancakes."

"Watch yourself, boy," said Sean. "Or I'll have you clean it afterward."

"I'd say that's poor compensation for one of your mouthwatering steaks."

"I taught you everything you know about surgical flattery," said Sean, shaking his head. "And it still works wonders." He laughed and got up to check the grill. Raising the stainless-steel lid of the wide bar-becue, he flipped a half dozen corncobs. The husks were blackened and smoking. The smell of singed fiber wafted around the patio. Satisfied, he returned to the table.

As Sean settled back into his chair, Dag examined his craggy features, abundant beard, and bright-green eyes. This man had single-handedly changed the course of Dag's life, picking him from the cadre of Georgetown wannabes and shepherding him up every rung of the Washingtonian career ladder. For years, Dag had appreciated Sean's efforts but viewed the relationship as a means to professional advance-ment. Guiltily poring through Sean's archive had forced Dag to face how wrong he was. Sean was supportive, not transactional, and Dag's selfishness blinded him to the genuine bond that had grown between them. Sean was more of a father to Dag than any of his foster parents had ever been. Sean could be harsh, but he was also direct and fair to those around him. As mentors went, Dag couldn't have asked for anyone better.

Sitting here with him right now, Dag had to present a facade of normalcy. He had spent the preceding day shuffling through Sean's private life in search of ammunition for distraction. They knew each other well, as well as Dag knew anyone. But exploring someone's feed was something else entirely. Dag had seen it before with Hsu. Private messages. Bank statements. Photos. Media preferences. Posts. Call tran-scripts. Metadata. Tax returns. Browsing history. Credit ratings. The accumulated detritus of a human life.

But Dag hadn't known Hsu. He was a stranger, an abstraction. Reviewing his archive felt like reading a background file on a new hire or the bio of a superstar. Sean was different. Dag had attended his nephew's bar mitzvah. Sean had helped Dag buy the condo. They'd flown together from one capital to the next and covered for each other whenever circumstances required. Dag might be discovering discomfort at the ethical compromises his career required, but he wouldn't have even had a career without Sean. So peeking behind the veil into his mentor's life had turned Dag's stomach. Not because Sean had any particularly nasty skeletons in his closet, but because Dag was sneaking off with his friend's omniscient digital diary.

Sean tapped the base of his beer bottle on the tabletop. "I'm going to be honest," he said, his expression turning serious. "I didn't just invite you here for a barbecue."

"I appreciate the interest," said Dag, hoping to lighten the mood. "But you're not really my type."

"Not quite," said Sean, face still grave. He leaned toward Dag, resting on his elbows. "This is an intervention."

"An intervention?" Dag had thought he was the one with the ulterior motive for this conversation.

"Look, you're the smartest kid I've ever worked with," said Sean. "And that's not just surgical flattery. I mean it. We burn through associates like a junkie through hits, and I've never invested the time or effort to groom someone like I've done for you." He leaned back. "But that can only go so far."

"Had you not scooped me up after Georgetown," said Dag, "I'd still be wandering this town with my head up my ass. I see alternative versions of myself roaming the Beltway every day, nothing but poor hacks in cheap suits. DC is an easy place to lose yourself. I count myself lucky to have you as my guide."

What did it mean when you realized that you truly appreciated someone only as you were preparing to double-cross them? Had Brutus felt this way while planning Caesar's assassination, or had he charged forward without a second thought, high on a heady cocktail of righteous anger?

Sean stared at him for a moment. Then he got up, bent over the cooler, and pulled out a plate supporting two thick T-bone steaks. Removing the plastic wrap, he placed them on one of the side tables that extended out from the grill like steel wings. Heat washed over Dag as Sean opened the grill, unloaded the corn, and jacked up the burners to the highest setting. He let the gas roar for a moment and then tossed on the steaks. They sizzled and hissed as marbled fat seared on cast iron grates. After a minute, Sean flipped them, reduced the heat, and lowered the hood.

He turned back to Dag and crossed his arms over his chest.

"You don't get it," he said, holding up a thumb and forefinger a few centimeters apart. "The partners are this close to firing you."

The muscles in Dag's neck stiffened. He knew he was on thin ice. But he hadn't expected cracks to be shooting out from beneath his feet. He had to revise his assumptions. Doubts exploded inside Dag's mind like angry wasps from a nest. Sean was a veteran lobbyist. He'd seen colleagues go off the rails before, and Dag had been throwing up red flag after red flag. Handing off Rachel without warning. Asking for leave. Returning with an enigmatic new client. Demanding access to VIP contacts. Getting fired by another major client. His own trials and tribulations had blinded Dag to the simple fact that his once-enviable career trajectory at Apex was coming apart like a defective nuclear rocket, showering debris and fallout over everyone close to him. And nobody was closer than Sean.

Dag pinched the bridge of his nose for a moment and then looked up. "I owe you an apology," he said. "I know I haven't been the same since shit went down with Federico."

Sean raised his bushy eyebrows. Then he turned back to the grill, cut the gas, and served the steaks onto waiting plates, which he carried over to the table.

"I know the shooting spooked you," said Sean. "I get it. When you dumped Rachel into my lap, I wasn't happy, but I accepted it. Then you disappeared for a month. That's fine, you'd asked me for a leave of absence. But then you come back with some big shot new client in hand? I mean, what am I supposed to think? If you needed R and R that bad, you got damn lucky with your professional networking on vacation. And if you were schmoozing with clients instead of trying to get your head straight, why not tell me about it? I mean, I was happy for you. I told you that over coffee. Nice way to impress the partnership and all, especially with Lowell asking after you."

"I—"

Sean held up a hand. "I can't really complain if you're bringing whales to the firm," he said. "But now Lowell calls me, says he's booting you off the team. Demands I step in personally. And this is right after the firm hooked you up with an emergency meeting with Hsu. And it fucking worked. Lowell got what he wanted. So why is he kicking your ass to the curb and forcing my hand? He's one of our most valuable clients—I can't very well say no. So now I'm personally running two major accounts that are supposed to be yours, and I don't even know why." He carved off a piece of steak. The chunk of meat on the end of his fork was seared on the outside and bloody in the middle. "The firm wants your head on a platter, and I'm feeling less and less inclined to deny them." He shook his head. "I'm sick of feeling like I'm driving an 18-wheeler with a blacked-out windshield, or living my entire life at Analog. Autonomy is one thing, mutiny another. If I didn't know better, I'd think you were trying to pull one over on me, align yourself with another senior partner."

Dag felt like he couldn't get enough air. How could he have been so stupid, so insensitive? Not only was his sloppiness endangering secrets he couldn't share, it was hurting a man he cared about, a man he had no choice but to lie to. His thoughts forked and multiplied before cascading into the well-oiled rut of self-recrimination. It was all his fault. He had been too slow to save Federico. He had been too confident to trick Lowell. He had been too foolish to win over Hsu. He had been too gullible to realize the extent of Emily's scheme. He had been too self-absorbed to understand Sean. He had been too scared to face his grief. He had been too proud to look within. He had been too weak to do what he knew was right.

He was nothing but an abject failure.

"When I was in Taiwan," said Dag, buying time. He thought back to reviewing Sean's archive, how he might be able to derail the line of inquiry. "I showed up at Hsu's house to meet him. But his staffer, Baihan, led me up the biggest damn mountain on the island. I was delirious by the time I found Hsu on the summit. And he was ready for me. He'd found out about my parents during the background check they ran." Dag gulped in a breath and tried to keep his voice even. "They dug up . . . details. Afterward, I visited the site. The street where they died. Between that and Federico . . ." His Adam's apple bobbed up and down. "You know Lowell. After Taipei, I just couldn't take it anymore, and I think he could sense that. Mortality has been on my mind a lot, and it's been impacting my work. I'm really sorry. I just keep letting you down over and over again." Dag stabbed the knife into the steak. It stood vertical and quivering. "You know what? You're right. I should resign. If I can't carry my own weight, I can't ask you to shoulder it for me."

Sean's hard expression held for an agonizing moment and then crumpled. He stood, pulled Dag to his feet, and enveloped him in an enormous bear hug. His beard scratched Dag's neck. Then he held Dag out at arm's length.

"Kid, you're not resigning," said Sean. "Not after the amount of work I've put into you. Look"—he flinched—"to be frank, it's a weird moment for me too. Last week I went in for my annual checkup, and the doc diagnosed me with colon cancer."

"What?" Dag put on his best semblance of shock as a lump rose in his throat.

Sean waved away the concern. "We caught it early," he said. "It's treatable with high success rates. Please don't pass that around—you're the first person I've told."

Dag nodded, despising himself for false sincerity.

"But it got me thinking too," continued Sean. "We've only got a limited time on this earth, you know?"

"Sean, I'm really sorry to hear that," he said. "Shit."

"Well," said Sean. "I know what I want to do with the days I've got left." He clapped his hands. "Eat the best damn steaks I can get my hands on."

Dag snorted as pathos evaporated like dew on a desert morning.

Mr. Snufflebunch yawned, and Sean pretended to ignore Dag sneaking him a piece of steak under the table. Just like that, the rapport that had waned over the past few months returned. Dag had never felt worse about succeeding at anything. He'd just used his mentor's stolen medical records to win him over.

"You know something?" said Sean. "I'm sorry about the whole 'ninja' thing. After you got caught up in that shitstorm in Tokyo, I figured it was worthwhile to send you over to commando camp. You get to play James Bond, the firm gets someone who can handle tough situations. But I know it was hard on you. All that shit up in the Arctic. I shouldn't have pushed you. I should have helped you transfer away from Lowell sooner, helped you find new clients, develop other strengths."

Dag flushed. "Nah, nothing to apologize for," he said. "Somebody needed to do it, and there were bright spots along the way. Lowell does have quite a bourbon collection."

Sean gave him a searching look. "I've been meaning to say something for years, but somehow just never found the right time. Then something like this happens, and you realize that the 'right time' is something you create, not something you wait on."

"Well, thanks," said Dag, wishing with all his heart that he could reciprocate Sean's authenticity. "Hearing you say that means a lot."

Sean nodded. "Now that I have you back," he said, "we can chart a new course. In fact, I need your help on something."

"Yeah?"

"As part of transitioning in to working with Lowell, I'm doing a holistic refresh on all energy-related initiatives on the Hill. I can't put my finger on it yet, but something funny's going on. Since the global carbon tax failed, I was expecting people to focus on other issues for a while. But there are a bunch of new proposals out, and I've heard staffers whispering off-record about more to come. It's all disconnected right now, just cross talk and rumor. But it's worth checking out, especially given the impact on our broader energy client base. I'm heading out this week to update Rachel on progress in Mexico. Want to do some sniffing around while I'm gone?"

Sean leaned back, and the golden light filtering through the branches of the dogwoods cast his face in dappled shadow. For a fleeting second, Dag could have sworn he was looking not at Sean but at the face of the little boy staring out from the depths of the kelp forest. He blinked, and the vision faded.

"Sure," said Dag, feigning a casual interest to mask his inner turmoil. "I'll see what I can dig up."

CHAPTER 39

The strategy was as detailed and actionable as Dag had come to expect from the Island. Efforts redoubled, and the entire staff was contributing to an intricate campaign to rip the subsidies out from beneath the feet of the fossil fuel industry. They were accessing, analyzing, and massaging the feeds of dozens of politicians, staffers, and civil servants. Top think tanks were drafting white papers and policy briefs to jumpstart action on the Hill, all funded by generous donations from various Island shell accounts. Journalists were rediscovering an interest in sifting through the oil pork barrel. It would take time for the scheme to bear fruit, but the seeds had been planted.

All they needed was for Sean to underestimate the scope of the threat his clients now faced. Lowell and his compatriots would rely on Sean's expertise to gauge their response to the flurry of activity. If he intuited the extent of the danger, they would pull out all the stops. And that would be that. It was far easier to stop something from getting done in Washington than it was to get anything done at all. But if Sean assured his clients that it was all bark and no bite, industry executives would be all too happy to avoid a new headache, especially given how close they had come to disaster in Taipei.

The Island needed air cover, and only Dag could provide it. Left to his own devices, Sean would surely find the signal in the noise and sound the alarm. But he trusted Dag. And if Dag could divert him, lead him down a few dead-end streets, their efforts would gain enough traction that once Sean realized what was really happening, it would already be too late.

They were going to disrupt the entire system that was pumping carbon dioxide into the atmosphere. They were going to rewrite the terms of the deal that the Industrial Revolution had forged with the devil. They were going to lay the groundwork for a saner world.

All Dag had to do was sacrifice Sean.

He was back in his condo, pacing the living room and rubbing pounding temples. Despite its gastronomic perfection, he had barely been able to stomach the steak yesterday and hadn't eaten since. Sleep had abandoned him after twenty fitful minutes, and thoughts waged war in his head like medieval fiefdoms for the rest of the too-long night. When dawn finally arrived, he was far too racy for his morning coffee.

"I can't," he said.

"Yes, you can," said Emily. She was beaming into his feed, a digital apparition in ultra-high definition. "It's an ideal setup. He's already asked you to play gofer. All you need to do is underperform."

"That's what I was supposed to do with Hsu, and look how well that worked out."

She shook her head. "Lowell is a paranoid bastard. You yourself told me that he's always playing games with his own people. But Sean isn't Lowell. You're his protégé, not his consultant."

Dag narrowed his eyes. "I got lucky yesterday. I was able to dodge his questions about you and Lowell. But there's still too much that doesn't make sense from his perspective. We put a Band-Aid on it, but it won't last. Eventually, he's going to get suspicious, and as soon as he does, the trust that we're relying on to pull the wool over his eyes will disappear."

"Sure," she said. "You might be right. But I can have Frances doctor his feed to try to keep those suspicions in check. This is a race against time. We don't need to keep him in the dark forever, just for long enough. And between you and us, I have no doubt we can achieve that."

Dag ran his hands through his hair. "You're asking me to stab my mentor in the back."

"Don't be melodramatic," she said. "You're just leading him on a small detour that gives us the opportunity to change the world."

"The reason that detour is so important is because we're abridging his ability to advise his clients. What do you think will happen after people figure out what's really happening? He'll be ruined. The trust clients have in Sean right now correlates perfectly with how fucked he'll be when it turns out he was so, so wrong. The firm will need to cover its ass, and his head will be the one to roll. No one in the industry will ever trust him again. He'll be a laughingstock in addition to a scapegoat. All because of me."

"So you're willing to stake our planet's future against one man's career," she said in a flat deadpan.

"Sean's not just his career," said Dag. "He's my friend."

Emily called up a cascade of images in their shared feed. Tent cities in the Yucatán. The dry bed of the Colorado River. Climate refugees fleeing Bangladesh. The tangled mess of mud, steel, and shattered concrete that was all that remained after the slide that killed his parents. An audio clip played. It was his aunt trying to hold herself together as she received the tragic call that would change the course of his life—and end hers prematurely.

Dag silenced it with a slashing motion. The vicious drumbeat in his temples threatened to crack open his skull. The raciness was making him light-headed. Insomnia had frayed the edges of his consciousness. *You must forgive my curiosity about what's going on inside the soul of a man who returns to the country of his parents' passing to petition on behalf of the very cause that contributed to their demise.* How the clouds had danced around them, shot through with the rose-gold kiss of dawn.

"You've spent your whole life preparing for this moment," Emily said gently. "Losing your parents, enduring the foster care system. No kid should have to deal with that, but you did. You survived it. You thrived despite it. You learned the skills you needed to change the world." She bit her lower lip. "But those lessons had consequences. You let hardship etch away weakness. Suffering became a friend, a tool with which to polish the diamond core buried deep within you. You built a fortress around yourself, succeeding in everything by trusting no one. But you're not alone, Dag. All of us here on the Island have had to push through to the other side of that. Trust is dangerous. But it's also beautiful."

Visceral emotion rose in Dag's throat, threatening to overwhelm him.

She leaned forward, voice urgent and eyes beseeching. "Dag, you can trust me. You can trust our mission. I invited you into our family. I gave you the chance to redeem your mistakes. We're all flawed, myself included, but we also get to choose what to do about it."

A single raw sob tore through Dag before he could master himself.

"Dag." Emily's gaze was pure, throbbing, incandescent energy. "You can do this."

"You're right," he said, wiping his eyes. "I can."

She smiled.

"But, I won't."

"What?"

It was the first time he'd seen her genuinely surprised. Then her expression shifted through frustration, rage, fear, and determination before returning to perfect serenity. Dag took a moment to consider the woman who had tattooed herself across his neurons. Emily had an almost childlike quality about her, an outlook that combined unerring faith in her own worldview and a fervent bias to action. That, paired with her innate ability to identify and manipulate other people's psychological triggers translated into an inescapable charisma. Even without root access to your feed, she was the kind of person who would reframe every conversation, defining the terms of engagement. Only once you were out of her presence might you discover that *her* reality wasn't necessarily *the* reality. The one thing that someone like that couldn't handle was when you decided to construct a parallel universe.

"It's one thing to accept what you've done to me," he said, "but it's something else entirely to ask me to turn around and do it to someone I care about."

"Humanity is more important than any one person," she said.

"No," he said. "How we treat people defines humanity."

"Don't force my hand," she said, shaking her head. "You know how high the stakes are, and you're mature enough to know better. We've bet everything on this. We can't afford to fail. Not this time. Don't make me do something I'll hate myself for. You owe me that much, at least."

He swallowed, took a breath.

"We have to find another way," he said.

Her sigh was pain distilled. That single breath of air somehow contained a lifetime's stories and grief.

Then something subtle changed in the quality of her attention. A switch flipped. It was like catching a passing whiff of something rotten in a five-star restaurant.

Dag was back in the kayak, blister bursting, hairs rising on the back of his neck, ambushed by the sudden certainty that a storm lurked just over the horizon.

She laughed, but it was sharp and humorless.

"Dag, Dag, Dag," she said, shaking her head. "This is just pathetic. I mean, your best friend is your *boss*? Really? I must admit, I am truly disappointed. I've invested an enormous amount in you over the course of your training and gave you every opportunity to excel on your own terms. I made a space for you here. I didn't even blink when you failed with Hsu. We had an entire backup plan ready to go. I wanted you to taste the joy of compassionate action. I wanted you to experience what it means to actually change the world for the better. I wanted you to discover that beautiful embryo that lives deep within us all." She threw up her hands. "But you leave me no choice."

Emily pushed her glasses up her nose and rubbed her eyes.

"All right," she said. "Gloves off. You want to find another way? We dox Sean."

Dag just stared at her, his brain clocking into overdrive.

"Yeah, you know what?" she continued. "It'll be simpler all around."

"You wouldn't." Dag was only able to summon a harsh whisper.

"Wouldn't I?" She cocked her head to the side. "This is more important than you, and it's certainly more important than Sean. Here's how it's gonna work. We'll start by releasing sensitive material from his feed to specific journalists in a steady drip to coincide with any major milestones on the policy front. Then right before we bring the big ones to the floor, we publish his entire archive. The scandal will dominate the news cycle and consume whatever attention Lowell and his colleagues are paying to Washington. Without their favorite political Sherpa, they'll bumble around the Beltway like lost toddlers anyway. They won't stand a chance in hell of mounting meaningful opposition."

"You'll utterly destroy him," Dag said, almost to himself, awed by the horror of her threat. Doxing was the nuclear option of information war. It would be like touring the entire world through Room 412, a thousand times over. It wouldn't just undermine Sean's professional future, it would eat away at his life like sulfuric acid.

"It's guys like him who are destroying our world," she said. "It's about time he gets what he deserves."

"No," he said. Memories surged. The feeling of her porcelain skin under his hands. Her low, urgent moans as their hips rocked ever faster. The thick smell of sex. Was Dag so easy to subjugate? "No, no, no. You can't. I won't let you. I'll—"

"You'll do nothing whatsoever," Emily cut him off. "Do you have any idea how trivial it would be for us to demolish your credibility? We know you inside out. So don't get any grand ideas like trying to go to the press. Your testimony would be less than worthless. And believe me, blowing up your reputation would only be step one. So don't consign yourself to a living hell. It would be too little, too late, anyway. We'll get our initiatives passed, Sean will, ah, *retire early*, and the world will be better for it." She rubbed her hands together. "Well, I think we're done here. Time to get to work."

"Wait," he gasped. His legs turned to jelly, and he had to catch himself on the doorframe. "I'll do it. I'll talk to him. Just give me some time."

She skewered him with a glare that could melt iron.

"I'll give you one week," she said, voice laden with disgust. "And from now on, you better not disappoint."

CHAPTER 40

Straps dug into Dag's shoulders as the hydrofoil sank and the hull of the boat hit the water. Only now could he feel the push and pull of groundswell. Unclipping from the harness, he made his way to the head on unsteady feet and emptied his bladder. He didn't want to risk having to pee once he was out there.

The stream of urine spattered around the metallic bowl before pouring down the drain. The toilet whooshed as Dag flushed. Lobbying had appealed to him because it promised to reveal how the world really worked and give him the tools to influence it. Years spent defending and enriching entrenched interests left him wanting more, a way to contribute to something larger than himself and right wrongs he'd helped inflict. But could a noble mandate require betraying a friend? If there was one lesson that Dag had learned from a career of political machination, it was the value of true loyalty.

Stripping off his clothes, he pulled on a thin, breathable base layer and then loaded the air-supply tank onto his back. It was heavy, and he took a moment to make sure it was correctly balanced across his hips. *This is just pathetic. I mean, your best friend is your* boss? Maybe Emily was right. Reflecting on his own life, Dag couldn't help but agree. He had no family to speak of. The last two women he'd slept with had seduced him only in order to use him. He devoted nearly all his energy to his work, and his most substantive relationships were with clients, colleagues, and competitors. He had once sought refuge from struggle in illustration. Lately, he had found solace only in ambition.

But just because something was pathetic didn't mean it wasn't true. Sean had given Dag a chance when so many others would have ignored a fresh grad with no family connections. He had taught Dag the craft and opened the door to a universe he could never have imagined. He had paved Dag's path to partnership in the firm and protected him against the slings and arrows of internal politics. Since the divorce, Sean had similarly pursued his profession with singular focus. That kindred spirit sparked a bond that was cemented by years of fraternal collusion and the occasional grilled steak. Though they often schemed together, their relationship was as yet untouched by scheming.

Dag couldn't forsake that. But neither could he allow Emily to dox Sean.

It was time for the hazmat suit. The aluminized fabric was thick and heavy, and it took a full fifteen minutes to stuff his body inside it, air supply and all. Had the rescue workers digging bodies from the Razif mudslide worn similar garb? The bulbous face mask layered a silver sheen on everything. By the time he closed the final zipper, he was sweating and breathing hard.

He could feel the growling marine-diesel engine downshift, and a notification sprang into his feed.

He had arrived.

Struggling to find his footing in the awkward suit, he shuffled to the main hatch. Without an airlock, opening it risked allowing contamination inside. But the boat's air-filtration system should be able to handle it. This wasn't Fukushima or Cofrentes, after all. Pulling up the dashboard in his feed, he hit the tender release, opened the hatch, and stepped out onto the deck.

The sky was low and oppressive, a uniform layer of pitch-black particulates that somehow managed to let through a weak and diffuse sunlight that cast no shadows. He should have known. Emily might act like a Good Samaritan, but she was just as willing to set morals aside to achieve her aims as any politician. Dag's refusal to divert Sean had pushed her over the edge, and she had an incomparable arsenal at her disposal to coerce him.

He was a fly caught in her spiderweb. And she was hungry.

With a splash, the pulley system deposited the dinghy off the stern. The hatch hissed shut behind him. Carefully gripping the rungs of the ladder, he lowered himself into the rocking dinghy, detached the lines, and goosed the engine. The small boat jetted out across the waves, gouging a wedge of wake as it curved in a wide arc toward shore.

Those who travel with the current will always feel they are good swimmers, while those who swim against the current may never realize they are better swimmers than they imagine. So this was how it felt to discover the difference. But the Island went further than controlling the current—they reached in to tweak the feel of the water on the swimmer's skin, the ache in their lungs, their choice of stroke.

The bow of the boat nudged up against land. Dag lumbered over the side and waded up through the shallows, tying the bowline to a bent parking meter. Then he looked up. The rising sea had claimed the low park, and the dinghy now floated a meter above what had once been lawns across which dogs chased Frisbees. Waves lapped at the curb where a few wrecked cars sat on their axles, windows shattered, paint bubbled and crumbling, tires long since disintegrated.

Frost might ruin one farmer and triple the price of his neighbor's harvest. Someone made a killing selling rubber gloves after each and every oil spill. One man's tragedy was another's boon. Dag had played both sides. He had helped Lowell expand global oil production and keep prices low enough that the world stayed drunk on combustion. And on the flip side, they'd invested in assets that would appreciate with climate change, creating a wildly profitable loop whose externalities they lobbied governments to ignore.

La Jolla smoldered before him. In his childhood memory of the cove, diners dawdled at fancy restaurants, concierges welcomed guests to posh hotels, and tourists delighted over baubles and silly T-shirts in one shop after another. Now the hill that rose above him was a burned-out shell. City blocks had been reduced to blackened squares on a barren landscape. I beams and rebar rose from the slag like skeletal rib cages. Brick structures had cracked and collapsed in the heat. Empty window sockets stared out from a partially erect concrete wall.

There had been a host of disasters that year, of course. Hurricanes, earthquakes, floods, and tornadoes galore. With resources spread so thin, something had to give. So Dag had pulled all the strings at his disposal to ensure that emergency-response capacity was deployed elsewhere, leaving the Escondido wildfire free to wreak havoc across half the state. If things had played out differently, maybe Louisiana would have suffered this fate instead. But things had worked out how they had, and what lobbyist wouldn't fight for the interests of his client? The media had painted Lowell a hero, the magnate who opened up high-rise after high-rise in unaffected areas for the refugees. The only niggling question they'd failed to pursue was exactly why the billionaire had bet so heavily on such developments in the first place.

Could it be called a crime if that was just how the world worked?

Carefully placing his feet to avoid debris, Dag shuffled up the sidewalk and away from the dinghy, following the curve of the hill as it rose from the shoreline and onto a bluff. The concrete he walked on was cracked but intact, covered in an ankle-deep layer of coal and carbon. The asphalt of the street itself had warped, flowed, and solidified again into a petrochemical glacier.

It was one thing to whistle while the world burns from the comfort of a luxury berth, quite another to summon the same insouciance amid the ashes. He had boxed up the pain, loss, and anger of the tragedy that had defined his childhood, channeling it into a certainty that the universe owed him something and that those in his way deserved their lot.

Staring out at the cinders, stale breath hot against his face, that seemed such a sad and petty outlook. The truth was that his parents' death was no one's fault, and everything he'd suffered through thereafter hardly made his experience unique. That's what he had found most compelling about the Island. Emily had assembled a team of people with personal histories far darker than Dag's who devoted their lives to causes larger than themselves—and actually got results. It had woken something inside him, shown him that realism and cynicism weren't synonymous.

A thousand questions pecked at his soul like crows in the heat of bloodlust. Was this new sense of conscience synthetic? His feed was his interface with the digital universe, his point of access to all information, his conduit to the throbbing heart of human culture. It was an external organ, one that he only now realized had been genetically engineered. If every digital experience had been carefully curated for years on end, then this soul-searching was simply the center of a manicured psychological labyrinth. They were fine-tuning his moral realizations as surely as his libido, all to fit into their larger scheme, to drive their mission forward.

The hazmat suit was stiff and claustrophobic. His muscles burned, and he couldn't wipe away the sweat that stung his eyes.

He had wanted to be a player of realpolitik. But once in the game, the prizes lost their luster. Without something personal at stake, it was just a bunch of blowhards in back rooms. Emily had served him a moral compass on a silver platter—he could play a key role in saving the world from the specter of climate change, help to offset the damage he'd done by championing those who profited by it.

Dag had watched with awe as Island staff demonstrated the tools at their disposal. The methods were disturbing, but were they justifiable? Falling victim to their program clarified just how wicked and powerful a weapon it really was. It highlighted Dag's own lackluster judgment. He had been so ready to take advantage of the benefits the Island offered, without pausing to consider the human impact it created. And where were the ethics in that? True justice didn't require a panopticon. If you made better policy via brainwashing, was that victory? Was that the world you wanted to live in? Maybe you'd have your way, but the political landscape would probably turn into something as dystopic as the street he now walked.

Ends and means didn't justify one another—they were two sides of the same coin.

Democracy was a messy business. Ugly, tired, and slow, it promised nothing but incremental change guaranteed to disappoint everyone. He understood what drove the Island crew. They were subverting a system they saw as fundamentally broken. But having seen the world through the lens of their engineered omniscience, Dag would take the frustrations of cooperation over the predations of coercion.

Critical thinking without hope was cynicism, while hope without critical thinking was naïveté. What Emily was doing appeared hopeful at first blush. Not just hopeful, effective. They'd secured political victories with unprecedented efficiency and instituted better policies. But the justice of their chosen causes belied a far deeper cynicism, a fundamental distrust in human integrity. Dag had been naive to think their solution might be a geopolitical deus ex machina. They won only by disenfranchising every person they touched, robbing them of their free will.

He remembered staring at himself down the barrel of the Tavor. Your feed was a mirror that reflected back your accumulated dreams, fears, whims, passions, and very identity. The Island subtly altered the reflection every time you glanced at it, until you no longer recognized yourself.

The memory was as faded as a twentieth-century sepia photograph. The charcoal ruins of La Jolla afforded no landmarks to speak of. But he found the spot.

Kneeling in the soot of civilization, Dag clumsily gripped the railing with the oversize silver gloves of his hazmat suit. He pressed his faceplate up to the bars and stared. Surfers carved turquoise waves that broke against a long curve of white beach that stretched to the very horizon. Dolphins breached in the thick kelp forests just offshore, sunlight glittering off their slick skin. A long pier jutted out from the famed Scripps Institution of Oceanography. Paragliders leapt from the bluff to spiral up and down thermals. Pastel estates covered the hills, and palm trees swayed in the breeze. On the rocky point below, sea lions snored and cavorted. Their submarine finesse had reminded a much younger Dag that there could be beauty amid the pain and inspired his first illustrations.

But that once-azure sky was now a low ceiling of smoke billowing out from where inland embers still burned. The homes were reduced to rubble. The beach was covered in wreckage. The ocean a polluted onyx tub. And below Dag, the point was nothing but a deserted pile of carbonized rock. This wasn't some clever fabrication. This was real. Time for Dag to follow suit.

And then huge snowflakes began to fall, filling his vision. He caught one in his glove and held it up to the faceplate in consternation. Not snow, ash. Ash rained down in a thick and silent blizzard, gently blotting out what little sun filtered through the smoke.

Who are you?

If his mind was not his own, how could he possibly know?

Anyway, it was the wrong question.

The only thing that mattered now was who he would become.

CHAPTER 41

"Is that 100gsm cartridge paper?" asked Dag.

Nell gave him an odd look. "Welcome back, Mr. Calhoun," she said. "If there's a member who would sponsor you, you may want to consider applying to join Analog. The waiting list is quite extensive, but you never know when a spot might open up." Her ocher skin shone in the warm light of the antechamber, and her formfitting but conservative dress matched the shade of her eyes exactly. "As for your question, my apologies, but I don't know the make of the paper. I can ask the manager, if you like."

"Not a problem," said Dag. "Just curious. Would you mind if I borrow a piece?"

Dimples formed on her cheeks as she smiled. "You may even have one to keep." She carefully tore a single sheet from the pad and handed him a fountain pen along with it. "Drafting a love letter?"

"If only," said Dag. "But unfortunately, it's nothing so romantic."

"Well, I'm sure whoever you're intending it for will appreciate the personal touch," she said. "I'll show you in."

Parting the thick red satin curtains with a slender hand, she stepped inside.

Hoisting his attaché case, Dag followed, making sure to keep her between him and the far corner booth.

He closed his eyes and took a steadying breath. From one moment to the next, his feed lifted like a parent releasing the hand of a trundling toddler. His mind was achingly quiet despite the hubbub of the club. Ever so slowly, he opened his eyes again. A lone pianist played in a far corner, reminding him of the hotel in Mexico City. One of the hounds raised its head and accompanied the bluesy riffs with a low howl. Dag smelled leather, oak, and a faint hint of lavender. Laughter and murmured conversation filled the air like champagne bubbles.

Lowell was a bastard, but Dag had been his wingman through enough escapades to learn that nobody really knew what they were doing. Everyone imagined their political opponents to be infallible leviathans who ruled with ruthless efficiency and relentless execution. But few plots survived contact with reality. The tangled network of human relationships that was the political arena was so complex that something inevitably went awry. It was through those cracks that new players clawed hand over bloody hand into the game. And once you were in, the only way to stay in was to throw yourself into the abyss of uncertainty with wild abandon over and over and over again. You had to risk everything every single day. Otherwise, someone willing to do so would topple you in no time at all. Winners didn't stay winners by staying cooped up in a fortress. They stuck their necks out so far that everyone else thought it was a bluff.

He touched Nell's forearm. Her skin was warm and silky.

"I'll start at the bar before joining them," he said.

As she walked him to an empty stool at the end of the massive bar, he asked, "Is there a physical courier service available?"

"Certainly," she said. "What priority level?"

"It has to be a dedicated courier, and I need it delivered this afternoon," he said. "Highest security. Absolute discretion. Interstate. Cost is not an issue."

She nodded as if the request wasn't at all unusual. "How large is the package?"

He held up the sheet of paper.

"Just this," he said.

She stared for a moment. "I'll send someone down right away."

"Thanks," he said. "I should have it ready by the time they arrive."

She slipped off to make the necessary arrangements, and he perched atop the stool and spun to face the bar. A dour mixologist poured him an incomparable old-fashioned. Savoring the butterscotch and citrus notes, Dag took a moment to compose his thoughts. Disparate components had lurked in the back of his mind for a while, but the idea hadn't clicked into place until he had returned the boat last night after a brooding cruise up the coast and out from under the unbroken ceiling of smoke. Tension hummed inside him like a charge in search of a grounding wire.

Like that golden retriever in La Condesa, he would make his getaway.

He uncapped the pen, placed nib to paper, and began to write.

CHAPTER 42

After dispatching the courier, Dag called over the bartender. The tall man had high cheekbones, black hair slicked back from his forehead, and the requisite bow tie and red suspenders. Under the sputtering light of the oil lamps, he could have stepped right out of a Prohibition-era speakeasy. He placed his hands flat on the bar, fingers splayed.

"What else can I get for you, sir?"

"Do you have any Casa Dragones?"

"An agave man, eh?" The man touched the side of his nose. "Indeed we do."

"Three glasses, neat, three fingers each."

The bartender raised his eyebrows.

"We'll need it," said Dag.

"As you say, sir."

Dag looked down the length of the bar. So much drama had played out within these hallowed walls. A refuge for the masters of successive technological revolutions, Analog was as jaded as a permanent expat. It was one of those special places that was somehow apart from the currents of history, a channel through which history flowed. Time for him to contribute to its legacy of intrigue. One way or the other, the world would be different when Dag stepped back out through its bronze-bound oak doors. He remembered the ribbon of orange peel falling from the peak of Yushan.

Niitakayama nobore.

A few minutes later the bartender returned carrying three long-stemmed, slender glasses that resembled champagne flutes. Each contained a generous pour of clear, fragrant tequila. Thanking him, Dag slid his left hand beneath the glasses so that the stems slotted in between his fingers and then lifted them slowly but steadily. The bases of the glasses sat against the edge of his palm, and the weight of the liquid they carried braced them against each other.

Reaching down with his right hand, he retrieved the attaché case and rose slowly from his stool. Weaving through the maze of tables was meditative. He had to focus his entire attention in order to avoid spilling the drinks as he dodged elbows, inattentive diners, and harried servers. It was a useful exercise, clearing his head before the most important negotiation of his career.

"May I join you?" he asked. "I believe I've exhausted the bartender's supply of small talk."

This wasn't strictly true, but thousands of illustrations had made Dag a sucker for symmetry. A strange lightheartedness overcame him, similar to the ephemeral but euphoric feeling he'd had on his stroll to meet these very same people at Analog only a few months before.

Sean and Rachel looked up in surprise from their booth by the hearth. The moment took on an almost cinematic quality. Dag wondered what secrets hid behind Rachel's wrinkled face, how many people she must have cultivated, cowed, and inspired on her quest to connect the world. Age had distilled rather than softened her. The kind of project to which she had dedicated herself required relentless ambition and inhuman patience. A pharaoh might have sensed a kindred spirit. The fire popped and roared. One of the vizslas arched its back and yawned.

"Dag." Sean's bushy eyebrows twitched, but he tried to cover his surprise in front of a client. "We were just reviewing the Mexico road map. Francisco Vasquez is on board, and his aunt is discreetly issuing talking points to her pundits. Between the Senate and the public, we should be able to squeeze concessions from the cartel bloc and start offering connectivity on a limited but expanding basis."

Dag managed to place the glasses on the table without spilling them and pulled up a chair so he sat at the end of the table, rather than sliding into either side of the booth. He took a deep breath and looked at each of them in turn. Beneath Sean's careful poker face, Dag could detect an undercurrent of concern. He regretted having to ambush his mentor like this, but there was no way around it. Any other path would have hurt Sean far more. Rachel stared back with perfect poise. Her one-eyed gaze sliced away any effort at spin, the product of a lifetime of corporate leadership.

"I'm sorry to interrupt," said Dag. "But this is urgent." He ran a hand through his hair. He was standing on the edge of an icy pond, about to take the plunge. "First things first. Sean, I formally submit my resignation. Effective immediately."

There. It was out in the open. Anxiety sloughed off him. No going back now.

Shocked emerald eyes stared back at him. Sean was, for once, speechless.

Dag turned to Rachel and said, "Ma'am, you can't let the Taipei decision stand. Commonwealth doesn't have the luxury of shortsightedness like politicians who prioritize reelection and financial contribution over policy."

Her eye didn't blink. He could drown in that purple iris.

"I don't think—" Sean began.

But Dag interrupted him, addressing Rachel. "Commonwealth's infrastructure binds the world together, but climate change is tearing it apart. Extreme weather, ocean acidification, forced migration, food-system risk, economic destabilization. All of it threatens your core business model as well as your most valuable assets. Disaster reduces feed engagement. Destruction rips components and users from the system. You simply can't afford the status quo."

"We are well aware of the risks," said Rachel, unruffled. "And we made our preferences known in Taipei. To be frank, I was disappointed."

"I read your op-ed, but disappointment won't solve the problem." The ash had fallen soft as snow. "Your personal majority stake and voting rights put you beyond the reach of quarterly pressure from shareholders."

The smallest hint of a frown flickered across her forehead. "There's nothing I can do."

"You don't have a choice."

"What are you implying?" Her tone was a drawn blade.

"Dag," said Sean, giving Rachel an apologetic glance. "Why don't me and you take a walk and go over this in private first?"

A political science professor had invited Sean in to do a Q&A with his Georgetown seminar to give the students a taste of what working on the Hill was really like. Dag still remembered how impressed he'd been with Sean's combination of Machiavellian sophistication and ability to make you feel like you were the most important person in the world just by looking at you. With those qualities, he would have made a great politician. But they made him an even better lobbyist. Dag had asked question after question, walking Sean off campus after the seminar ended. A few months later, his continued persistence landed him a job. That job had been his first break. It had given him a path, a cohort, a future to plan for. Now he was leaving it behind forever, in part to protect the man who had hired him in the first place.

"I'm sorry," said Dag. "I didn't want to spring this on you. But there was no other way to guarantee infosec." He turned back to Rachel. "Ma'am, the international community failed to pass a global carbon tax into international law. But the Commonwealth terms of service are more enforceable than any piece of international legislation. No country can function without the feed. Even places like Mexico and China that maintain their own fiber would collapse without the software. It's like electricity, it powers everything."

"I came here for a campaign update," said Rachel, "not to be berated by my lobbyists."

"I'm no longer your lobbyist. I'm an individual activist," said Dag. "And I'm not here to lecture you. I'm here to offer you a deal."

Her frank stare declared her incredulity. Rachel oversaw an empire that would have made Genghis Khan blush. The world economy depended on Commonwealth infrastructure. The feed was like air, something so essential you took it entirely for granted. Governments depended on Commonwealth just as citizens depended on governments. And Commonwealth depended on Rachel.

"A simple trade," said Dag. "That's all."

Her wrinkled face was an indecipherable map.

"And what do you have to offer?"

He remembered the taste of fried chicken and waffles, the smell of the breeze fresh off the strait, the blisters from a clandestine paddle.

"What if I could tap into your entire feed archive? What if I could tweak the parameters of your every search, read your every message, individually manipulate your every interaction? What if I controlled every single aspect of your digital life and shaped your experience to serve my own ends?" He paused. "It seems to me that you might want to stop me. In fact, your entire business depends on stopping me. Commonwealth is like currency—without trust, its power evaporates." Dag snapped his fingers.

"I'm very sorry," said Sean, face as red as his beard. He gripped Dag's forearm and began to slide out of the booth. "I'll get rid of him."

But Dag never broke eye contact with Rachel, and Sean froze when she raised a finger.

"Mr. Calhoun," she said. "Get to the point. What have you brought to trade?"

"The biggest security breach in Commonwealth history," he said. "A small group of hackers has root access to your system, and they use it to manipulate the feeds of high-level politicians and business leaders."

"Impossible," she said.

He shrugged. "They've been doing it for years."

"We have the tightest cybersecurity on the planet," she said. "The best minds, the best practices, the best tech. There's no way an exploit like this exists. You're concocting a conspiracy theory."

"Well, it certainly seemed so when they targeted me," said Dag. "But I assure you that this conspiracy is far more than mere theory."

"You have evidence?"

"I do."

"Let's see it."

"I said this was a trade," said Dag. "Not a gift."

It was as if Rachel had been carved from solid marble.

"What is it you want?" she said at last.

Just like that, Dag knew he had won. It was like the moment the Arctic Council cast their votes. He remembered the unassuming Taipei city block. The onslaught of Razif images. The disbelief and terror that laced his aunt's voice when she received the fateful call. The difference between the Arctic Council victory and today was that, this time, he was championing his own cause.

"Take the Taipei proposal," said Dag, "and bake it into your terms of service. Implement the global carbon tax, enforceable via immediate refusal of Commonwealth services. Announce it tomorrow morning."

"Impossible," she repeated. "Even if we could roll something like that out so quickly, it wouldn't work. Governments don't like the rug being pulled out from under them. They'd become a direct threat to Commonwealth."

If he'd learned anything from Emily, it was that the world was far more pliable than everyone assumed.

"More of a threat than the vulnerability I described?" he asked. "More of a threat than inaction?"

A moment of stony-faced silence passed.

"You better not be bullshitting me."

"I won't give you names," he said. "But I'll provide the full exploit architecture so you can lock the back door. Commonwealth will trundle along, and nobody need know about this awkward little episode."

"Are you *insane*? You won't give me names? You're claiming someone's hijacked the feed, and you're asking me to let them run free?"

"They figured out pretty quickly that material gain was easy," he said. "They could tap as much wealth as they needed by gaming hedge funds against each other. What does anybody do when they have more money than they know what to do with? They either obsess over it, implode, or discover philanthropy. This group is trying to save the world in their own way. They don't deserve to be crucified."

"If they've accomplished even one percent of what you describe, they're terrorists."

Terrorists. He remembered walking the perimeter of the bucolic paddock with Javier, how his dark slender hands had trembled when he told the story of Emily rescuing him and his sister from a Houston hellhole. If Rachel only knew she was condemning a man who had helped her build Commonwealth in the first place. But now that he was finally throwing off every tether, Dag wasn't going to define himself by denouncing others.

He shrugged again. "Do you care more about solutions or revenge?"

Her pupil dilated.

Never sell past the close.

It was time.

"Do we have a deal?"

He stood and held out his hand.

She rose slowly to her feet. Her expression was simultaneously serene and homicidal.

"If your information is good," she said, "I'll do as you say."

They shook, and Dag tried to assess the gravity of the gesture from the warmth of her small dry hand. This legendary grip was a covenant more sacred than any contract on earth could guarantee. It was the very foundation upon which Commonwealth was built.

"Pleasure doing business with you," he said.

Reaching down, he hoisted the attaché case onto the table. "In here, you'll find precise records of exactly how my feed was commandeered, together with notes on the perpetrators' approach. It's quite elegant. You can correlate across your user base to determine where else the same techniques have been applied. Revert the changes. Clean the code. Close the loophole."

The black leather hissed against the wooden tabletop as Rachel slid the attaché case to rest in front of her. She sat and popped the clasps, opening it to reveal Diana's detailed trove of intel. Rachel removed sheets of diagrams, reports, graphs, and annotated code, stacking them into neat piles and shuffling them back and forth in an arcane and compulsive system that got progressively more frenzied as she absorbed their contents.

Dag and Sean sat in tense silence, trying not to disturb Rachel. But she was devouring the material with such a monopoly of attention that she wouldn't have noticed a grenade going off in the middle of the bar. Her absolute focus lulled them into a strange sense of timeless stasis, as if awed into submission by an implacable bureaucracy.

All of a sudden, Rachel surprised them by scooping up the paperwork without a word, piling it back into the case, and slamming it shut. She stood, reached for the glass, and downed the tequila in a single gulp. She came up from the shot coughing and spluttering, then looked at Dag.

For a fraction of a second, her poise evaporated and her watering eye betrayed a naked combination of outrage, fear, and determination. And then the armor slid back into place.

She was, once again, a master of the universe.

"If you'll excuse me," she said. "It appears I have a busy night ahead."

Dag raised his own glass.

The pianist built to a crescendo.

History wasn't linear. Radical change happened only in fits and starts, separated by fallow periods of relative stability.

The tequila set his throat ablaze.

He couldn't yet divine its shape, but it was an achingly beautiful feeling to trace the line.

CHAPTER 43

"Is this déjà vu, or do you intentionally wait until we meet Rachel at this godforsaken place to spring things on me?" Sean tugged on his beard. "I'm not even angry. That was too . . . insane to inspire anger. I'm just . . . I don't even know. You know I can't get you your job back after that, right? Even my sway over the partners has limits, and this is so far out in left field it's not even in the ballpark."

A chuckle escaped Dag. Maybe this is what those sea lions felt like. For so long, his career had defined his identity. Sacrificing it was strangely liberating, as if a weight had been lifted from his shoulders. He had faced down the ghosts of memory, dispensed with the mission he'd agreed to carry out on the Island, and disarmed them at the same time. For the first time that he could remember, there was nothing he had to do, no party line he had to toe.

He could just be.

"You're a madman," said Sean with more awe than animosity.

"If I hadn't resigned," said Dag, "Apex would have been ruined. I meant what I said. Lobbyists aren't activists. We elevate the clients' goals above our own, rather than trying to impose our wills on them. With your energy portfolio, it's especially important that the firm not be implicated. This way, I'm out of a job, but you're going to have more work than you can handle once Rachel makes her announcement. Nobody will know what to do. Everyone will need counsel."

Sean cocked his head to one side. "You quit to save my reputation?"

"You make a damn good steak," said Dag. "And I hope to taste one again someday."

Despite himself, Sean grinned.

"And what you told Rachel?"

"All true," said Dag.

A tide was rising inside him, dark, frothy, and immutable.

Sean's massive shoulders shuddered. "Fuck," he said.

There was a long moment of silence. Dag remembered how he felt when Emily had first explained the scheme to him and when Diana had revealed the full extent of it at this very table. Matryoshka dolls all the way down.

"If people knew . . ."

"If people knew, it would be the end of Commonwealth," said Dag.

"It would be the end of far more than that," said Sean, half-horrified, half-wistful. "The whole damn world relies on them."

"And now they'll do their part to protect the whole damn world in addition to profiting from it," said Dag. "We see how guys like Lowell work. We help them do it. They claim to play by the rules and fight tooth and nail to buy up the umpires. Should be fun to see the reaction to a new playbook. I'd be useless to the firm now anyway." He shrugged. "I caught a bad case of conscience."

"The cancer has made me rethink some priorities as well," said Sean. "The threat of impending mortality can give us rationalizers a hard time."

Sean had intended it as a joke, but Dag nodded solemnly.

"This whole mess?" said Dag. "It's not even the worst part."

He was a dam about to burst.

The look Sean gave him was quizzical and unnerving.

Dag took a deep breath and let it out slowly. There was no turning back.

"Look," he said, "you asked if this was déjà vu. Last time the two of us were sitting here in this booth, I lied to you."

Once Dag started to tell the story, it poured out of him in a flood. He told Sean about stumbling back from Federico's assassination and meeting Emily in the bar. He told Sean about Room 412, about Emily cracking his feed, about his first visit to the Island. He explained how their efforts had inspired him in a strange way, revealing the reservations he'd been harboring about his work at Apex. He shared the vestigial sense of belonging he'd felt when Emily made it clear that they needed his help, that he could be a part of something bigger, that he could make a difference. He admitted to using his role at Apex, his relationship with Lowell, his access to Hsu, all to help achieve the ends the Island sought. He described how Diana, right there at Analog, had crushed him with the revelation that Emily had been targeting him for years, curating his digital life, cultivating his psychology with a steady drip of manipulation. He reported how fundamentally disorienting it was not being able to trust yourself, second-guessing every part of your identity, trying to find something, anything, to grasp on to. He confessed to pillaging Sean's feed, using their illicit knowledge of the cancer diagnosis to distract him, Dag's own refusal to continue, and Emily's ultimatum.

The tale was steam escaping from a pressure cooker. It hissed and spat with pent-up shame and regret. But it was also the first ray of light entering a boarded-up house in a condemned neighborhood as a hopeful squatter adjusted his sweaty grip on a crowbar and pried the plywood from a broken window. As a child, Dag had learned that love led to nothing but pain. He proceeded to seal himself off from authentic relationships as he learned to navigate a hostile world. That savvy and independence had served him well, earning him a gilded ticket to a life of privilege, accelerating his rise at Apex, and allowing him to rationalize his initial alliance with Emily. But her threat to ruin Sean had cracked something inside Dag, forcing him to acknowledge the cost of his studied detachment. Choosing not to care might mitigate the risk of pain, but in doing so it destroyed the capacity for joy, for finding meaning. Emily had known that, even as she was trying to convince him to betray Sean. *You built a fortress around yourself, succeeding in everything by trusting no one. Trust is dangerous. But it's also beautiful.* She was right about that, even if she'd been wrong about where that realization might lead him.

Dag told Sean all this and more, about what their relationship meant to him, how their friendship had changed his life, and why it had taken him so long to recognize something so simple.

And then, suddenly, Dag was done.

Sean was pale behind his beard. His hands rested on the table, fingers interlaced and trembling. His green eyes were strangely blank.

Then, slowly, Sean reached out and raised his glass. Lamplight painted the clear liquid amber, sparkling off drops falling to the table as Sean's shaking hand spilled some of the liquor. Downing the tequila, he wiped his mouth.

"You're a sneaky motherfucker, you know that?" said Sean, voice catching.

"That's why you hired me," said Dag.

"I always suspected you would go off on your own one day," said Sean. "Your pitches to clients were so crafted, the visions you laid out for them so compelling. You hated the overhead of managing the other partners, relied too much on me for that. I thought you'd run for office. Snag yourself a Senate seat. Put what I taught you to work. But this . . . I don't even have words for this."

Abruptly, Sean slid out from the booth and stood up.

Dag stood to face him.

"Look," said Sean, peering at Dag as if through heavy fog, "everything you said. All this. I—" He faltered. "I need some time to process. It's hard to know what to think, what to feel. I—"

Reaching out, he crushed Dag in a bear hug. He smelled of pine, freshly laundered wool, and tequila. "Let me know next time that fridge runs empty," he said into Dag's shoulder, "and I'll fire up the grill."

And then he was gone, striding off through the tables without a second glance.

Dag's head spun, and his legs threatened to give way. He slid back into the booth and tried to slow his pounding heart. These were uncharted waters, and he didn't even have a compass.

"Sir, are you okay?"

It was Nell. She looked down at him, concern written across her elegant features.

"Why?" asked Dag. "What do you mean?"

"Ahh," she said, visibly uncomfortable. "I'm sorry, Mr. Calhoun, but . . . you're crying. Is there anything I can get for you?"

Dag touched his cheeks, shocked.

A laugh bubbled up from deep inside him.

"Why am I crying?"

"Umm." She bit her lip.

"I'm sorry," he said, laughing again. "What a stupid question."

"Are you sure you're okay?"

"Honestly," he said, surprising himself, "I think I am."

CHAPTER 44

As soon as the red satin curtains fell back into place behind him, Dag's feed hit him like a tsunami. Notifications crashed into his mind like artillery. Messages piled up in every queue. The digital fire hose pounded him with merciless force, demanding his attention.

"Mr. Calhoun?" Nell looked up from the podium.

"Yes?" said Dag, gritting his teeth against the onslaught.

"I'm glad to see you're feeling better," she said. "I asked the manager. And you're right, it's 100gsm cartridge paper."

A window opened automatically, filling his entire visual field with a view of the living room in the main house on the Island. Audio piped in at full volume, grating and painful. Emily was there along with Javier and everyone else. They were working with adrenaline-fueled intensity. Shouted instructions and arguments shot back and forth. The courier's pouch sat open on a coffee table with the letter he'd written on a page torn from the very pad Nell was holding up in front of him.

"Finally." Javier looked up at Dag. "I've got him."

"Dag," said Emily. "What the fuck is going on?"

He tried to exit, mute, minimize—anything to get him past Nell and out the door. But his feed wouldn't respond. The live audiovisual stream was force-feeding itself into his system. He lost his balance and managed to grab the edge of the podium for support.

"Mr. Calhoun." Nell's concern deepened. "Should I call someone? What's wrong this time?"

"What have you done?" asked Ferdinand.

Everyone was standing now, moving closer together, staring at him, demanding answers. But Nell was also there right in front of him, looking like she was afraid he might keel over. He couldn't dial down the visual opacity or the volume. Nausea churned his stomach. Unable to control their relative priority, he was stranded between the digital and physical worlds, his attention vacillating and his brain rebelling. It was the mental equivalent of the medieval rack, stretching him until tendons severed, joints popped, and bones fractured.

"I can't answer your questions until you let me get out of here," he gasped.

"Mr. Calhoun?" Nell stepped around the podium.

"Is this really a conversation you want to have with witnesses? Just give me back intensity controls."

Javier looked at Emily, then nodded. His fingers twitched, and suddenly Dag had control of his feed again. He immediately turned down the volume and marginalized the video stream so he could focus on Nell.

"I'm very sorry," he said. "Too much tequila."

He attempted a rakish smile, but it didn't land.

"Are you sure you don't need help?" asked Nell. "We always have a doctor on call."

For half a second, he considered accepting the offer. If he ducked back through those curtains, he would be off-grid, beyond the Island's reach. He could find an excuse to hide out there until Rachel sealed Commonwealth off from the Island. Nobody would be able to seize control of his feed. But he needed to fill them in before the gate came crashing down, and he wasn't about to attempt a second kayak infiltration into hostile territory.

"Thanks, but I'm fine, really. Just enough liquor to embarrass myself twice in a row, that's all. I'll get out of your hair. I promise not to be a bother next time."

Before she could ask more questions, he shouldered through the oak doors and stumbled between the two bouncers and out onto the street. His ears still rang, and the world seemed to spin slowly around him. Disoriented, he managed to make his way to a small park bench overlooking a lawn covered in bald patches and pigeons.

The line to the Island had been open the whole time, and now he brought it front and center. A dozen angry faces stared back, Emily and Javier in the foreground.

"Who the hell do you think you are?" she asked.

"You posted a similar question on the wall of Room 412," said Dag. "And I think I'm finally starting to work my way toward an answer."

"Care to explain yourself?" Sarcasm dripped from Frances's words. "We're on red alert here, pulling out of every hard-earned position because of your warning."

"I accomplished the mission," said Dag.

"What are you talking about?" demanded Emily.

"Tomorrow morning, Rachel will announce that a global carbon tax has been added to the Commonwealth terms of service," said Dag. "Every country will be forced to comply or lose feed access."

Stunned faces stared back at him.

"Why would they do that?" asked Ferdinand.

"I handed over the exploit architecture," said Dag. "Rachel had no choice. But I didn't reveal your identities. That's why I sent you the warning. As long as you pull out fast enough, there won't be a way for them to determine attribution. You'll still have your facilities and your money, but your back door into Commonwealth is over. We should keep this conversation short. I assume her engineers will be tracking my account closely for any possible links to you."

Frances snorted. "The connection is cloaked, and the buffers clear immediately—there won't be a log."

"Doesn't matter to me," said Dag. "I'm the one who brought her the data. But if I were you, I'd err on the side of caution."

"Five minutes," said Javier, brushing hair from his face with a slender hand. His tone was curt, facing crisis with efficiency. "I know Rachel. She'll move quickly. It's not worth the risk."

"What makes you think she won't just shut us out and renege on changing the terms of service?" asked Ferdinand.

"I don't think she will," said Dag. "We shook on it, and the value of her word is too intimately tied to people's trust in Commonwealth for her to go back on it. But even if she does, I can take everything public. She knows that, so I'm betting she'll stick to it."

"You're *betting*?" spluttered Ferdinand. "You—"

Javier silenced him with a gesture. "*Why*, Dag? Why do this at all? We had a plan, a good one. Even if the carbon tax works as we hope, now you've disarmed us. We've lost our secret weapon, but there are so many problems that need our attention. You *know* that. That's why you joined us."

"Are you fucking kidding me?" said Dag. "You threaten to dox Sean when I refuse to destroy him, and you think I'm just going to kiss ass and thank you for it? Fuck you." He gripped the cold iron armrest of the bench. "You told me we were a family. If this is how you treat family, then I'll take the foster care system any day. If you're this cruel and this blind, maybe I should have given Rachel your names after all."

A frown creased Javier's high forehead. "Dox Sean? What are you talking about?"

"Bullshit," said Ferdinand, aghast. "We don't blackmail."

"I told you that when we met," said Frances.

Dag was taken aback. Why would they lie? Were they covertly recording this session and wanted to express their innocence for anyone playing it back later? But how would that benefit them? They would never want evidence of their own culpability to be made public, so what possible motive could they have for denying the doxing threat?

And then he noticed Emily.

Before, she had been standing next to Javier. But she hadn't said anything in a while, and now she was edging toward the side of the frame and the French doors that led out onto the deck. Could there be honor among all thieves save one?

"Emily told me three nights ago that you would dox Sean if I failed to distract him from our subsidy-reduction initiative," said Dag. "And that was the least of it. Ask her, if you don't believe me."

"She would *never* do that," said Ferdinand. "None of us would."

"You're just trying to make excuses for demolishing everything we've worked for," said Frances. "Don't try to make this about something else."

But Javier's expression frosted over, and righteousness fled his wide dark eyes, leaving them gaping and empty. It looked like he was living through a long-anticipated nightmare. He turned to Emily, and she froze, looking suddenly terrified.

"Is this true?" asked Javier quietly.

She couldn't meet his gaze. Her imperial authority withered. She looked like a little girl who wanted to disappear through a hole in the floor. Ferdinand, Frances, and others were silent, looking back and forth between them like a tennis referee following the ball.

"This is the future of the biosphere we're talking about," she said at last. "It's not a straightforward change in domestic legislation—it's the planet itself. Nothing is more important than that."

"I see," said Javier coldly.

Palpable currents ebbed and flowed beneath the exchange. Dag could sense years of fraught debate under the surface, countless late-night arguments unresolved and festering. This line of reasoning was a geological fault in their friendship, in their cabal. It reminded him of Gretchen.

"We didn't have another contingency," she said, desperate. "This needed to work. Too much hung in the balance. I couldn't let Dag betray the mission to save face with a man whose entire job is helping fossil fuel interests game the system."

"So you decided to overlook everything we stand for?" asked Javier.

"Dag fumbled Hsu. He was about to fumble Sean. I had to do something. If Dag would have just followed through, none of you would ever need to know. It was never supposed to be this way."

"You're right, it wasn't," said Javier, his voice strained and exhausted. "We would have found another way."

"There was no other way!"

"And you never even thought to ask us first?" Javier looked around at the group. "You never considered whether a decision this important was one we would need to make together?"

Her questing silence was its own answer.

"I see," Javier said again, incomparable angst underlining the simple words.

"I had no choice." She was at once vehement and resigned.

"There's always a choice," Javier said gently. "You taught me that. You taught us all that."

Tears began to stream down her cheeks and drip onto the thick rug beneath her feet. The people nearest her sidled away, distancing themselves from the chieftess turned pariah. A rush of vertiginous empathy overcame Dag. Emily had altered the course of history through sheer force of will, and now her very ambition had torn the effort apart.

"I'm sorry," she whispered hoarsely. "I'm so sorry."

"It's a little late for that," said Javier.

"I broke it," she said to no one in particular. "I broke us."

Javier hauled himself back from the edge of an abyss and seemed to return a changed man.

"Those five minutes are up," he said to Dag. "I can't guarantee the security of this connection any longer. We have a lot of work to do to make sure the Island is protected from tracking or incursion from Rachel's cybersecurity teams. There isn't much of a window, and we need to make the most of it. The rest will have to wait. For now, congratulations on getting the global carbon tax implemented. Despite everything, that's our biggest victory yet."

Dag nodded, thoughts whirling through his mind. He had assumed Emily had been at the vanguard of a unified front, that everyone on the Island was complicit in her threat. But she had gone rogue and broken faith with Javier and the rest in order to secure the victory she sought. The team's anguish was palpable through the feed. In contrast, Dag felt numb. Emily's excess had shown Dag the rotten core of the entire enterprise. Had he known she was operating alone, he would not have done anything differently.

"And thanks for giving us this chance even though you thought we'd screwed you," continued Javier. "We may not have a back door into Commonwealth anymore, but we still have a lot of resources and good people to dedicate toward building a better world. For what it's worth, you always have a home with us, no matter what."

"Emily gave me a second chance once," said Dag. "I figured this was the least I could do." He remembered her hand gripping his throat, the electric intensity of her eyes. "Try winning hearts and minds the old-fashioned way. Get out there and appeal to people's better nature. Who knows? They might even surprise you."

He cut the connection.

Home.

Reaching into the inside pocket of his jacket, Dag removed a folded piece of paper and opened it. He stared down at the last sketch he'd drawn. He had been sitting on a foreign curb opposite the site of his parents' demise, lost in a wilderness of regret.

Home wasn't always a place.

CHAPTER 45

The mottled gray boulder was rough and warm beneath Dag's hand. The winds had shifted, and the clear sky was mercifully free of smoke from Southern California. Shingle and tile roofs of wealthy Berkeley homes turned the hill below him into a mosaic that stretched out to encompass the university and reach all the way down to the encroaching bay.

Indian Rock.

Places like this were nodes around which human cultures ebbed and flowed. The Ohlone tribes had gathered acorns from the once-abundant oak trees, ground them into flour in specially carved pits in the rock, and subsisted on the bitter porridge as a staple. Today, the Bay Area relied on imported foodstuffs genetically engineered and carefully cultivated to endure the erratic and extreme weather patterns that had long since become the new normal.

Rachel had made the announcement yesterday, and the feed was ablaze with commentary, analysis, and contention. Once the dust settled, enforcement by Commonwealth would surely be more effective than the UN. But even if the tax worked as well as economists hoped, it would take decades for changes to pay off. Success would be bequeathing a world to their great-grandchildren that was no more unstable than it already was today.

But the well-worn appeal to future generations rang empty to Dag. It was a balm for the conscience, but if he was honest with himself, it hadn't really driven his decisions. He was a different person from the overcaffeinated man who had scrambled up from the blood and dust outside that Mexican café. The past few months had shaken him to his core, body and soul.

Abstract altruism hadn't fueled that change. Cantankerous climate models didn't galvanize behavior. It was how the real outcomes of those projections affected people's lives. Seeing that carbonized La Jollan rock with nary a sea lion in sight meant more to Dag than a thousand news reports.

It forced him to reevaluate his closest relationships.

Sean.

Lowell.

Emily.

His parents' ghosts.

Himself.

He had built his life on the assumption that people were fundamentally selfish and that influencing them required quid pro quos. It had seemed a truism growing up in the system. The K Street world teemed with professional game theorists. The Island's techniques were a subtler implementation of the same tactics. Emily's last-ditch coercion had taken it one step too far.

But perhaps the best example was what Dag had done to Rachel. Leveraging the privileged information at his disposal to force her onto a path she would never have otherwise taken. It had felt good to finally do something on his own account, instead of serving some magnate. But it had also been the culmination of a career spent manipulating people.

If he believed everyone was only out for themselves, then manipulation justified itself. But applying that same logic to his parents had always kindled a deep-seated resentment. If only they hadn't decided to go on that vacation, he would have had a family. It was that slow-burning anger that allowed him to ignore the connection between his work for Lowell and disasters like Razif.

Over the windblown water, San Francisco rose from behind the dikes and dams protecting downtown from the rising sea. The Golden Gate Bridge was a vermillion arc through which he could just catch a glimpse of the Pacific. Puffy cumulus clouds sat on the horizon like celestial sheep. Sir Francis Drake had explored this coast on behalf of the European superpowers. Now the bay he'd tacked his twenty-two-gun galleon by was the throbbing heart of the world's information infrastructure. Dag's feed hummed on the edges of his consciousness just as the teams that built and maintained it labored nonstop in plush offices on the shores of this storied inlet.

Discovery consisted not in exploring new lands but in looking at the world through fresh eyes. Emily and Javier had spent ten years crafting his feed to incite desire for a higher purpose. It had worked, if not in the way they intended. His mouth twitched in a shadow of a smile. You might have the best tools in the world, but shaping someone else's behavior was still a fool's errand. Rather than making him a peon to their schemes, their interference had awoken in Dag the possibility of assuming the best of others. And if he chose to see the best in people, then he could no longer rationalize blaming his parents for his bereavement.

They were a couple of good people who had gotten unlucky.

Emily believed in things so deeply she'd cross lines to achieve them.

Javier stood by his code, both of honor and algorithms.

Sean saw loyalty and service as ends in themselves, even if they required taking actions he disagreed with.

Hsu would sacrifice everything to safeguard his nation.

Rachel refused to see any problem as insoluble.

Lowell delighted in the untempered chaos of life.

Dag had spent his life playing zero-sum games.

But if you chose to love instead of fear, the spoils lost all meaning. And without the spoils, there was nothing left to justify what he'd helped Lowell do. The only prize he'd won was regret.

Squatting on his haunches, Dag plucked a blade of grass off a tuft sprouting from a crack in the rock. The sharp smell summoned his conversation with Emily under the Island's starry sky. *Understanding how things came to be frees us to imagine new possibilities.* She might have hijacked his feed, but that didn't mean she was wrong about everything.

We are the stories we tell ourselves. The world existed at the cusp of history just as Dag lived at the cusp of his feed. Collective and individual identities might be shaped by circumstance, but only acquiescence guaranteed them to be determined by it.

Dag could take some satisfaction in the elegance of the Commonwealth deal. Hopefully it might start to offset the damage he'd done. But it was also the last deal he'd make for a long while. It was possible to negotiate for fairness instead of advantage. But Dag's obsession with gaining advantage had been what put him on this path in the first place.

The way you looked at the world manifested what you saw in it.

It was time to get beyond that and figure out what true generosity meant.

CHAPTER 46

Dag yelped and jumped forward as a firm palm spanked his ass.

"Gotcha!"

"Damn it, Diana," he said, rubbing his smarting butt. "That stings like hell."

"You were staring off into the sky all doe-eyed and melancholic," she said, laughing. "I figured you'd appreciate a little wake-me-up."

"Ah, I see. You snuck up from behind and smacked me for my own benefit."

She assumed an expression of heartfelt compassion. "I've always been a true humanitarian," she said. "Bleeding heart, the whole hog."

"I've never met a humanitarian with the CIA on their résumé."

"Well, you learn something new every day, right? Rules are there to be broken."

"Which is why you started this encounter by practicing your BDSM technique?"

Her eyes flared wide. "Ooooo," she said. "Is that an invitation? My place is only a few blocks away. You have no idea what I could do to you with nothing but a forty-centimeter silk cord. *Ravish* wouldn't even begin to describe it. It's applied quantum physics, opening up entire parallel universes of tantric bliss."

"You do this thing," said Dag, "where whenever I say something, you take it five levels further."

"It's called intelligence," said Diana. "It's a rare condition. You wouldn't have heard of it."

"Exactly."

Reaching a temporary stalemate, they stepped to the edge of Indian Rock and watched the sun dip behind the mountains of distant clouds, suffusing them with deep orange and purple hues. The soft light made the entire Bay Area appear to glow from within. San Francisco's skyscrapers glittered and shone. A flock of sparrows zigged and zagged. Sailboats scudded back toward the marina.

"So," said Diana, "what have you got for me this time, cowboy? Another first-of-its-kind conspiracy that upends everything we know and trust in the universe? I couldn't help but think that Commonwealth taking a steaming shit on the geopolitical world stage must have something to do with your little escapade." She shot him a glance, then shrugged. "But honestly, I'm not sure how you're going to top these last few assignments. My other clients are so boring by comparison. It's like trying to go back to vanilla ice cream after you've tried pistachio saffron. No dice."

Dag let out a breath. He felt unaccountably nervous.

"I don't have a new assignment," he said.

"Aha!" she said, clapping her hands. "I knew it. You've finally fallen for my feminine charms."

When he didn't immediately respond with repartee, she looked at him quizzically.

"I have something for you," he said.

Reaching into the inside pocket of his jacket, he pulled out an envelope and handed it to her.

She accepted it with a slight frown.

"Another portrait of dear old Emily?"

"Go ahead," he said. "Open it."

239

Slipping a finger under the flap, she tore open the envelope and removed the folded piece of paper Dag had carried with him since Taipei. Her eyes flicked up to him, then back. She unfolded the paper and sucked in a tiny sip of air in surprise.

The foreign capital had buzzed around him. The curb dug into his ass right where Diana had slapped it. Drones danced between skyscrapers. Pedestrians decked out in the latest fashions gossiped and laughed. Garbage trucks did their rounds, playing "Für Elise" on repeat to call residents down to dispose of their rubbish. The air was hot and heavy with humidity, tasting of peanut and vinegar. On the other side of the city, delegates from around the world were casting votes on the historic global carbon tax initiative that Emily had tried to summon into law.

But, for once, Dag hadn't been consumed with geopolitical maneuvering.

Hsu had sent him down a dark alley into memories he'd rather forget. Tiptoeing toward introspection, Dag nearly drowned in the violent juxtaposition of the peaceful, extant brightly lit apartments against the mud and madness in his feed's chronicle of Razif destruction. But a momentary prescience had sent him into that bookstore, armed him with the weapons he needed to escape the shadowy depths.

Putting pencil to paper, Dag had reached for something *normal*.

And he found an anchor amid the chaos. Something solid. Something secure. Something safe.

Actually, not some*thing*. Some*one*.

He'd been so immersed in the creative process, so consumed with every stroke, that he hadn't truly been cognizant of the subject of the sketch until after it was complete.

Diana was staring at a portrait of herself.

Wide brown eyes under tight brown curls.

You can trust me.

When his work erred toward espionage, he relied on her. When he thought he might be going insane after discovering his life plastered across Room 412, he came to her. When intuition teased him with the suspicion that maybe, just maybe, Emily hadn't just jacked his feed but was also administering it, he offered something to Diana he had never considered giving to anyone. Root access to his feed. There was nothing more intimate. He thought the extreme vulnerability would eat him up inside, but it had been a release, not a burden.

Diana was a nut. But she came through. Every time.

It was the most difficult piece he'd ever drawn. His illustrations brought to life kingdoms of the fantastic. But Diana's face was average in every way. Her eminently forgettable appearance had been a serious asset as an intelligence officer. Her countenance was the essence of normal, belying the uncommon brilliance and profound weirdness that lay behind it. Sketching her required capturing the former while hinting at the latter.

And then her arms were around him, squeezing him in a hug so tight he couldn't breathe.

"You motherfucker," she said into his shoulder, emotion displacing sardonic flair. "Nobody's ever made anything this nice for me."

He hugged her back. Then leaned back to look at her.

She wasn't his type.

His type had been carefully engineered by a remote team of hacker psychologists.

Fuck them.

He kissed her.

She tasted of cloves and rosewater.

After what might have been a few seconds or an eternity, they broke apart.

For no reason he could fathom, the first words out of Dag's mouth were, "I can make pancakes."

Her giggle was a truer salve than prayer.

"If that's your version of a pickup line," she said, "then you're the man for me."

CHAPTER 47

Dag returned to consciousness slowly, like a bear emerging from hibernation. Pale morning light angled in through the bedroom window, transfixing Diana's avian shoulder blade. She was half under the covers, curled up, and snoring softly. She had been surprisingly small in his arms, her body a tiny home for a big personality.

Luxuriating in the sloth of inching toward wakefulness, Dag took pleasure in the mild soreness, the cadence of breath. The walls and ceiling of Diana's bedroom were covered in stars, five-pointed glow-in-the-dark stick-ons that had made the room come alive in the darkness of night and that dawn now dimmed. Before falling into bed with him, she had carefully leaned the portrait up against a simple vase on the wooden dresser from which a vivid bouquet of tulips sprouted.

It was good to be alive.

Careful not to disturb her, he slipped out of bed and pulled on his clothes, padding out barefoot and quietly shutting the door behind him. Diana did indeed live quite close to Indian Rock. It was a cozy one-bedroom cottage tucked away in North Berkeley, not the kind of place he'd assumed an ex-spy would seek out.

Unlike his apartment's granite-and-stainless-steel theater, her kitchen looked well used. Tile-and-grout countertops. Blood oranges in a bowl. Four-top gas range. A fading photograph of a blue-and-white

Greek village against the electric turquoise of the Aegean. Ceramic sink stained by water rings.

He opened the fridge, the cool air raising goose bumps. An assortment of cheeses and fresh produce. Butter, eggs, and a tub of yogurt. Smoked salmon, mustard, and a variety of artisan hot sauces. Moving on to the cupboards, he found flour, salt, sugar, baking powder, a measuring cup, a mixing bowl, and a whisk.

He rubbed his chin. Most of the way there, but two key ingredients were missing.

Noticing something that hadn't been visible last night, he peered through the window over the sink, then opened the back door of the cottage beside it. Humid air rolled over him, rich with the smell of soil and pollen.

The wonder of unexpected discovery thrilled through him. He was standing in a greenhouse built to match the full size of the residence. The walls and roof aligned with the back of the cottage, covered most of the backyard, and turned the square floor plan into a single rectangular building divided to house humans in the front half and plants in the back.

And what plants. It was as if he had just stepped from a quiet Californian neighborhood into a dense tropical jungle. Vines climbed into the rafters. Enormous leathery leaves the size of elephant ears drooped over the small mosaic footpath. Flowers of every size, shape, and color gave the place a festive air while hairy-trunked saplings reached toward the glass ceiling. Pushing through the undergrowth, he stepped into a small circular opening in the middle of the primeval tangle. A small bistro-style table marked the center of the space, accompanied by two chairs. Enclosed on all sides by lush greenery, it was a world within a world. A pocket universe. Diana's passion project.

It was marvelous. Here. This is where he'd lay out breakfast.

Diana went deep. She had been a colleague, a friend, for years, but Dag would never have guessed at what lay beneath her particular flavor of coy audacity. He spent so much time being the person the situation required, honing every aside and microexpression, that he couldn't help but wonder whether that came at a cost. Did his own life lack depth and texture because he invested so much in external effort? It was never too late for reflection.

Returning to the house, he left an automated note to ping Diana if she woke before he returned. Then he found his shoes, checked the location of the nearest market, and set off walking.

It was still early, and the neighborhood was quiet. Strolling down the tree-lined residential streets, a basic sense of humanity began to seep back into his soul. He felt more grounded than he had in months. Who knew what the future might bring, but right now he was looking forward to making breakfast for a woman he'd known for years and had only just discovered was irresistible. Thinking of her made him want to turn around, snuggle back under the sheets, and make love to her again. But his tumescence was softened by a certain joyous incredulity. He didn't just lust after Diana, he genuinely liked her.

That was scary. It was a feeling he'd normally flee but was now determined to run toward.

It wasn't the culmination of a drawn-out courtship, a tumultuous romantic drama that mended broken hearts with happy endings. That stuff was fodder for the feed, not real life. Fermenting inside Dag was something that had more in common with nostalgia, a fleeting glimpse of wondrous beauty momentarily restored.

Something to treasure.

A bell tinkled as he entered the market. A wizened Japanese man sat on a high stool behind the counter. Assorted customers browsed the aisles. There was a surprising amount and diversity of fresh produce, but Dag made his way to the dry-stuffs section. He scanned the shelves. It had to be here somewhere.

There. Maple syrup. He double-checked the label. The real stuff, not drummed-up agave hogwash. Now time for the final ingredient.

Moving to the back corner of the market, he sought out the refrigerated section. Dairy. Dairy. Dairy. Bingo. Pulling open the large refrigerator door, he retrieved a slim carton of buttermilk.

Mission complete.

But as he straightened back up and the door suctioned closed, something hard jammed into his back and he bumped up against the cold glass.

"Easy now, Mr. Calhoun," a voice rasped into his ear. "Just do what I tell you and this'll all be over in a minute. No dramatics, no soft shells to the gut. Get me?"

"Diana," Dag said after a quarter second's shock, dispensing frisson with a chuckle. "You got me. But is this any way to treat a gentleman out getting you groceries?"

The briefest of pauses.

"I don't know what you're on about," said the voice. "So just shut up and stay casual. We're just two friends picking up eggs or whatever."

Diana was really good at disguising her voice, probably another skill learned at Langley, so Dag glanced back over his shoulder to call her out. And his heart skipped a beat. Instead of a sprightly brunette, a squat moonfaced man stared back at him with eyes that weren't so much hard as bored. A professional doing his job, Carhartt jacket over jeans. He jammed what must be a gun into the small of Dag's back, the weapon concealed inside an innocent canvas shopping bag.

Pulse pounding like a jackhammer, Dag followed his instructions, shuffling down the row of refrigerators, pretending to browse. Careful not to turn his head, he looked sidelong down the aisles, trying to judge his chances of breaking free and dashing down one for the exit. There were other shoppers in the market, though none close by. Dag tensed up. Would this guy really gun him down with that many witnesses? Was the canvas bag large enough to cover a silencer? If he chucked the syrup into the wine section, could he shatter enough bottles to draw attention?

"Don't even think about it." The man's voice was blasé.

So much for that. If he was going to die today, at least he'd gotten laid last night. But that line of thought led him back to Diana, surprising her with a romantic breakfast that now seemed like an impossible dream. Had she woken up? Read his note with a yawn and a smile? Would that simple missive be the last she ever heard from him? He couldn't remember the last time he'd been so excited to share a meal with someone. Now he was heading toward a body bag while she was sleeping in. No. Stop that. Stay focused. Make it to the next moment, and then the one after that.

They reached a set of service doors in the back corner of the market. They were gray plastic on top and black rubber on the bottom with big dual-direction hinges.

"Push slowly," the man continued with efficient disinterest. "If you try to swing them back to hit me, you'll regret it. Just step through and then into the office on the left."

Dag pushed through them, making sure his movements were slow and deliberate.

"That's it," said the man. "The office on the left."

This was the warehouse, crates of produce stacked to the ceiling, fluorescent lights, scuffed floors, carts for moving stuff around.

Dag didn't bother to stifle a morbid smile. This was his life. One back room after another. He'd had enough of seeing how the sausage got made.

As promised, there was a door on the left that looked like it led into a small office.

"Inside," said the man. "We don't have all day."

Dag gripped the door handle, wondering whether the cool aluminum was the last thing he'd feel. Sucking in a shallow breath, he opened it and then froze on the threshold.

Stilettos. A midnight-black suit perfectly cut to tantalize and intimidate. Freja stared back at him imperiously. She wore an expression of mild distaste, as if considering an unavoidable mud puddle in her path. Dag was too stunned to speak, but his chaperone jabbed him in the kidney and he stumbled into the cramped room. He desperately tried to weave together some semblance of logic that would place her here in front of him.

Before Dag could gather his wits, Freja stepped aside, revealing a tchotchke-covered vinyl desk behind which sat Lowell, a predatory grin spread across his baby face.

"Freja, if you'd be so kind as to give us the room?" said Lowell. "I promise this won't take but a minute."

With a disapproving grunt, Freja exited along with the lackey, leaving Dag alone with his former client. Any lingering hope that he might make it back to Diana vanished.

Dag slowly lowered himself onto the hard plastic chair across from Lowell, placing the syrup and buttermilk on the floor beside him. Questions bred like rabbits in his fraying mind. He wanted to summon his feed, but didn't dare miss a beat.

"I've always been fascinated by places like this," said Lowell, gesturing around the shabby little office. The fiberboard grid-panel ceiling reminded Dag of county office buildings. The walls had once been white, but dust and grime had turned them gray. "Seats of power. The Oval Office is just the same. The only difference being that one commands turnips and the other a nation."

"What do you want?" asked Dag, trying to keep despair out of his voice.

Lowell rapped his fingers on the desk. "You're more resourceful than I expected, my boy. I'll give you that. You flubbed Hsu, and after our little chat down in Mexico, I figured you'd skive off. But you seem to have taken it as more of a pep talk. Good for you. Nice to see the next generation grow a pair."

Absentmindedly, Lowell picked up a snow globe from the desk, shook it, and watched the contents settle. "Then again, maybe I'm not giving myself enough credit. I did train you up myself. It shouldn't surprise me that even a failed student might actually go on to make something of themselves."

"Why am I here?"

"The most delicious part is that I'm not even precisely sure how you did it," said Lowell. "You were repping Rachel before I hired you back, helping Commonwealth replace the Mexican cartels' bandwidth monopoly. Then you throw the carbon tax fight to doom my business, but your bid fails by the grace of darling Freja and a hellishly steep bounty for Hsu. I'm safe. Bailed out. Home free. Champagne. Hookers. Cue drumroll."

He tapped out a beat on the desk with his forefingers.

"But then, out of nowhere, Rachel decides to swoop in and uni-laterally implement the godforsaken carbon tax anyway," continued Lowell. "I'm halfway through my victory march, and someone tears my pants down and starts pounding me up the ass with a spiked dildo. No lube. Ouch."

Lowell formed a loose fist with his left hand and jammed his right thumb into the opening.

"So." He smacked his hand on the desk hard enough to make it jump. Dag twitched, and Lowell smiled thinly. "I know you're behind all this somehow. I've been doing this too long to believe in coincidences."

Lowell narrowed his eyes. "I'm reviewing my portfolio, and Freja's freaking out. After Rachel's announcement, our share price plummets like a head off the guillotine. That tax is steep enough to eat more than our margins—it's going to force whole countries to find immediate energy substitutes. Solar is going gangbusters. Battery stocks have never been better. But this doesn't just fuck our E&P business. It under-mines the entire investment thesis on our coastal property play. Folks don't know it yet, but those assets are now stranded. Which, of course, nobody would know better than you."

Panic spread through Dag like the ash falling over La Jolla.

"Now we have two options," said Lowell. "I could call Emmanuel back in here and put you out of your misery. You look like a drowned rat right now. He'd do you clean. The man's a pro. It's his daughter's fifth birthday party later today, but I'm sure he could dispose of the body en route to pick up a present."

This was how it was going to end. Executed by a hit man in the back of a grocery store. At least they didn't have Diana.

"Or"—Lowell brushed back his light-brown hair—"I could thank you kindly and let you go on your merry way."

Dag's mind went blank. He had sabotaged the source of Lowell's power. Nobody got away with that.

"I'm not going to lie," said Lowell. "I've been thinking about the first option. Nice sense of closure. But"—his expression turned feral—"but, but, but." Gripping the edge of the desk, he leaned across toward Dag, eyes gleaming. "What have all my businesses been based on? Each and every one?"

Dag thought the question was rhetorical until Lowell hissed, *"What?"*

Another game. Games within games within games. Thoughts, angles, and contingencies tumbled through Dag's head. If they were still playing, then there might yet be a way out.

"Second-order effects," said Dag, throat dry and tongue thick.

"Eureka! You were always a sharp student. So while you were busy convincing Rachel to save the world, did you stop and think about those oh-so-lovely second-order effects?"

Lowell wanted an answer. Dag racked his brain. He had been seeking redemption, not leverage. "You already listed most of them. Capital migration from assets hit by the tax to those that escape it. Down-line impacts on assets more or less exposed to risks from the new emission profiles. General market adjustment."

Lowell's face lit up as if appraising a masterpiece. "But you're missing the forest for the trees," he said. "No, my boy. The elephant in the room is *sovereignty*."

"Sovereignty."

"Rachel just upset the global balance of power," said Lowell. "Commonwealth provides the infrastructure the world depends on. But they've been able to establish and maintain their monopoly because they're a toolshed. They're the stadium, but governments are still the umpires. Rachel didn't just issue a press release—she started a goddamn war. She announced Commonwealth isn't just handing out tools anymore, it's making *policy*. Policy enforced by denial of service, which in this case means access to the global economy. In one fell swoop, she transformed herself into Big Brother. Or in this case, Big Sister. But they're not the only ones with muscles to flex. Governments might depend on Commonwealth, but they've got assets too, like armies. And if anyone is finely attuned to the tiniest ripple in the separation of powers between public and private, it's the folks megalomaniacal enough to snatch political seats for themselves in the first place. Commonwealth is encroaching on the sovereignty of the nation-state, and you can bet your ass that every national leader is going to fight back with every dirty move in the book. You've created a monster, and every Goliath needs a David. That's where I come in. You're looking at the brand-spanking-new king of government contracting. We're liquidating our books and putting everything into helping countries nationalize local Commonwealth assets, create alternative access points like the cartels, and fight off the specter of unchecked corporate power. It's boom times again. Creative destruction and destructive creation, baby."

Lowell raised two fingers. "And that's where the second option comes in." He stroked his fingers down his jawline. "Much to my surprise and your relief, while Freja tracked you down, I realized that I wasn't actually going to have you killed. Weird, I know. Instead, I'm here to *thank* you. I'm always grateful when someone does me a favor, even if they're an opponent. It's only fair."

Lowell stood, the chair clattering over behind him. Stepping around the desk, he placed a hand on Dag's shoulder and leaned down to whisper in his ear. "A little bird told me you recently became unemployed. Well, you ever need a job, all you have to do is ask." He guffawed. "Hell, I should cut you in right now. You've created almost as many opportunities trying to screw me as you did trying to help me. Keep up the good work."

Striding past Dag, he opened the door.

"Oh," he said over his shoulder. "Do me a favor, will you? Let your fuck-buddy Rachel know I'm coming for her. We don't need Commonwealth, we need common ground. Catchy, right?"

The door snicked shut, and Dag was alone. After a few minutes of terrified silence, he started to believe that maybe he wasn't in fact going to be executed this morning. His teeth began to chatter. His armpits were soaked with sweat. It was all he could do to keep his bowels under control.

Lowell was right, of course. Yesterday's announcement upended the entire modern geopolitical playbook. The closest analogs might be the British East India Company or the Verenigde Oostindische Compagnie, global firms with private armies and absolute power over their holdings. Dag had forced Rachel's hand. In order to protect the integrity of Commonwealth, she had launched it into direct competition with governments the world over. Worse, the opening salvo was over an issue that the international community had just voted down.

It was a slippery slope to tyranny.

Schemes begat schemes begat schemes. Outside the false constraints of sport, there was no such thing as decisive victory. There was only the blind fumbling of the fallible, of which history was its record.

Dag closed his eyes. Once again, politics swirled around him, threatening to suck him in. The metallic smell of blood and propellant filled his nostrils. Federico's body twitched on the pavement. A life snuffed out so easily, and for so fleeting a benefit. Was his son still at Oxford? Was his daughter pursuing her burgeoning athletic career despite the family tragedy? Did their father's ghost regret the years he'd spent away from them buttressing his Senado position? Emily and Javier had infiltrated the feed to pursue causes they deemed important. But the most important things were right there all along.

Dag opened his eyes. This time he would swim against the current.

That old couple from the café materialized in his mind's eye, coffee stain on napkin, the ineffable bond that was as obvious as it was invisible. Not love per se, but the loam of trust in which love might sprout. Dag had cast vulnerability as weakness and excised it. But impenetrable armor cut you off even as it protected you from harm. He didn't know whether they had survived the attack, but at least they had something worth living for. It might stay forever beyond his reach, but there was only one way to find out. Just a single step. And then another. And another after that. One day, you might look back and realize you had blazed a new trail through the existential undergrowth.

Breathe in. Breathe out. His galloping heart slowed.

Power was indeed a fickle bitch, so why must he be steadfast in its pursuit? For good or ill, this could wait. He had higher priorities. Retrieving the syrup and buttermilk, he set off to make the best damn pancakes a certain girl with tousled hair and sleepy eyes had ever tasted.

The End

AFTERWORD

Although the idea for *Bandwidth* had been gestating for a while, I had a number of false starts. Did it focus on Emily's formative teenage years? Or perhaps Javier's courageous attempt to build a new life for himself and his sister? Was this a contemporary tale, or would it take place decades hence? What might that future look like?

At one point, I thought that the protagonist might be a stand-up comedian. I am so glad I didn't go down that route. I'm not nearly funny enough to do justice to a comedian's inner life. But the jump from comedian to lobbyist was shorter than you might think. Both professions require a finely tuned sense of observation and an intuition for the invisible systems that shape our world and lives.

It was from that milieu that Dag began to emerge. A striver with a keen eye for the dynamics and incentives that guide and warp society. A survivor who was willing to do what it took to win. A seeker who couldn't deny his own failings once he finally achieved true introspection.

Characters rarely stride onto the page fully formed, like a stage actor entering from the wings. Instead, they start as a blurred sketch, and only become more solid, more real, as the story progresses. Like all of us, they define themselves through their actions, and I always know that a character is becoming a human being when they start doing things that surprise me. By the end of the rough draft, Dag and the rest of the cast had become dear friends.

That rough draft grew in fits and starts during late 2016 and early 2017. This was a turbulent time in the United States, and it was impossible to escape the chaos and outrage of the presidential election. Technology played a disturbing and divisive role in that election, defying the utopian pronouncements all too common in Silicon Valley. Let's just say there's ample material for investigative journalists to dig their teeth into.

But great novels offer something different from great reporting. Fiction shines when it entertains and challenges us at the same time. It transports us. It offers an opportunity to move beyond intellectual debate and play out ideas in the gritty, intimate, messy context of people's actual lives. It forces us to put things in perspective and to ask hard questions even if we don't have ready answers.

If we are the stories we tell ourselves, what happens when someone else controls the narrative? What does it take for a cynic to rediscover authenticity? How is technology changing the structure and exercise of power?

These were some of the recurring questions that surfaced again and again as I worked my way through *Bandwidth* chapter by chapter, scene by scene, word by word. They are questions I am forced to consider every day when I succumb to the distraction of social media, find myself ignoring injustice because it all just seems to be too much, or contemplate just how out of touch our social institutions are from a world of accelerating innovation.

These are dark thoughts, and there is a dark vein running through *Bandwidth*. But whenever I struggle, I try to channel Dag's passion for history. I'd rather live in 2018 than in 1918. Or 1818. Or 1718. Or any other time. Dag would never trade his future for our present.

By historical standards, most people alive today enjoy miracles that the emperors of old could only dream of (and likely didn't). We are a lucky and privileged few, and whatever corruption and injustice we seek to overcome isn't new or unique. And that leads us to a challenging conclusion.

The world is what we make it.

If we throw up our hands when the going gets tough, we get what we deserve. So take a deep breath, do some gentle stretching, and make the world a better place. Do a favor for a stranger. Be kind when instinct calls for harshness. Question your assumptions. Make good art. Tell your loved ones how grateful you are to have them in your life. Lend a hand to those in need. Take real risks to do the right thing.

Oh, and remember that in an age of acceleration, contemplation is power. The feed can only define you if you let it.

Thank you for reading. I poured my whole self into *Bandwidth* and it's an honor that you made time to read it. If you enjoyed the story, please leave a review and tell your friends about it. These may sound insignificant, but you'd be amazed at the difference every little thing makes. Books succeed or fail based on word of mouth. I may have written the story, but Dag's future is in your hands.

Onward and upward.

Cheers,
Eliot

FURTHER READING

People often ask about the writing process, but I find the reading process much more interesting. Reading is a superpower that we too often take for granted. It is telepathy. It is a time machine. It is a magic door into countless new worlds, hearts, and minds.

I am a reader first and a writer second.

Ever since I can remember, I've loved books. When my parents read me stories as a child, I would stare into the middle distance and lose myself in them indefinitely. Growing up, I would hide among the dusty library stacks until closing time. When high school English teachers passed out assignments, I ignored the curriculum and ventured off on my own. Curiosity is my drug of choice.

Sometimes reading a book stokes my enthusiasm so much that I simply can't wait to dive into a new story. My dearest hope is that *Bandwidth* did that for you. There are so many incredible books out there, fiction and nonfiction, that can entertain, inform, and transform us. Read. Read. Read some more. Oh, and please share your favorites so we can benefit from your discoveries.

After finishing a great book, I often wish I could ask the author what they are reading. What books touch their very core? Where do they find inspiration? Where does their enthusiasm lead them? I've found many of my favorite books thanks to recommendations from my favorite authors.

I'm sure you've realized it by now, but I'm a little crazy. Obsessed, even. But if you just happen to be a little crazy too, then I've got a secret for you.

Every once in a while, I send a simple personal email sharing books that have changed my life. Because reading is such an integral part of my creative process, I often find gems in unlikely places. The goal of the newsletter is to recommend books that crackle and fizz with big ideas, keep us turning pages deep into the night, and help us find meaning in a changing world.

I also share writing updates and respond to every single note from folks on the mailing list, so joining is the best way to get or stay in touch with me. There's nothing I love more than hearing from readers.

Oh, and if you decide to join our little gang, promise me this: When you come across a story that moves you, pay it forward and pass it on.

Sign up here: www.eliotpeper.com

ACKNOWLEDGMENTS

There's only one name on the cover, but *Bandwidth* was a team effort from start to finish.

Adrienne Procaccinni and her team at Amazon Publishing transformed a raw manuscript into a beautiful book and shared it with the world.

DongWon Song at Howard Morhaim Literary offered invaluable counsel and tireless support as my agent and champion.

Jesse Vernon and Tegan Tigani whipped the book into shape. Any errors are mine alone.

Kevin Barrett Kane created a gorgeous and evocative cover.

Josh Anon, Lucas Carlson, Martha Millard, Tim Erickson, Nick Farmer, Eric Raab, Craig Lauer, Josh Elman, Nell Pierce, and Danny Crichton contributed notes that vastly improved the story.

Tim Chang, Virginia Heffernan, Brad Feld, Malka Older, Berit Anderson, Brett Horvath, Cory Doctorow, Katie Moran, William Gibson, Lavie Tidhar, Ramez Naam, Hugh Howey, Craig Mod, Tim Urban, Ben Casnocha, Kim Stanley Robinson, Barry Eisler, Kevin Kelly, Alexis Madrigal, Reece Hirsch, William Hertling, Chuck Wendig, Tim O'Reilly, Paolo Bacigalupi, Michael Crichton, Ryan Holiday, Kevin Bankston, Maria Popova, Neal Stephenson, John Underkoffler, Andrew Chamberlain, Ev Williams, and Ada Palmer were constant sources of inspiration as role models, mentors, and friends.

Odesza and Ramin Djawadi made the music that became my *Bandwidth* writing soundtrack.

Erik and Karen Peper taught me to love learning and stories.

Andrea Castillo is my constant creative partner and the love of my life. Our sheepadoodle, Claire, provided welcome companionship and distraction.

Finally, you brought *Bandwidth* to life by reading it. Stories exist to be experienced, enjoyed, and shared. You are the fire in its belly and the wind in its sails.

To all, a thousand thanks.

ABOUT THE AUTHOR

Photo © 2014 Russell Edwards

Eliot Peper is the author of *Cumulus*, *True Blue*, *Neon Fever Dream*, and The Uncommon Series. His near-future thrillers have been praised by *The Verge*, *Popular Science*, *Businessweek*, *io9*, and *Ars Technica*. Eliot is an editor at *Scout* and an adviser to entrepreneurs and investors. He has helped build various technology businesses, survived dengue fever, translated Virgil's *Aeneid* from the original Latin, worked as an entrepreneur-in-residence at a venture-capital firm, and explored the ancient Himalayan kingdom of Mustang. His writing has appeared in *Harvard Business Review*, *TechCrunch*, and the *Chicago Review of Books*; and he has been a speaker at places such as Google, Qualcomm, Future in Review, and the Conference on World Affairs.

Visit www.eliotpeper.com to get personal reading recommendations from Eliot and learn more about him. He is also active on social media at twitter.com/eliotpeper and facebook.com/eliotpeper.